LIFE
IN
A
FISHBOWL

LIFE
IN
A

FISHBOWL

LEN VLAHOS

BLOOMSBURY
NEW YORK LONDON OXFORD NEW DELHI SYDNEY

This is a work of fiction. All of the events, incidents, names, characters, companies,
businesses, executives, and organizations portrayed in this novel are either the
products of the author's imagination or are used fictitiously.

First published in the United States of America in January 2017
by Bloomsbury Children's Books
www.bloomsbury.com

Bloomsbury is a registered trademark of Bloomsbury Publishing Plc

For information about permission to reproduce selections from this book, write to
Permissions, Bloomsbury Children's Books, 1385 Broadway, New York, New York 10018
Bloomsbury books may be purchased for business or promotional use. For information on
bulk purchases please contact Macmillan Corporate and Premium Sales Department at
specialmarkets@macmillan.com

Library of Congress Cataloging-in-Publication Data
Names: Vlahos, Len.
Title: Life in a fishbowl / by Len Vlahos.
Description: New York : Bloomsbury, 2017.
Summary: Fifteen-year-old Jackie is determined to reclaim her family's privacy and dignity
by ending a reality television program about her father's terminal brain tumor.
Identifiers: LCCN 2016022364 (print) | LCCN 2016030157 (e-book)
ISBN 978-1-68119-035-8 (hardcover) • ISBN 978-1-68119-036-5 (e-book)
Subjects: | CYAC: Family problems—Fiction. | Brain—Tumors—Fiction. | Cancer—Fiction. |
Terminally ill—Fiction. | Reality television programs—Fiction. | BISAC: JUVENILE FICTION /
Family / General (see also headings under Social Issues). | JUVENILE FICTION /
Performing Arts / Television & Radio. | JUVENILE FICTION / Social Issues / Friendship.
Classification: LCC PZ7.V854 Li 2017 (print) | LCC PZ7.V854 (e-book) | DDC [Fic]—dc23
LC record available at https://lccn.loc.gov/2016022364

Book design by Jessie Gang
Typeset by RefineCatch Limited, Bungay, Suffolk
Printed and bound in the U.S.A. by Berryville Graphics Inc., Berryville, Virginia
2 4 6 8 10 9 7 5 3 1

All papers used by Bloomsbury Publishing, Inc., are natural, recyclable products
made from wood grown in well-managed forests. The manufacturing processes
conform to the environmental regulations of the country of origin.

In loving memory of Patrick A. McCartney, Patti Girvalo Neske, Avin Mark Domnitz, and my uncle Charlie Vlahos

LIFE

IN

A

FISHBOWL

Prologue

Thursday, September 10

Jackie Stone loved her father. She loved him a lot.

She kept a photo of her dad, Jared, taped to the inside of her locker at school. It was a recent selfie of the two of them on a ski lift. Wisps of Jackie's blond hair poked out from beneath her hat but did nothing to obscure the smile stretching from one side of her face to the other. Whenever the day got rough, which for Jackie was more often than not, she would sneak a peek at that photo. It had become a kind of visual security blanket.

On the days Jackie's father wasn't in Salem, where he served in the Oregon state legislature, she would find him barricaded in his study. Jackie suspected he was just as likely playing games on his Wii as he was working. The joy her dad took in beating Tiger Woods at his own game, even on a virtual golf course, made her love him even more. Either way, she knew better than to interrupt her father when that door was closed.

But Thursdays were different.

It was her father's day to run errands for the household— the grocery store, the post office, the dry cleaner's—and then head to the gym. On returning home, he'd drop his bag of sweaty workout clothes just inside the front door, take the stairs two at a time, and squeeze in next to Jackie on the top step. They would talk for a bit, eat a family dinner with Jackie's mother and sister, and then snuggle on the couch and channel surf the TV. She and her dad called it "father-daughter date night," and it was Jackie's favorite time of the week.

Even at fifteen, curling into the warmth and safety of her father's shoulder gave Jackie a feeling of peace and comfort that she found nowhere else in the world. She knew he felt the same.

But the wait for her father to come home on this Thursday was interminable.

He was late.

**

Jared Stone liked his brain. He liked it a lot.

Sure, there were times—the monotony of the evening commute, the late innings of a lopsided baseball game, the comforting repetition of the weekly church service—when it would seem to shut down, switch to some kind of autopilot. But for the most part, Jared's brain was hard at work.

It helped him navigate the halls of the state capitol, where he was serving his fourth two-year term representing the good people of Portland. It told him how to read the inscrutable faces of his wife, Deirdre, and his two teenage daughters, Jackie and Megan; to know when they needed him or when he should give them a wide berth. It knew which foods tasted good, which women were attractive, and which colleagues had a problem with body odor. And it seemed, generally speaking, to know right from wrong. Jared's brain, you could say, was his best friend. Which is what made it so hard to hear that his brain had a high-grade glioblastoma multiforme—or would have made it hard had Jared known what a high-grade glioblastoma multiforme was.

"A glio what?" he asked.

The doctor, a gray-haired woman with a square jaw and white sandals like Jared's aunt Eva used to wear, looked at him for a long moment. "I'm sorry, Jared. It's a brain tumor."

He let the words roll around his brain: *I'm sorry, Jared. It's a brain tumor.* Was she sorry that it was a tumor, or sorry that she hadn't made herself clear when she used the term "high-grade glioblastoma multiforme"? Was the part of his brain that he was using at that very moment the part with the tumor?

"And?" he asked.

"And it's not good news," the doctor answered.

"Not good news?" Jared heard the words but was having trouble following the conversation. He knew he needed to focus, knew it was more important now than ever that he focus, but he just couldn't seem to do it. It was this intermittent lack of focus, these spells of confusion and memory loss, along with the persistent pain in his right temple, that had brought him to the neurologist in the first place.

"No," the doctor said. She waited for Jared to catch up.

"Not good news," he said, now understanding.

"It's inoperable."

"Inoperable," Jared repeated, this time understanding immediately.

"The only course of therapy I can prescribe is palliative."

"I'm sorry, Doctor. I don't know that word." Though he didn't know if that had always been true, or if he had once known the word and had forgotten it.

"It means we can try to alleviate your suffering, but we can't do anything about the growth. It's going to stay."

"The growth is going to stay?"

"Yes."

He let this roll around his brain, too, and again wondered if the thought was rolling over, under, around, or through the tumor itself. "Can I live with a tumor?" he asked.

The doctor let out a sigh. She hadn't meant to and stopped herself mid-breath, so it came out as an "ahh" and sounded more like a noise of agreement than sorrow. Then she said, "No."

"No," Jared repeated.

"No," the doctor said.

She delivered this news as a matter of fact, as if she were reporting the temperature and humidity, but Jared could see her eyes welling up, and he felt sorry for her. Empathy was central to his nature, or at least he thought it was. He couldn't be sure of anything now.

***

The high-grade glioblastoma multiforme tumor liked Jared Stone's brain. It liked it a lot. In fact, it found it delicious.

Like most living things, the tumor had no idea how it had come into being. Much as a baby emerges from the womb and finds its mother's nipple, the glioblastoma simply woke up one day eating its way through the gray matter in Jared's frontal lobe and knew that it was pleased to be there.

To the tumor, this was a normal existence. It's what tumors did: they consumed their hosts' memories until they both—the host and the tumor—ceased to be. As the glioblastoma imbibed the seemingly endless expanse of neurons, subsumed the very essence of its host's mind, it would, over time, become more Jared than Jared. That's when it would be game over. But the tumor didn't know that. It only knew it had to keep eating, that Jared's memories tasted wonderful, that they were things to be savored.

On the morning of Jared's visit to the doctor, the Thursday Jared learned he had a brain tumor, the glioblastoma was watching the memory of Jared's older daughter, Jackie, enter the world.

Deirdre, Jared's wife and Jackie's mother, was lying on an operating room table, her head and shoulders on one side of a blue sheet, a surgeon and nurses hovering over her body on the other, their work obstructed from the glioblastoma's view. The tumor took in every detail. The sparkling white sheen of the floor and walls; the odors of blood and disinfectant mixing together in a way that suggested something of great importance was afoot; the sounds of beeping equipment and inhaling and exhaling respirators. The tumor absorbed the sights, smells, and sounds as if it were experiencing them itself, which, in a manner of speaking, it was. To the tumor, the memory of the event was no different than when Jared had lived it.

From the flavor and construction of this particular memory, the glioblastoma knew that Deirdre was having an emergency C-section, that the umbilical cord was wrapped around the baby's neck. Jared, and now the tumor, was sick with anxiety.

Jared, seated by Deirdre's head, hunched forward and held her hand, offering a series of bromides. *It's going to be okay* and *The doctor said this sort of thing happens all the time*. Jared tried to make each statement heartfelt, but the tumor knew that its host didn't believe his own words. It knew because the tumor didn't believe them either.

Deirdre was crying. More than anything, the glioblastoma wanted to stop her from crying.

And then, new crying.

Different crying.

Crying replete with all the mysteries of the universe.

At first, the crying was centered over Deirdre's body, but the sound quickly traveled farther away, and Jared—and now the tumor—had a moment of panic.

The anesthesiologist, who the tumor hadn't even noticed sitting next to Jared, must have sensed Jared's unease.

"It's okay," she said. "They're just cleaning her up and giving the Apgar test."

"Apgar test?" Jared asked.

"They give the baby a once-over to make sure everything is in the right place. It's routine."

A moment later, a nurse in mint-green scrubs, a mask covering all but her eyes, showed the baby to Deirdre, and then handed her to Jared.

"Congratulations," she said. The tumor could see that beneath the mask the nurse was beaming. It wondered how she could muster such sincere emotion for something she did every day.

"Well, hello, Jacquelyn," Jared began. "You are so small." The tumor could sense the muscles in Jared's arms and neck tense; it savored the fear that Jared felt, fear that he would somehow manage to drop this newborn human.

"I want to see," Deirdre said. Jared got down on one knee and held the baby in Deirdre's field of vision. Then Jared did something the tumor didn't understand at all: he began to sing.

The song was so soft at first that the glioblastoma was

certain no one else, not even Deirdre, could hear it. It was a private lullaby for his new daughter. But the tumor could hear it and thought it was beautiful: Willie Nelson and Ray Charles's "Seven Spanish Angels." The title popped into the tumor's head, or would have if the tumor had had a head, which it did not. But the experience was just the same.

"She stopped crying," Deirdre said, her eyes so filled with joy that the tumor thought its host's wife might burst.

Jared smiled, leaned forward, and kissed Deirdre on the forehead. Then he leaned forward and kissed Baby Jackie in the same spot. Where Deirdre's skin was rough and covered in sweat, Jackie's was smooth and smelled of hope and promise. The baby let out a small coo.

In that moment, the tumor knew, the bond formed between father and daughter was unbreakable. It paused to savor that feeling, letting the unbridled happiness envelop it.

Then the high-grade glioblastoma multiforme devoured the memory whole.

***

Jackie's younger sister, Megan, had a gaggle of her school friends over that Thursday afternoon and had made it clear that Jackie's presence was not welcome. Jackie was more than happy to oblige. The last thing she wanted was to watch reruns of *The Bachelor*, or some other moronic reality show, while Megan and her friends clucked at the television like a brood of hens.

After her father had failed to come home at the appointed hour, Jackie retreated to her room to do homework. She stepped around the pile of crumpled laundry in the middle of the floor, patted the oversize *Mean Girls* poster for luck (as she always did), and pushed aside the textbooks and mystery novels scattered on the desk to get to her schoolbag. She flopped on the bed facedown, her schoolwork resting on the pillow.

A pencil in one hand, a finger twirling her hair with the other, Jackie smiled when she came across her tenth-grade English vocabulary "word of the day":

fatuous (fach-oo-uhs) 1. Foolish or inane

That summed it up nicely: Megan and her gang of eighth-grade celebrities were certainly foolish, and almost entirely inane.

Not that it mattered. Jackie would have been holed up in her room even if Megan and her friends hadn't invaded the first floor of the house. Jackie's room was her sanctuary. It was the only place in the house where she felt completely at ease.

The only place *outside* the house where Jackie felt comfortable was on the Internet. To be connected to the world, she often thought, was a lot better than actually venturing into it. For one thing, she loved the anonymity. You could lurk on web pages or in chat rooms, and no one cared. No one called attention to you, and if they did, you were gone in a click. It was like she had her own pair of Ruby Red Slippers and could teleport from Oz to Kansas to Hollywood to Tokyo in the blink of an eye.

The only person she ever spoke to online was Max. Jackie wanted to talk to him now but knew he wouldn't be there so late in the afternoon.

Jackie heard the front door of the house open and close, heard the entire pack of Megan's friends offer a "Hi, Mr. Stone" in unison and then laugh for no reason whatsoever. That was one of the things that bothered Jackie most about Megan's friends: the laughter without obvious cause.

But that didn't matter; her father was home. Jackie was off the bed, out the door of her bedroom, and sitting on the top step in an instant.

Jackie heard her dad say something—she couldn't hear what—to her mom, and then saw him round a corner and head up the stairs. Her ear-to-ear grin faded when she noticed her father was mumbling to himself and seemed more than a little distracted. Bewildered, Jackie watched as he walked right past her.

"Dad?"

Jared stopped in his tracks and turned around. "Oh, hey, Jax, sorry. I didn't see you there."

This was not their normal routine. Far from it. For him to walk by, oblivious to Jackie's presence, was akin to the president of the United States absentmindedly walking past the podium at a press conference. It just didn't happen.

"Dad, are you okay?"

"Huh? Oh, yeah, just a lot of work today."

Jackie could tell it was a lie.

"I'm going to get cracking," he added before entering his office and closing the door behind him, leaving his daughter staring after him in confusion. He didn't invite Jackie in.

***

Jared wasn't ready to say anything to his family. He couldn't tell them what the doctor had told him; that his episodes of confusion and his headaches would get worse, and that in three months, maybe four, he would be dead.

As bad as he felt about what had just happened with Jackie on the steps, he couldn't worry about that now. He needed to think.

The doctor had told Jared he could keep the feelings of confusion at bay, at least a little, by reducing the number of "external stimuli" his brain was forced to parse. Jared surveyed his office looking for external stimuli. He turned off the computer, the monitor, and the printer to remove any background hum. He turned off the overhead lights and the desk lamp. Feeling silly standing in the dark, he lay on his back on the floor.

Jared was lying there for several minutes before he said "death" aloud.

He was startled by his own voice, so he said it again. "Death."

Trebuchet, the family dog, who had been napping in the office, looked up for a moment, and then, in a way typical of black Labs in their sunset years, put his head back down and heaved a heavy sigh of exhaustion.

Death is an anagram for hated, Jared thought. He realized the quiet room was, in fact, helping him think more clearly.

"I'm going to die," he said aloud. *That's an anagram for* goodie timing, he thought. *Strange.*

The more he thought about it, the less afraid Jared was of dying. He had bigger fish to fry. Like most state legislators,

Jared needed a second job just to survive. Unlike most state legislators, Jared was not a lawyer; he was a graphic designer. The limited income provided by his two jobs, even with Deirdre's salary, was going to leave his family in a bad financial state. He had life insurance, but it was only a $500,000 policy, purchased on a twenty-year term just after Jackie was born. The mortgage alone would eat through that amount of money like a worm through an apple, *or a tumor through a brain*, he thought. He stretched every corner of his mind looking for a way to fix the problem, but the harder he thought, the more his head hurt. He didn't know if it was the tumor or the situation that was causing him distress, but it didn't much matter.

"I need money," he said aloud. *Die enemy no*, he thought. Jared wondered where all these anagrams were coming from. Wordplay wasn't something he'd ever had an affinity for, or at least not that he could remember. Maybe it was a result of the tumor, maybe it was making parts of his brain more clever while it was killing him.

He thought of more anagrams as he "drifted off to sleep" (*edited effort flops*) among a sea of "words and letters" (*trestle and sword*).

***

Over the next few days, Jackie noticed her father keeping mostly to himself. She tried to talk to him, but each conversation was more baffling than the one that came before.

"Hi, Daddy," Jackie said one day.

"Huh? Oh, hi, Peanut. I'm good, thanks." And he walked away.

Not only was the length of the conversation uncharacteristic and troubling to Jackie, and not only had she not actually asked how he was, but "Peanut" was her dad's nickname for Megan.

"Dad," she asked on another occasion, "can you help me with my math homework?"

"Sure, Jax, but maybe later, after we watch *Jericho*."

That would have been normal if *Jericho* hadn't been canceled years earlier.

To be sure, not all their encounters were out of the ordinary—Jared still remembered to ask about school, and even managed to give the appearance of listening to Jackie's answers—but there were enough signs for Jackie to wonder if something wasn't right.

She tried asking her mom, but Deirdre was distracted in a different way, in the way that suburban moms are always distracted. They have too much to deal with to worry about anything that isn't a three-alarm fire. And while Jared's brain tumor was most certainly a three-alarm fire, it had yet to be phoned in.

Jackie figured her dad was just stressed about work or something and put it all out of her mind, unwittingly enjoying a last few days of blissful ignorance.

***

Jared kept the news of his brain tumor to himself for four days, spending most of that time lying on his office floor, trying to think. He came out just often enough to make sure his family wouldn't suspect anything was amiss, going right back in once he was convinced they were thrown off the scent of trouble.

Jared tried hard to think of a way out of what he saw as his financial predicament. There was college to pay for soon. And cars and spring break vacations and whatever else kids needed money for. But mostly he was just trying to think. When he was bored with lying in the dark, he would turn on his computer and click from one cancer website to the next. The grim news he read about high-grade glioblastoma multiformes made his head hurt, and he found himself linking instead to news and entertainment sites.

That was how he happened on a strange article from a few months earlier:

Divorced Man Auctions His Life Online

March 14—Worldwide News Now

When Jens Schmidt realized he needed a fresh start, he auctioned his material possessions online. From an unused tube of toothpaste to a 2002 Toyota Camry, Schmidt put his entire life up for sale to the highest bidder.

The thirty-four-year-old Dutchman, a successful attorney who likes to hang glide and ski, seemed to have it all. But then his wife of seven years, an Italian woman named Anna Mazzucchi, filed for divorce, and Schmidt decided it was time to move on.

"I just didn't want any reminder of my life before," he said.

Schmidt's listing includes his house, his hot tub, his clothes, his television, his cat, and his car. He also notes: "My friends are included in the package. If you win the auction, they promise they'll be nice to you."

Jared looked up from the article on his computer screen, and the world froze for a moment.

An idea started to percolate in Jared's brain. A crazy idea. An idea only a man with a high-grade glioblastoma multiforme could possibly have. He would auction his life—not his things, but his actual life—on eBay. The euthanasia lobby was pressuring him to take a position on a proposed expansion to Oregon's right-to-die laws; he would become their poster boy. Jared Stone, for sale to the highest bidder—do with him as you please.

PART ONE

Meet the Bidders

Tuesday, September 15

Hazel Huck liked games. She liked them a lot.

She liked games of skill (chess and crossword puzzles), she liked games of chance (Yahtzee and Risk), but the games she liked best of all were role-playing games. From the off-line worlds of Dungeons & Dragons to the online universes of EverQuest, Dark Age of Camelot, and World of Warcraft, Hazel liked nothing better than to lose herself in someone else's skin. To be a giant elf warrior with 150 hit points was to be invincible; she spent every free moment she was allowed living in those worlds. It was how she fought against the ebb and flow of her daily grind.

Hazel was a square peg in a round hole. From a well-to-do family in Huntsville, Alabama, she should have, at seventeen years old, been preparing for her debutante ball. Her classmates at the Florence Nightingale School for Young Women seemed obsessed with their coming-out parties. But not Hazel. To her, the notion of officially entering society seemed anachronistic at best and embarrassing at least. Her parents, attorneys with a practice focusing on maritime law, were disappointed but respected their daughter's independence.

Other than schoolwork and family obligations—chores, visits with aunts and uncles, mandatory attendance at church on Sundays—Hazel lived in a virtual world. Her closest friends were members of her Warcraft guild. And why not? They were interesting. She'd never met them, but she knew more about them than she did any of the girls at school. One was a middle-aged businessman from New York; another a high school girl from Bolivia; another claimed to be a published science fiction author, though he (she?) would never reveal the names of his (her?) books, stories, or publishers. It didn't matter. You could be who or what you wanted in that world, not only in the characters you played but in the stories you told.

In her first foray into online gaming, Hazel was nervous about her own story—or what she thought was her own lack of story—so she made one up. She claimed to be in graduate school studying English literature at a university "somewhere in Europe." Other people seemed impressed, and before she knew it, there was no escape from her lie. To make her online persona seem plausible, she conducted exhaustive research into the most important English lit doctoral programs in the UK and France. She was always ready with some new tidbit of information to support her tale. Over time, she came to believe that this character—whom she publicly called Tess—really did exist. It was too late to tell people she was a high school student—a freshman when she first spun this particular yarn and now a senior—from Alabama. She embraced the fiction and let the lie stand.

Hazel was casting a Circle of Healing spell when an instant message from a Warcraft friend popped on the screen. The IM said:

Can you believe this? ROTFL!

and included a link to Jared's eBay listing.

But Hazel wasn't laughing.

***

Ethan Overbee liked his executive assistant, Monique. He liked her a lot.

He liked the way she would anticipate his need to reschedule a meeting. He liked how she knew which of his underlings were allowed access to him, on which days, and how long they were to be left waiting in his anteroom. And he liked how she always seemed able to deflect calls from his girlfriend, or his mother, or his sister. But most of all, Ethan Overbee liked the things Monique would do for him when he closed the door to his Santa Monica office.

It never occurred to Ethan that he made Monique feel like a high-priced prostitute, and that her sense of self-worth was so permanently destroyed she couldn't even look in the mirror without wanting to throw up. It never occurred to him because it couldn't. Unlike Jared Stone, Ethan Overbee was a man completely and utterly devoid of empathy.

In later years a team of geneticists would discover a particular DNA marker (on chromosome 15q) that was responsible for human empathy. A subsequent study would determine that successful heads of state, corporate CEOs, and avid weekend cyclists were missing this particular marker in a much higher proportion than the rest of society. Ethan, it would turn out, could be counted among their ranks.

So it was no surprise then that Ethan was not only obsessed with his bicycle but, at thirty-two years old, was the youngest man to ever hold the position of deputy executive in charge of programming for the American Television Network. ATN was the crown jewel of a media empire—comprised of television, radio, and newspaper outlets around the world—that managed to offend just about everyone, but also managed to draw record numbers of viewers, readers, and listeners year after year. A *New York Times* op-ed referred to ATN as a "mirror reflecting the darkest parts of the American soul." If Ethan had bothered to think about it (he didn't), his pragmatic side might have agreed.

What he lacked in empathy Ethan made up for in appreciation, lavishing luxurious gifts on those people who treated him well. He was feeling especially appreciative of Monique—who was, unbeknownst to Ethan, still in the bathroom crying—as he browsed eBay listings in search of the perfect gift.

He knew that Monique "simply adored" the actor Heath Ledger. Normally, he would just make a few phone calls and Ledger would appear in his office ready to take Monique out to lunch. But the guy had overdosed on drugs, so Ethan was reduced to actual shopping. *Talent*, he thought. *They're all the same.*

There were nearly two thousand items listed on eBay, but none of them seemed right. Ethan felt that a signed photo or a piece of a movie costume that Ledger had worn was too mundane. A thought occurred to him: perhaps there was some piece of memorabilia connected to Ledger's death. He wondered if that was too morbid but couldn't see how it would be.

The press said Ledger's death was an accident, but Ethan didn't believe it; he searched for "Ledger suicide." As he was perusing the few macabre items that the search results returned, he saw a "People who viewed this item also viewed" link. One of them had the curious tagline, "Human Life for Sale." He clicked it.

And that was how Ethan Overbee came to see Jared's listing.

**

Sister Benedict Joan liked the Internet. She liked it a lot.

She liked the way it helped her spread the Word of God through her blog, christscadets.blogspot.com. She liked how it allowed her to stay connected with the other warriors in Christ's army from around the world. And, most of all, she liked how the Internet allowed her to see and fight against the never-ending stream of smut, irreverence, and blasphemy that was determined to destroy decent society. A less optimistic woman would have been overwhelmed by the pornography and violence that seemed to fuel the pulse of the World Wide Web. Not Sister Benedict; it gave her purpose.

As prioress of the Sisters of the Perpetual Adoration, she was a leader in her community, and she felt a personal responsibility to protect the nuns and novices under her care. This meant much more than providing food and shelter; it meant doing everything in her power, small though that was, to help fashion a world informed and infused by the teachings and love of Jesus Christ. You could say that the only thing Sister Benedict Joan liked more than the Internet was Christ himself.

The Sister was a throwback. Since Vatican II, most nuns had kept their given names, becoming Sister Ella, or Sister Casey, or Sister Jordyn. To Angela Marie Taggart, keeping her own name seemed anathema to true Catholicism. The nuns she idolized as a little girl—with their piety, their obedience, their almost martial beauty—had taken the names of male saints, a tradition she felt bound, at least in part, to uphold. She saw her name as both a stern and a reassuring presence for the young women of the convent, not to mention the students at Annunciation Catholic School, where she taught third grade. You just didn't question someone named Sister Benedict.

Her earliest childhood memory was of a Catholic Mass, and she knew from that moment, as a four-year-old, she would devote herself to Christ. What she didn't understand then, and still didn't understand now, was why she was the only one. Week after week parishioners would line the pews of St. Mary's Church and sit reverently beneath the high stained-glass windows, standing, sitting, and kneeling when told, and opening their wallets and hearts when asked. They would smile with visceral sincerity as they said, "Peace be with you; and also with you," to one another. If they all believed in the Lord and in his teachings, that what was in the Bible was true, that it was God, the King of Kings, the Creator of All Creation, the Master of their collective fate they were there to celebrate, how is it that they could only be bothered to worship once a week? Shouldn't this be a full-time job?

This is what Sister Benedict Joan was thinking about as she powered up her laptop. Like always, she had no answer. She shook her head and sipped her Earl Grey tea.

The Sister liked to watch the computer go through its electronic ablutions: loading Windows, loading the antivirus software, checking for updates, and checking e-mail. She imagined it was guided by the hand of God, though she knew it was the minds of the men who created such technological wonders, and not the wonders themselves, that were the real evidence of divine grace.

She opened her browser and checked her blog. She never liked the name Christ's Cadets, but all the good names—Christ's Warriors, Christ's Knights, and Christ's Soldiers—were already taken. There was one new comment, which was a bit unusual. While Sister Benedict felt certain that people read her blog, they rarely left comments. When they did, they usually took the form of "Get a life, you f***ing joke," only the "uck" wasn't blocked out.

This new post, like the few others, was anonymous, and it simply said, "This must not be allowed to happen." Beneath that plea was a link to Jared Stone's eBay listing.

***

Sherman Kingsborough liked life. He liked it a lot.

At twenty-three years old, Sherman was already stinking rich. He was the happy recipient of a trust fund bequeathed to him by a father who'd made millions war profiteering during Vietnam, and who had died on Sherman's eighteenth birthday.

Sherman's mother had returned to her native Korea when he was a little boy (his father had more or less dispatched her like she was an unwanted employee), and he never had contact with her again. Sherman was, incorrectly, led to believe that his mother had abandoned him. With no siblings and no parents, and having grown up in a world of excess and extravagance, Sherman's moral compass was left to drift unchecked. It spun round and round, never quite finding north.

It wasn't surprising, then, that Sherman used his newfound millions to indulge every whim and fetish imaginable. From sexual encounters too deviant to name or number to keeping the most exotic endangered animals as pets, only to eat them for dinner, Sherman had denied himself nothing. If his brain thought it, he did it.

It wasn't all depravity and debauchery, though. Each time Sherman found himself plumbing the depths of his darkest impulses, he would follow it with a noble gesture. When he fired his father's entire household staff because of a spot on a wine-glass, Sherman spent two months working at an ashram in India. A week after he told a fifteen-year-old high school girl he loved her just to get her into bed, ditching her in a seedy hotel room the next morning, he flew to the Bering Strait to clean oil-soaked gulls that had been caught in the wake of a tanker spill. And after evicting a poor family from one of his father's many real estate investments—a dilapidated apartment building in Queens, New York—Sherman climbed to the top of Mount Everest as part of an expedition that was raising money for Habitat for Humanity. Each gallant act a counterbalance to atone for one of his sins.

It was an unbreakable cycle that seemed to be (like Sherman actually was) on methamphetamines. He never stopped to catch his breath, never took stock of who he had become; he was afraid of what he might find.

After six years of living such a high-octane life, Sherman Kingsborough was bored out of his freaking mind. For the man who had everything, or at least had access to anything, there seemed to be nothing left.

But Sherman had felt this way before. After he summited Everest, he was sure he had peaked, a pun he repeated to himself through the entire descent, but found traveling with opium smugglers in Pakistan to be a whole new high (the latter pun unintended). It seemed that whenever he was out of new things to try, a previously unknown path presented itself. It's better to be lucky, he liked to say, than good. It was the guiding principle of Sherman Kingsborough's life.

It was also the first thought that came to his mind when he saw Jared Stone's eBay listing.

***

Jackie was lying on her bed staring at her new iPhone, scrolling through Neil Gaiman's Twitter feed. In the few weeks she had owned the phone—she and Megan had each received phones as gifts for the new school year—it had become an extra appendage for Jackie, never more than a few feet away, almost always in her hand. She was already plugged into every social network she could find—Twitter, Facebook, Instagram—but almost never participated. She was a lurker, a voyeur.

That's just how she was wired. Jackie was not the kind of student who raised her hand in class, she was (usually) not the kind of daughter who questioned her parents, and she was not the kind of Internet user to voice her opinion. Jackie was perfectly satisfied to troll without ever reeling in the net, though she wondered if her failure to participate made her a troll of a different kind. The only person with whom she interacted online was Max, and he lived in Saint Petersburg, Russia.

She and Max were participating in a social media exchange program through their respective schools. Jackie didn't want a friend in another country—she had enough trouble with friends in the good ol' U. S. of A.—but the teacher made it a required assignment. When she found out that her randomly assigned partner was a boy, she had a bit of a meltdown.

But Max turned out to be nice. He was fascinated by American culture and would pepper Jackie with questions when they were online together, which was usually during her morning free period in the computer lab. He was most interested in American movies and seemed obsessed with American directors like Martin Scorsese, Cameron Crowe, and Steven Spielberg.

So far they hadn't talked about anything really serious, mostly just music and movies and what kids wore to school. Max had already dated three different girls, which made Jackie embarrassed about her own nonexistent love life, but luckily, Max never asked. He also played the guitar, which she thought was pretty cool.

Maybe it's because she knew they would never meet, but somehow talking to Max felt safe. Jackie found herself stepping out of her comfort zone with him, and she liked it. Plus, she couldn't help thinking that, maybe, he had a little crush on her.

She was just starting to get lost in a daydream about Max when the doorbell rang, pulling her back to the moment. Jackie being Jackie figured someone else would answer it.

***

Jared Stone read his listing for the fourth time. He couldn't shake the feeling that he'd forgotten something:

HUMAN LIFE FOR SALE

Forty-five-year-old man with four months to live is
selling his life to the highest bidder. You may do with
him as you please—slavery, murder, torture, or just
pleasant conversation. A human life, yours to control,
yours to own. Buyers must live in a state or country
with a law allowing assisted suicides, and the buyer
bears the cost of transportation and tax. There is a
reserve for this auction.

If there was something missing, he couldn't put his finger on
it. He'd worked on the listing in a moment of true lucidity, so
maybe the feeling tugging at the corner of his consciousness
was just the tumor. But still . . .

The listing had been live for only five hours, and already
there were seven bids. These early bids were from a collection
of society's fringe actors. Their purchase histories showed a
fondness for Nazi artifacts, medieval weaponry, and Hello Kitty
collectibles. The highest bid from this group was $900, so far
from the reserve of $1,000,000 that Jared had to laugh.

The doorbell rang, and he heard his daughter Megan scream,
"I'll get it!" as she thumped down the stairs, taking the steps
two at a time as she always did.

Megan was a strong, self-sufficient girl, and he had no
worries about her ability to accept, understand, and process his
death. It would be traumatic, no doubt, but she would perse-
vere. She was one of those kids who moved through life with a
natural ease.

His older daughter, Jackie, was a different story.

Jackie allowed herself to exist in the shadow of her younger sister, never stepping into the light, never establishing who she was. She was small and tender, and Jared loved her more than life itself. It was worry about Jackie more than anything that propelled him to roll the dice with the eBay listing.

Jared heard a group of muffled voices at the front door, followed by "Mom! Dad!" from Megan. He pushed himself back from his computer and went to find out what was going on.

"Um, honey," his wife, Deirdre, was saying, having reached the door a few seconds before he did, "is there something you want to tell me?"

Right, Jared thought on seeing the half-dozen camera crews and twice that number of reporters, *now I know what I forgot.*

***

Just as Jared was being besieged by the media at his front door, the glioblastoma was feasting on a memory from Jared's second Christmas, when he, Jared, was one and a half years old. The memory was hidden so well that the tumor had to drill down through a rarely used sector of Jared's brain to find it. The drilling was such a shock to Jared's system that it caused the tumor's host to stumble forward and fall into the arms of his wife.

The tumor was oblivious to what was going on in the world outside Jared's brain. It was too enamored with the "snow boat"—the name with which Baby Jared referred to his first sled—to pay attention to anything else.

Unmarked, shiny, and red, like a mid-life crisis convertible, the sled was a thing of beauty. Baby Jared did his Baby Jared dance, basically running in place and laughing, as he held the sled's yellow string. He didn't know that it was meant to be used in the snow, but it didn't matter. It was, according to his scale of the world, huge, and it was his.

The feeling was pure unadulterated joy. The tumor was so happy it thought it would cry, if it had eyes, tear ducts, or tears, but it was just the same. The experience was as tender as if it were happening in the present, in the physical world.

For her part, Deirdre caught Jared and helped him to the floor. He collected his thoughts, such as they were, pushed himself up, managed to stand without falling over, and turned back to the throng at his front door.

The tumor didn't even notice.

***

"There's something wrong with Dad." Megan burst into the room, stopping in the doorway, breathing hard. Jackie kept her eyes glued to her phone.

Megan cleared her throat. "Did you hear me?"

Jackie had heard Megan but just figured that her little sister was trying to find a new and sinister way to torture her. For reasons Jackie never understood, it had become a favorite pastime of Megan's. She'd find the one thing that mattered most to Jackie and use it as a weapon against her.

Once, years earlier, Megan had asked: "Is there a boy in your class named Kevin something or other?" She was in fourth grade, Jackie in sixth; and the question made Jackie's heart stop.

Kevin Memmott sat in front of Jackie. He was an ordinary boy with an easy way about him, and he was Jackie's first real crush. Each morning when he entered the class and said hello to her, Jackie's palms got sweaty and her stomach felt like it was shrinking. She would put her head down and mutter hello from beneath her bangs. He would shrug and take his seat, and they wouldn't talk again during the day. To Kevin, it was a forgettable routine. For Jackie, it was *their* routine.

"There is a boy named Kevin," she told Megan. "Why?"

"Oh, no reason, just that I heard him talking to another boy . . . about you." Even at nine years old, Megan was as good at baiting her sister as a professional fisherman was at tying a fly on the end of his line.

"What were they saying?" Jackie asked, looking at her feet and twirling her finger through her hair, trying but failing to pretend like she really didn't care.

"Well, I heard them saying . . ." Megan paused, and even though they were in the privacy of Jackie's bedroom, she lowered her voice, like she was telling a secret and didn't want anyone else to hear. "I heard them saying that he likes you!"

Every person who has ever had a crush believes, in their heart of hearts, that the object of their affection feels the same way, even though there has never been any outward sign of it. Jackie spent so much time imagining that she and Kevin were girlfriend and boyfriend that Megan's lie was just too easy to believe.

Megan could see that she had the hook in her sister's mouth, and all she had to do was reel her in.

"He was talking to some other boy in your class, Scott something or other." *Scott Yee,* Jackie thought, *Kevin Memmott's best friend.* "He said he really likes you, and wants to ask you out, but just wished you would dress nicer."

The next day, Jackie, who never wore anything other than blue jeans and loose-fitting sweaters, donned the same dress she had worn to church on Easter Sunday just a few weeks before. It was faded pink, hung down just above her knees, and had a big bow in the back. Her parents were so happy to see Jackie come out from under her shell that they couldn't help but ooh and aah over her at the breakfast table.

When she got to school, Jackie waited out front for Kevin Memmott, just standing there in her pink dress, everyone doing a double take as they passed by. When Kevin finally arrived, Jackie lit up like a high-powered flashlight.

She mustered the courage to say, "Hi, Kevin," as he and Scott Yee approached.

"Huh? Oh, hi," he said, not even noticing her.

An instant later, another boy, Jason Sanderson, with his thick glasses, uncombed hair, and a prematurely pockmarked face, walked up. "Boy, oh boy, Jackie, you look pretty today!"

Jackie liked Jason well enough. He was a nice boy, though utterly unaware of his surroundings, as if part of his brain was always somewhere else. The frumpy appearance combined with the absentminded-professor demeanor made him a favorite target of the other children. It made Jackie angry that they picked on Jason; once she even stepped outside her comfort zone and came to his defense. But on this day, the day of the Easter dress, Jason Sanderson was the last boy on Earth she wanted to see.

Then, from somewhere behind her, Jackie heard giggles and snorts; both she and Jason turned around. Megan and her friends were standing nearby, doubled over in laughter. Jackie knew right away that, though they usually brayed like hyenas for no reason at all, this time their laughter had purpose.

She turned and ran all the way home, staying in bed for two days pretending she was sick but mostly just crying under the covers, partly from embarrassment and partly because she couldn't understand how her sister could be so mean.

So when Megan came into her room now and said, "There's something wrong with Dad," Jackie's guard was already up.

"Uh-huh," she answered.

"Look outside. We're on TV."

Jackie was skeptical, but there was something different in her sister's voice. She went to the window.

A throng of reporters was dissipating on her front lawn. Some were packing up sound equipment, some were capturing a last shot of Jackie's house for network news B-roll, and some were walking to their cars. It was like a flash mob had met, played their prank, and were now heading home.

Jackie started for her door to go downstairs, but Megan caught her arm.

"Jax," she said, her voice catching, "don't."

Then the two sisters sat on the bed together, something they hadn't done in years, and Megan told Jackie everything she'd heard.

"Wait. Daddy's dying?" Jackie asked when Megan finished.

Megan nodded and burst into tears. She flung herself into Jackie's arms, sobbing into her big sister's chest. Jackie was too stunned to react right away. But crying is like yawning; once one person starts, the other person can't help but join in.

***

The defining emotional moment of Hazel Huck's life happened when she was seven years old. Her dog, Boots, was drinking out of his bowl, lapping mouthful after mouthful of water while Hazel waited patiently behind him. It was a well-rehearsed script they acted out with glee each morning.

Boots would lick Hazel's hands and face until she woke up and then lead her to the door. She'd let him out, watch him do his business, let him back in, and feed him. Hazel would then stand exactly nine steps behind him (nine was her lucky number) and watch him eat. Each morning Boots would assault his kibble as if it were his first meal in weeks, making sure he chomped every last piece, and then drink half his bowl of water. When he was done, he would turn around, see Hazel, wag his tail, and nuzzle his wet face into her belly.

On this one morning, after he was done with his water, Boots turned around, wagged his tail, took a step toward Hazel, and fell over. Hazel screamed.

The vet, a tall thin man with a tall thin nose, a wide thin mustache, and a high thin voice, said, "Brain tumor." Hazel, a precocious seven, was pretty sure she knew what that meant. A lump was growing on Boots's brain.

"Can you scoop it out?" she asked.

Her mother burst into tears when she saw the hopeful look on Hazel's face. The vet got down on one knee so he could look Hazel in the eye. "I'm sorry, precious, I don't think we can."

The day they buried Boots in the backyard, Hazel did all she could to fight back the tears. She didn't think Boots would want her to cry. When the last shovelful of dirt was thrown on his grave, Hazel let go, and it all came out. She ran into her house, flung herself on her bed, and didn't come out of her room again that day.

When she saw Jared Stone on the news ten years later, with his wife and dog, talking about his brain tumor, the memory of Boots came flooding back. She went straight to her computer and sent a message to her fellow Warcraft guild members with the subject: "Alert! Alert! We have to help Jared Stone!"

***

The evening Ethan Overbee saw the news clip of Jared, any thought of his assistant, Monique, went right out of his head. His first thought was, *Holy shit.* This was followed by his second thought, *Holy FUCKING shit!* These two thoughts were followed by a complex series of thoughts that formed the basis of a new idea in Ethan's head. He needed to act fast.

Ethan had only been at the studio for three years, but already he felt he was languishing in the shadow of the executive in charge of programming, Thaddeus St. Claire. Thad had taken Ethan under his wing and was grooming him for the top job a decade or so down the road. But young people, especially young, rich people, and especially young, rich people missing a certain marker on chromosome 15q, don't wait years—let alone decades—for things to go their way. Ethan saw an opening now and was going to take it.

"Monique," he barked into his speakerphone. "I need to find someone who just posted something on eBay. It's urgent. Do we have any contacts there?"

"I'll check, Ethan," she answered, betraying no hint of the revulsion she felt in simply hearing his voice. "Can I ask what this is in reference to?"

"I've just discovered the reality TV series of the century."

***

Sister Benedict Joan had her doubts about the veracity of the eBay listing. Certainly no one could be foolish or Godless enough to sell himself into oblivion. But that night she saw the man on the late news.

She was surprised at how young, nice-looking, and reasonable he seemed to be. He stood nearly six feet tall and had hair the color of apple pie, a pleasantly wide mouth, and caramel eyes. He even professed to have faith in God.

He did seem a bit confused during the interview, and when asked why, he claimed it was the result of the tumor growing in his head.

Of course, the Sister was not pleased to hear Mr. Stone's views on euthanasia.

"Until this happened, I honestly didn't know which way I would vote," he told the reporter, referring to the bill before the Oregon legislature. "I only hope I live long enough to cast a yea vote."

An evil thought flashed through the Sister's mind: she felt satisfaction that God would strike Mr. Stone down before he could use his legislative power to wrap man's greatest sin in the cloak of governmental protection. Of course, the Sister's brain didn't seem to process the paradox of its own thought, that Jared was being swayed to vote in favor of euthanasia by the very tumor the Sister believed to be an instrument of God. In any case, the Sister knew enough to recognize a wicked thought for what it was; she crossed herself three times and turned her attention back to the TV.

What caught the Sister's attention most was that Mr. Stone lived in her parish. She didn't know if he was a Catholic, but one needn't start out a Catholic to die a Catholic martyr. And if Sister Benedict had anything to say about it, Mr. Stone wouldn't be dying for a very, very long time.

She reached for the phone to call the monsignor.

***

When Sherman Kingsborough first saw Jared Stone's listing, he knew he had to bid, but he didn't quite know why. When he saw Jared on the news, a face now given to what had merely been a notion, his interest bloomed into an obsession. His brain went through a kind of mental gymnastics as it considered what to do with Jared:

Maybe I could perform brain surgery, he thought. *I can be the first man to execute a full-brain transplant, maybe replace his sick brain with a healthy monkey's brain. That would be funny.* But even Sherman realized he would need so much training that he wouldn't have time to succeed. He filed the idea away for future reference.

Maybe he could turn the man into a suicide bomber. But Sherman didn't have anything he wanted to bomb, and that seemed kind of pointless.

Maybe, he thought, *I could just kill him.*

Sherman let that roll around his mind for a bit. *Yes, kill him. What would that be like? Would I feel powerful, like a god? Would I feel sad?* Not knowing what he would feel like was all the impetus Sherman Kingsborough needed. This was something new, and that made it desirable.

For the record, Sherman's brain didn't have any damage to the anterior prefrontal cortex, nor did he have an excess of monoamine oxidase-A—two of the more likely indicators of violent behavior or lack of a conscience. No, Sherman was just bored to tears and desperate for a new experience.

He began to contemplate how best to murder someone, and none of the options felt quite right. Guns weren't sporting, lethal injections were boring, and while drowning had a certain appeal, it seemed as if it would be over too quickly. *Maybe*, Sherman thought, *bidding on this guy's life isn't really worth the trouble.*

He spent time surfing the Web for ideas and was about to give up when he came across a reference to a 1932 film called *The Most Dangerous Game*: a *shipwrecked man washes ashore on a remote island owned by a deranged Russian who plays a game hunting humans.*

"Hunting humans," he said aloud after reading it. "Hunting humans." Sherman's brain conveniently ignored the part about the "deranged" Russian, seeing only what it wanted to see.

He knew that the man who had posted the eBay listing had a brain tumor—it was a central point of the news story—but he didn't really know what that meant. What if, by the time he purchased his prey, the guy was comatose? No, he needed a victim who would run, hide, and fight back.

As he had learned from his father, when you need a piece of information, go to the source. Sherman composed a note to Jared using eBay's contact form, sent it off, sat back, and waited.

***

Jared was still reeling from his encounter with the media. They'd descended on his house like the Portland rain. The lights, cameras, and blitzkrieg of reporters felt like a vise grip on his right temple. Or was it the tumor making his head hurt? Or did the lights and cameras and reporters make the tumor hurt, which made his head hurt? Whatever the case, his head was throbbing, again, and his focus was all but gone.

When he finally closed the front door, he hardly noticed Deirdre and Megan standing there, both crying. He half crawled, half stumbled up the stairs, Trebuchet trailing at his heel, and practically fell to the floor in his office lair, nudging the door shut with his foot.

The part of his mind that was aware of the outside world expected Deirdre to follow him, but she didn't. Jared and Trebuchet were alone in the dark. He could hear the dog panting, could feel his breath on his arm. This, more than anything, helped to center Jared. He reached in the direction of the dog's warm breath, felt for his ear, and gently scratched just behind it, Trey's favorite thing in the world, or at least Jared thought it was.

Butch tree, Jared thought, making an anagram out of his dog's name.

Trebuchet licked his lips and put his head down with one big sigh, his panting calmed to an even measure, a metronome of the living. The two of them, Jared and his faithful companion, drifted off to sleep at almost exactly the same time.

8d 11h 39m

Jackie woke up next to Megan, the two of them snuggled together on Jackie's twin bed, Megan snoring gently.

Everything came flooding back to Jackie: Megan's report of what her father had told the newspeople at the door; how her father had collapsed; the fact that her father was dying of a brain tumor. She understood precious little of what was happening and wanted more than anything to talk to her dad, but she couldn't.

For her entire life, Jared had been Jackie's anchor. No matter how bad things got for Jackie, her dad was there to make it better, even if only a little. But now, the bad thing *was* her father. The realization was paralyzing.

Jackie didn't know what else to do, so she sought solace in the one place she felt safe: the vast, anonymous ocean of the Internet. The clock on her computer said it was nine p.m., much earlier than she thought.

First she looked for her father's eBay listing. Jackie didn't believe this part of Megan's story; it just couldn't be true. Her father would never do anything like that. How could he?

But there it was. "Human Life for Sale."

She read it once and started to well up. She quickly clicked back to Google, which helped to bring her to a state of equilibrium. Little did Jackie know that each click on the World Wide Web released a microscopic hit of dopamine, anesthetizing her brain and dulling her senses. It was as habit forming as smoking.

Next she needed to sort out the part of Megan's story that made the least sense. *What the heck is "Youth in Asia"?* Jackie wondered. She'd made her sister repeat the phrase three times. Jackie typed it into Google.

The first result was for a 1980s British band that Wikipedia called "anarcho punk," whatever that was. They had only one record, and that was something called "a cassette album," whatever *that* was.

The second result made a lot more sense. It was also a Wikipedia entry, and it was for euthanasia, which was apparently pronounced like "youth in Asia." Jackie had heard of euthanasia. She knew it had something to do with a person deciding to end her own life, usually because she was really sick. The article said it was also sometimes called physician-assisted suicide.

The main thrust of the argument in favor of euthanasia, Jackie read, seemed to be that people had the right to make up their own minds about when they lived and died. Jackie had never given it any thought before, and her immediate reaction was that any kind of suicide was wrong. They had taught her at Sunday school that life was precious; it was God's greatest gift. Suicide, she'd learned, was a sin.

But her gut reaction was different. In her heart, Jackie believed that people should be able to make up their own minds about anything they wanted, as long as it didn't hurt anyone else. That should include when they lived and died, shouldn't it?

But the most interesting part of the Wiki entry was the role Oregon, her home state, played in the history of euthanasia. She clicked a link for something called the Death with Dignity Act. She was surprised, and maybe a little proud, to learn that Oregon was the first US state to protect doctors who helped terminal patients end their lives. She was even more surprised to learn that the state legislature, her father's legislature, was considering a major expansion to the law right now that would also protect family and friends who played a role in helping the terminally ill end their suffering. That meant that her father, who was dying of a brain tumor, was also voting to make it legal to die a little sooner. Unbelievable.

Jackie's head started to swim; it was all too much for her to process. She was already fifteen years old and had stellar grades, but her emotional experience did nothing to prepare her for this.

Jackie's eyes nearly popped out of their sockets when she saw that her father's quote to the reporters—from just a few hours earlier on her front stoop—was already referenced in the article. The speed at which information traveled was mind-boggling to Jackie.

Retreating to the safety of Facebook, Jackie looked for Max, but he wasn't online. It was twelve hours later in Saint Petersburg, so she didn't really expect to see him.

Jackie needed to tell someone about what was happening with her father, and Max seemed like the safest bet. Maybe it was because he was so far away, almost like he wasn't real, like he couldn't hurt her. Whatever the reason, she decided to send him a message:

> **Jackie**
> I know it's the wrong time for you to be online, but I just wanted to say hi. So, hi. Okay, really, there's more than that. Maybe I'll look for you tomorrow.

She read her note over and smiled at the thought of how her father would send her Facebook messages addressed to "Dear Jackie," with a closing of "Love, Dad," never really understanding that you didn't need to identify yourself in a world where your identity traveled with you.

Thoughts of her dad brought Jackie back to Earth. She tried to put those thoughts aside until she could figure out how to process them. She went back to mindlessly scrolling through her news feed, letting the dopamine wash over her frontal lobe. After a while, she crawled back into bed with Megan and drifted off into an uncomfortable sleep.

***

Jared opened his eyes, but the room was trapped in darkness. There wasn't even light seeping in from under the door. He knew he'd been having a dream, but he couldn't remember any of the details. (The glioblastoma had eaten it.)

The total absence of light made Jared realize that he'd slept for hours. *Our shelf sport,* he thought, making another anagram. At least he seemed to have his faculties.

He knew his first order of business was to find his wife and daughters, explain everything, and try to set things right. But he wasn't quite ready. He reached for Trebuchet and felt the fur on the dog's abdomen, once black, now mostly gray, rising and lowering in time with his own rhythmic snoring. Trey grunted, acknowledging his master without fully waking up.

Pushing himself up on his elbows, Jared made it to his desk and brought his computer back to life. *Time to see if there are any new bids*, he thought.

There were none. But he did have a new message in his eBay in-box.

Dear Sir—I'm interested in placing a bid on your auction titled "Human Life for Sale." I'm a serious bidder with sufficient resources to meet your reserve and more. My question is this: Are you physically and mentally fit? Are you able to run, jump, crawl, climb, and react to new circumstances? Have you ever used a gun, knife, or bow and arrow? I'm interested to know what kind of life I'm bidding on. Thanks in advance for your answer, and sorry about your predicament. I hope I can help. You can respond to me via eBay, or you can send an e-mail to SKingsborough92@gmail.com.

Jared had to read the note five times before he was convinced he had read it correctly. "Ever used a gun, knife, or bow and arrow?" he asked the still-sleeping dog. "What the heck am I getting myself into here?"

Frightened, he lay back down and closed his eyes.

***

Ethan Overbee was the first to place a real bid.

Technically, he didn't have the authority to spend $100,000 of the studio's money, but in the world of television networks, a hundred grand was how much meeting planners spent, not programming executives. No one would question it. No one except Thad St. Claire, and that was exactly the point. In Ethan's mind, this was the beginning of the end for his mentor.

Thaddeus St. Claire was an old-school network executive who had clawed his way to the top. His first job for ATN had been forty years earlier, in the ad traffic department. He worked long and thankless hours to make sure advertisements for Tide and All laundry detergent didn't run in the same commercial break. From ad traffic, he moved to a junior position in network operations, to a junior position in programming, to a senior position in programming, to the deputy executive in charge of programming.

The executive in charge at that time was a septuagenarian with a penchant for Soupy Sales–variety hour specials and gin and tonics. Thad did the network and the world a favor when he ended the career of his predecessor. It's true he did it by exposing his boss's weaknesses to the network president and board of directors, but it was long overdue.

The move gave Thad, somewhat unfairly, a reputation for being ruthless. (Thad's assault on the character and behavior of his boss was more an act of mercy than of aggression.) But reputations become reality, and Thad's reputation was all the justification Ethan needed; ascension by assassination, he convinced himself, was morally acceptable.

Never mind that Ethan had been out of Wharton for only three years. And never mind that Thad had handpicked, trained, and groomed Ethan for the top job if Ethan would only wait.

Not wanting to leave it to Monique to enter the bid—Ethan wasn't about to trust something that would change his career to a glorified receptionist—he entered it himself. He saw right away that he hadn't met the reserve.

He still hadn't made contact with the seller, some guy named Jared Stone up in Portland. Monique had tracked down his home number and address but had been unable to reach him. Ethan, who was working long past dark and was alone in the office, decided to try for himself.

Answering machine.

He put the phone down and considered his options. As he did, a new idea started to take root.

***

Sister Benedict had never met a Cardinal before, which was funny, as she had already met two Popes. Of course, those "meetings" were actually mass rallies where she was lucky enough to have been granted a spot on the rope line so that she might have a chance to kiss the Pontiff's ring. At the time, she thought of it as the Rope-a-Pope Line, and then immediately crossed herself for blaspheming. Today's meeting with Cardinal Trippe was a face-to-face, sit-down affair, which, of course, began with the Sister on her knees.

It hadn't been easy for the Sister to gain an audience with the Cardinal. The officious priest who served as a buffer between Cardinal Trippe and the world was more than a little skeptical when the Sister first called to request the Church save Jared Stone's life. The priest had dismissed her with grace and not a little condescension, the way a parent dismisses a child angling to stay up past his bedtime. The priest denied her request. But Sister Benedict would not be deterred.

She and the Sisters of the Perpetual Adoration spent most weekends in service to the community. On one such weekend, they had painted the interior of the rectory of a nearby parish. The presiding bishop was so appreciative that he kept repeating, "If there's ever anything I can do for you, Sister, just ask."

She called in the favor, and the audience with Cardinal Trippe was granted.

Sister Benedict Joan's mind was racing as she kissed the Cardinal's ring. She'd spent hours finding out everything she could about the man and was going over her mental notes, steeling herself to the mission at hand.

Cardinal Matthew John Trippe, whose name was pronounced "Trippy," was the archbishop of the metropolitan province of Portland, which included dioceses in four northwestern states, and he was everything Sister Benedict was not. He was young and charismatic, and, far worse, he eschewed tradition, believing the Church should start down a path of change. He embraced Portland's LGBT community, welcoming them to the flock; he wanted to see women take more leadership roles during mass; he believed in climate change and the need for conservation; and while Sister Benedict knew the Church had a true and deep-seated responsibility to care for those in need—as she herself had often done—this man actually seemed to believe that wealthy people should be *compelled* to share their hard-earned gains with the indigent. To the Sister, this was anathema to the entire idea of charity; it was socialism.

As she knelt before the Cardinal and thought about these things, Sister Benedict almost shivered with disgust. Cardinal Trippe was like one of those awful Protestant priests who play guitar from the altar and sing "Kumbaya." She secretly thought of him as Cardinal Hippie.

From her research, she could see only two things she and the Cardinal had in common: their innate sense of piety and a shared belief in the sanctity of life. At least Trippe, liberal fool that he seemed to be, still opposed abortion. It was this last fact on which the Sister was counting.

Sister Benedict stayed on one knee until the Cardinal bade her "get up, Sister, get up. Have a seat."

They were meeting in the office of the Portland diocese, where the Cardinal performed mass each Sunday when he wasn't traveling. It was a modest, plainly decorated space. The only sign of opulence was a solid gold crucifix on the wall behind the Cardinal's desk.

"Tell me, Sister, what urgent matter brings you to this good office today?" Sister Benedict had to admit that the man did exude a kind of charm. His teeth were unnaturally bright, making her wonder if he'd had them whitened. *The sin of vanity*, she thought to herself. The truth was that the Cardinal came from a long line of people with very strong tooth enamel and he had been a near fanatic about oral hygiene from the earliest age.

"Life itself, Father," she answered. Trippe cocked an eyebrow and waited for her to continue. "The man on the news, the one with the brain tumor. The one who has put his life up for sale on the Internet. He's here, in Portland! And unlike that unpleasant incident with that Schiavo woman in Florida, where the family intervened, it appears that the only issue here is money."

"And tell me, Sister," the Cardinal asked, "how do you propose we intervene?"

"Simple, Your Grace. We buy him."

"Come again?"

"We bid on his eBay auction, and we buy him. And once he's ours, we use all means at our disposal to keep him alive."

"Sister, I'm fairly certain the Holy See would not look kindly on nuns buying and selling human lives with church money. That went out with the Inquisition." His smile suggested that she would see the wisdom of his words and that this meeting would end. Cardinal Trippe, a good and decent man, was not prepared for the depth of Sister Benedict's resolve or for her growing obsession with Jared Stone.

"Not buying and selling, Your Eminence. Buying and cherishing. There are any number of Catholic hospitals in the Northwest. Surely a man of your influence could persuade one to take this man as a patient."

"I see," Cardinal Trippe said, sounding as if he did not see. "And how does keeping this one man alive benefit our Church?"

"Because, Your Grace, all human life is precious. We honor the Lord with every soul we save in this world and prepare for the next."

The Cardinal nodded as he fished an almond out of a small bowl on his desk and chewed it slowly, carefully. Sister Benedict sensed that she had piqued his interest and decided to go for broke.

"And because, Your Eminence, saving this man, keeping him alive, will be a news story to end all news stories. The press will camp out in this man's hospital room for months, perhaps even years. All the world will look to our province, to your province, as a shining example of true divinity." The Sister knew it was a bit of a Hail Mary, a term she had once thought blasphemous but now understood. She hoped that she was interpreting the whiteness of the Cardinal's teeth correctly, and that an appeal to his vanity would be the deciding factor.

"Tell me, Sister, have you ever used eBay before?" the Cardinal asked, sitting back in his chair. He was swiveling it slightly from left to right, making the Sister feel as if she and the entire room were in motion.

"No, Your Grace."

"I have. My mother is a big Frank Sinatra fan, and I was able to find an original pressing of his 1955 album *In the Wee Small Hours*. Not my cup of tea, but Mother loves it. I got it for fifteen dollars, including shipping. A bargain. It's really a remarkable use of technology."

The Sister had not counted on this, on the Cardinal sharing her fascination with technology, and it made her light up. "Yes,

Your Grace, I couldn't agree more. And now it will afford us an opportunity to do the good work of the Church. If we can win the bid—"

Cardinal Trippe held up a hand, indicating the Sister should stop. "I'm sorry, Sister, we cannot, as I'm sure you will understand, actually appropriate the money to bid on a human life." She started to protest, but the Cardinal cut her off again. "I understand what you're trying to do, and it is laudable. The circumstances really do afford us a chance to demonstrate our commitment to life, to all life. But we cannot spend so many of our resources to save a single life when that money can help so many others." The Sister was crestfallen, her mind racing for a way to sway the Cardinal, when he continued. "However, there is a much smaller sacrifice we can make that can perhaps stop this troubled young man—what was his name?"

"Jared Stone, Your Eminence."

"To stop Mr. Stone from going through with his ill-guided attempt to sell himself, while also accomplishing your goal of shedding light on the sanctity of life."

"A smaller sacrifice?"

"Yes, Sister, a much smaller sacrifice. You will sacrifice your good standing on eBay." The Sister looked perplexed, so the Cardinal leaned forward to explain his idea.

Seven hours later, Sister Benedict Joan bid on Jared Stone's life. The $1,000,000 was exactly enough to meet the reserve and to make the Sister and her Mother Church the leading bidder.

***

Deirdre Stone liked her house. She liked it a lot.

She liked the garden she and her daughters had planted under the bay windows in the front yard, with roses, hydrangea, and a holly bush; she liked the pale green color she and Jared had painted the living room walls when they first moved in; she liked the way that color had aged and matured with the house, with their relationship; and she liked the worn, comfortable couch that was her spot late at night to unwind from the day, after the girls went to bed and Jared had fallen asleep in his office.

On this night, Deirdre spent what felt like an uncountable number of hours curled up on that couch, crying.

After she watched Jared retreat to his office, stumbling up the stairs following the onslaught of media, she slammed the front door shut and collapsed on the sofa. Megan ran upstairs, no doubt telling Jackie everything that had happened. The girls stayed up there, never calling out for her, never asking about dinner.

Deirdre finally cried herself to sleep, woke up, and cried some more.

She tried to distract herself with television and work e-mail—Deirdre was the executive assistant to the CFO of a multinational insurance company with a West Coast office in Portland—but she couldn't concentrate. She put her head back down and sank into a restless sleep, her dreams a jumbled narrative about cancer, coffee, and New York City.

When she came to in the middle of the night, there were no more tears. She felt hollowed out, like there was a big, gaping, sucking hole at the center of her being. The only thing left to fill it was anger. Deirdre didn't cry anymore because she was too mad to cry. She stomped up the stairs and practically kicked in the door to her husband's office.

"I just have to know, what the fuck were you thinking," she barked into the room. She stopped short in the doorway. Every other time she opened this door, Jared was either sitting cross-legged in the desk chair in front of his computer or napping on the futon that doubled as their guest bed. He wasn't there now, and for a minute Deirdre thought he wasn't in the room. That's when she noticed him lying on the floor.

"Oh my god!" she cried and dropped to her knees. "Jare?" She shook him, and his eyes flicked open.

"Oh, hey, D." He smiled up at her. "I must've dozed off again."

"What are you doing on the floor?"

"Reducing external stimuli. Helps me focus. I think."

Deirdre lay down on her back next to Jared and stared at the ceiling. It was hard to see any detail in the low light.

"Does it hurt?" she asked after a long minute of painful silence.

"Does what hurt?"

"Your tumor."

"Oh, right, of course. Sometimes. Yes. Headaches. Mostly, I just feel confused. And I'm starting to forget things."

"Like what?"

Jared propped himself up on one elbow and looked at her. He pursed his lips and tried hard to concentrate on Deirdre's question. "I'm not sure," he answered.

"Oh, sweetie," she said, tearing up. "I was just making a joke."

Jared paused for a second and then smiled. "Oh, I see. That is pretty funny." He put his head back down.

They lay there for a while, like two kids in a summer field looking up at the stars.

"Why didn't you tell me?" she asked, keeping her eyes focused on the ceiling.

"I don't suppose you'd believe me if I said I forgot."

"Is that true?"

"No," he said quietly. "I suppose it's not. I guess I wanted to figure out how to make everything okay first."

"And selling yourself to some psychopath on eBay was your answer?"

"Like I said, I'm confused. I'm not even really sure what I'm saying to you right now. Am I making sense?"

Deirdre rolled over to look at her husband to see if he was serious; she didn't see a hint of irony or mischief on his face.

"Don't you think the girls and I can take care of ourselves?"

"I guess I didn't think," he said. They were both quiet for a while before Jared added, "Although, you know, I did get a bid for a million dollars. I think it's from a hooker or something. The name is SisterBJ143."

Deirdre rolled onto her side, facing away from Jared.

"What?" he asked, taking her hand. "I won't do anything you wouldn't want me to do."

"Then don't die." She said it so softly she wasn't sure Jared had heard her. When Deirdre rolled back over, she saw serpentine streaks of tears carving rivers on her husband's cheek.

"Oh, Jare," she said and took his hand.

They both cried and hugged and hugged and cried.

Then their lips met, and they began to kiss.

***

Jackie was sitting in the back of the class, her usual spot, slumped down in her seat, trying to evade the notice of her chemistry teacher. Maybe if she had been more nonchalant about it, the teacher wouldn't have noticed, wouldn't have zeroed in.

Esther Markowitz stood five feet two inches tall but still managed to tower over every one of the students in her class, including Jackie, who was a good three inches taller. Patches of pink scalp showed through the teacher's short, frizzy hair, and she had some kind of monstrosity—a mole, a wart, a boil—at the corner of her right eyebrow. Her demeanor matched her appearance to a T.

"Miss Stone," she boomed, walking toward Jackie. "Perhaps you can tell us how many joules are in a mole." She arrived at Jackie's desk, standing ramrod straight and perfectly still.

Jackie kept her head down.

"Look at me, Miss Stone."

Jackie looked up, but she couldn't make eye contact with Mrs. Markowitz. She wondered how the woman had managed to become a "Mrs." Who would marry such a witch?

"Well?" the teacher asked.

Jackie had no idea; she never had any idea.

"Jackie?" Mrs. Markowitz said.

Jackie didn't answer.

"Jackie?" she said again, this time louder.

Jackie just stared at the front of the class, her eyes searching for some clue to the answer to the question, searching for some way out.

"Jackie!" Mrs. Markowitz yelled, grabbing Jackie by the shoulder and shaking it with more force than such a diminutive person should have been able to muster.

"JACKIE!"

Jackie opened her eyes and saw her sister. Megan was gently shaking Jackie's shoulder and whispering her name, trying to wake her from a dream.

It took a minute for Jackie's head to clear and to remember where she was and what was going on.

"Huh? What time is it?"

"It's like two in the morning," Megan whispered, "but listen!"

Jackie went still and listened. She heard laughing. No, crying. No, something else. "What is that?"

"I think it must be Dad. I'm scared."

"C'mon," Jackie said, taking her sister by the hand. They slunk out of the bedroom into the pitch-black hallway. They edged along the wall, moving closer to the sound until they were outside their father's study. As soon as they got there, Jackie recognized the noise for what it was. Her parents were making love.

Jackie wasn't sure how she knew, since she had never even kissed a boy, but there was no mistaking it. She looked at Megan and saw that her sister had figured it out, too.

"Gross!" Megan said.

"Sssh," Jackie told her, and led them both back to Jackie's room. They crawled back into bed together, and in a matter of moments Megan had fallen back asleep. Jackie lay awake for a while longer and smiled for the first time in that long, miserable day. If her parents were still able to make love, maybe her father's illness wasn't as bad as it seemed. Maybe everything would be okay.

***

Glio—the name by which the high-grade glioblastoma tumor now thought of itself—didn't know what was happening, but it was lighting up Jared's brain like a football stadium at night. Glio really, really, really liked it. He stopped to watch.

It was the first time Glio thought of itself in the masculine. "I am he," it said, or *he* said, to no one in particular. Or would have said had he been able to form words or even make sounds.

The show ended in one ginormous explosion of color and light, then faded like the evening sky on the most perfect night. Glio sat in wonder for a moment before returning to the work at hand, picking off his host's memories one by one—the sheriff's badge Jared got for his third birthday, a big dog biting him on the cheek when he was six, running away from his family at an amusement park when he was ten because his cousin was teasing him about his fear of roller coasters. Buoyed by the light show, Glio's hunger intensified. It was a feast to end all feasts.

The pièce de résistance was Jared's first real kiss. He was thirteen years old, on vacation with his parents at some long-forgotten resort in the Berkshires. The girl's lips were covered in a fruity gloss that surprised Glio, just as it had surprised

Jared. He expected them to be moist with saliva, not sticky with raspberry. He could feel the gloss adhere to his own lips, or Glio's idea of lips, holding him in place, making the kiss last. The girl's name was lost to Jared in the ebb of time, but Glio found it. Gail.

He could see her face: a wide mouth, eyes so rich in color they were almost lavender, and a button nose. Glio had no way of knowing that the memory had been enhanced by Jared's brain. But it didn't matter. It was like manna from heaven.

After the kiss was over, the memory consumed, Glio drifted off into the hypothalamus and, like his host, fell asleep.

***

Hazel Huck's shoulders sagged as she stared at her computer screen.

"A million dollars," she said aloud to her empty bedroom.

From the very beginning, Hazel's plan had been to raise money to purchase Jared on eBay and then return him to his family, to allow him to die with dignity, comfort, and cash. She had succeeded in getting pledges totaling $15,000 from her online gaming friends. She had called in every favor—sold every piece of handcrafted virtual jewelry, hired her level sixty-five druid out for future quests, and sold every ingot of gold in her war chest for pennies on the dollar. It was a remarkable feat for a seventeen-year-old girl.

And then it went viral.

All of a sudden, Warcraft characters Hazel had never met were wearing "Save Jared" T-shirts over their chain mail and leather armor. There were player vs. player melees in which the losing party would agree to donate X dollars to the cause.

Blizzard Entertainment, the über gaming company behind World of Warcraft, caught wind of what was happening in Azeroth and pledged to match whatever funds were raised. The money was collected in an account set up by one of Hazel's guild brothers who, in real life, was a banker. Hazel's $15,000 swelled to $150,000 almost overnight, and then doubled with the Blizzard match. But it was still many, many leagues from the million-dollar reserve and opening bid. The effort, spectacular though it was, failed.

Hazel couldn't explain why Jared's cause had become so important to her. Yes, it started with Boots, but now it was something more. Her life needed meaning. Jared Stone's plight made her realize that fighting imaginary monsters to get to virtual treasure was a pleasant diversion, but not something to aspire to. Here was a chance to help a real human being.

In the end, though, it turned out to be moot.

"A million dollars," she said again.

Hazel turned off the screen, flopped on her bed, grabbed her weathered copy of *The Fellowship of the Ring*, and fell asleep reading.

***

Sherman Kingsborough saw the $1,000,000 bid and panicked. He hadn't yet received an answer to his query about the seller's physical and mental state, but he had so worked himself up about the chance to kill another human being that he had to get in the game. His bid was $1.2 million.

It was a worthwhile gamble. Besides, to Sherman, it was really just pocket change.

He had settled on a *Hunger Games*–like test of skills in which he and Jared would be turned loose in an enclosed wooded reserve. They would be given scant supplies, minimal survival gear, and neither would be allowed to leave until the other was dead. He had already begun scouting locations and hiring staff to make it all happen.

But without Jared, it would all be academic. Sherman needed to win that auction.

***

Sister Benedict couldn't tear herself away from the computer. She had been sitting there for ten hours, only getting up once to use the bathroom.

She refreshed the page every two or three minutes, a solemn promise to herself that each click of the mouse would be the last, that she would turn the computer off and tend to her duties, returning to the auction later, closer to its scheduled end time. But, despite her best efforts, Sister Benedict was human, and she simply could not look away.

Since the auction began, three different young nuns in training had entered the Sister's office seeking guidance in resolving personal disputes. With each interruption, Sister Benedict looked up from her computer and said, "God gave us brains and hearts to figure out how to fix our own problems. Don't come back until you can tell me what path the Lord has shown you to solve this crisis," the word "crisis" dripping with the sarcasm of absolute authority. The Sister was so lost in the world of the Internet that she had no idea what any of the novices had said to her. For all she knew, one of them was pregnant. (None were.) But still, she couldn't stop clicking that mouse.

The Sister was aware that her bid was a canard, a red herring, and that she and the Church had no intention of paying the money. Cardinal Trippe's plan was for the Sisters of the Perpetual Adoration to make sure that they won the bid. When the auction ended and it was time to pay, they would simply renege. In this way, they would block Jared Stone from going through with his plan.

"But aren't we committing a kind of sin?" the Sister had asked the Cardinal, confusion etched on her thick brow. "If we do not intend to complete the auction, then bidding on the auction is a kind of lie, is it not?"

"Do you know the story of Rosa Parks?" Cardinal Trippe asked.

"Of course, Your Grace."

"Then you know that Ms. Parks broke the law by sitting where she sat on that bus. Yet what she did was still right." While Sister Benedict grudgingly acknowledged that the law restricting where black people could and could not sit was wrong, she still thought that Rosa Parks should have followed the rules. Though she, the Sister, was politic enough to know to keep that to herself. She also had to bite her cheek to stop herself from correcting the Cardinal from using "Ms." when he should have been saying "Miss," something she did with her students at the Annunciation school.

"It was a form of civil disobedience," the Cardinal said. "What we're doing is the twenty-first-century version of the same. Call it social disobedience. It is wrong that this man can sell his life on eBay, so we will block him from doing so, peacefully, passively."

Dear Lord, the Sister thought, *give me the strength to deal with this fool. Next he'll be talking to me about that Indian martyr in the diaper.*

When Sherman Kingsborough's bid came through at $1.2 million, the Sister immediately bid it up to $1.5 million. Even though the bid wasn't real, she couldn't help but revel in the appropriation of such a large sum of money. *Perhaps,* she thought, *I can still convince the Cardinal that when we win the auction, we should pay the price and bring this man under our care.* The Sister had, unknowingly, become intoxicated with a feeling of power.

***

Ethan Overbee watched the bidding war heat up. He watched, and he waited.

***

Sherman Kingsborough had barely finished submitting his bid when his offer was trumped. The original bidder had upped the ante to $1.5 million.

"Son of a bitch!" he said to an empty room. Or not so much empty, as filled with garish trinkets designed to flaunt his wealth, including a life-size replica of Michelangelo's *David*. The truth was Sherman hated art. But an older woman he had lusted after a year earlier convinced him that all men of wealth and power covet great works of art. "It's a measure of one's place in the world," she had said with an air of certainty.

Sherman never really got it but indulged the woman's passion for sculpture and painting. She seemed worldly and wise, and for a brief time he thought he was falling in love. He wasn't.

Not to be outdone on eBay, Sherman immediately raised the going price for Jared Stone's life to $2 million. "Take that, bi-otch," he said to an original member of the Terracotta Army, smuggled, or so he was told, out of China on a rickshaw. (If his paramour—with whom Sherman had grown bored and dumped—had done her homework, she would have known the clay soldier was a fake by the decidedly angled features on its face, and the "Made in Taiwan" scrawl etched on the sole of the soldier's left boot.) Sherman didn't know that his competing bidder was a woman, and he definitely didn't know she was a nun. He just called everyone "bi-otch." It had become his thing.

He, too, watched, and he, too, waited.

***

Sister Benedict Joan said five Hail Marys and crossed herself twice as she increased her bid on Jared's life to $2.5 million. The Sister had deluded herself into believing that she would prevail with the Cardinal and that Jared Stone would be hers. The irony of it was lost on her completely.

"Ha!" she cackled when she saw that she was once again the auction's new top dog, immediately covering her mouth and giggling, looking around to make sure no one was there to witness this act of hubris.

***

When Jared woke up, he was lying on the floor of his office, covered with a blanket. Sunlight bent around the edge of the curtain, leaving two long, white stripes on the carpet.

"The White Stripes," Jared said aloud. *Seethe with trips*. He looked around the room. "Deirdre's gone, if she was ever here." He couldn't be sure. Trebuchet was gone, too, and he realized he was alone and talking to himself.

Jared had been dreaming about something, but he couldn't remember what. It might have had something to do with his first kiss, but as he sat on the floor and racked his brain, or what he feared was left of his brain, he couldn't remember any details. At that moment, he wasn't entirely sure he'd ever been kissed. But then the memory of the previous night came flooding back. That, at least, was still intact.

Stretching his back and neck, Jared eased himself up and over to his computer. The high bid was now $2.5 million, still from SisterBJ143. "Are there really one hundred forty-two other SisterBJs?" he asked the computer screen.

When he looked at the bidding history, Jared saw that one other bidder—the man who had submitted the unsettling questions about his physical and mental acuity—had come in at $2 million.

A bidding war was exactly what Jared hoped would materialize. He hadn't answered the man's letter, and now thought it wise that he had not. To Jared's way of thinking, this was an "as is" purchase. He didn't need to give anyone a leg up.

Then a strange thing happened.

Jared refreshed the page, hoping to see the two bidders egging each other on, but when he did, his auction disappeared. At the same time, he saw a flag on the page indicating that he had a new e-mail message in his account. Figuring there was a connection, he opened his in-box. This is what he found:

Dear Seller—We regret to inform you that your auction, "Human Life for Sale," violates eBay's usage policies against listing humans or human remains as sale items, and as such, the listing has been removed. All bidders have been released from their obligation, and you are hereby prohibited from listing this or similar auctions in the future. Should you have any questions, please address them to <u>Customercare</u>. Any subsequent violations of our usage policies could lead to your immediate suspension from eBay. Thank you for your time.

Jared didn't know if he should laugh or cry, if he was relieved or distraught. It's not that he was caught between conflicting emotions—though he was—it was that the tumor, at the very moment, happened to be sampling the part of Jared's brain responsible for emotional comprehension. It was both amused and touched by the conflict going on around it. Synapses were firing and misfiring like a bad cell-phone connection. To Jared, it just registered as more confusion.

Either way, his eBay experiment was over and he was none the richer. He let out a long slow sigh.

And that is exactly when Jared's cell phone rang.

PART TWO

A Deal Is Offered

Friday, September 18

Ethan Overbee was not a man who left things to chance.

When he was in middle school, Ethan was caught red-handed selling bootleg cassette tapes on school property. He'd been in the fiction aisle of the school library selling a scratchy copy of Bon Jovi's *Slippery When Wet* to another student. To make matters worse, the library was supposed to have been closed at the time. To make matters much worse, the principal was giving a tour of the school to a group of visiting dignitaries from the Board of Education, and he and his guests rounded a corner just in time to witness the exchange of goods for money. It must have looked like a drug deal, because everyone gasped. When Ethan let the cassette tapes fall to the floor, making it clear that there were no narcotics involved, the school brass exhaled a collective sigh of relief.

The principal smiled broadly at Ethan and his customer, a fellow eighth grader at Henry Wadsworth Longfellow Middle School in suburban New York, and said, "Boys, why don't you drop by my office when you're done here." And he and his guests carried on. None of them looked back.

Ethan's partner in crime, an honor student named Winston Swale, bounced from one foot to the other as he wondered how to explain to his parents that he was being suspended from school for sponsoring an illicit music-copying ring. This is exactly the scenario the principal was laying out for the two boys as they stood before him an hour later. The principal was a humorless man whose ears turned red when he was angry, and on that day they were the color of a dodgeball from the school gym.

But Ethan was Ethan, and he had stacked the deck.

Unbeknownst to the principal, and unbeknownst to Winston, Ethan had a hall pass from the school librarian. The pass gave the boys permission to use the library during their free period to work on a report about Marco Polo and the Silk Road.

When the principal called and questioned the librarian about the permission slip, she acknowledged its legitimacy. She, of course, didn't know the boys were going to use the library to buy and sell black market goods, but the truth was, she liked Ethan and didn't want to see him get in trouble.

"Honest, Mr. Finn," Ethan began, almost slipping and calling the principal "Mr. Fink," the nickname students more commonly used, "we were just taking a break from the report to swap music tapes."

Ethan then produced a half-finished report with the title "Marco Polo and the Silk Road" emblazoned across the front page. Winston, who knew for a fact that no report writing had been attempted in the library, managed to keep his astonishment in check. Had Principal Finn flipped through the report, he would have spotted it for the fake it was. Other than the title page, it was a report about the differences between igneous, sedimentary, and metamorphic rocks.

Viewing the hall pass and report like pieces of surprise evidence presented by lawyers for the defense (in this case, Ethan representing himself and his friend), the principal decided it was just easier to declare a mistrial and let the boys off with a warning. Ethan made out nicely. He escaped without a blemish on his record and earned a reputation for outsmarting the principal. He became a kind of cult figure in his school.

Now, nearly two decades later, Ethan had once again stacked the deck. Getting the auction delisted was easy. The eBay rules on selling humans and human remains left no room for negotiation. It only took a complaint from another user to bring it to the attention of the eBay goon squad.

Getting Jared's cell phone number was also surprisingly easy.

Because each state had its own arcane laws governing the ownership of media outlets, the network employed paid lobbyists in all fifty state capitals to protect its interests. It was a stroke of luck that their lobbyist in Salem had worked with Jared on a bill a year earlier, and that the two had hit it off. When Ethan called, the lobbyist gave him Jared's cell number without skipping a beat.

By the time Ethan dialed Jared's phone, he knew exactly what he was going to say.

***

"Hello?" Jared said as he answered the cell phone, a ring of uncertainty in his voice.

"Hello, Jared," said the voice on the other end, and Jared wondered if it really was a voice, or if the brain tumor was trying to talk to him. "May I call you Jared?"

"Sure."

"Do you know why I'm calling?"

"That depends," answered Jared. "Are you real, or are you my brain tumor?"

The voice on the other end of the line hesitated but only for an instant.

"No, Jared, I'm not a brain tumor. I'm a man. Same as you."

"You have a brain tumor, too?" Jared asked.

"Well, no. But I'm a *man*, same as you." Jared didn't know what to say, so he waited. "My name is Ethan, and now that your eBay listing has been removed, I think I can help you."

"Help me how?" Jared knew he should be suspicious, but at that precise moment, Glio was consuming a memory of Jared bathing Jackie when she was a toddler—the warm water, the soap bubbles, her toy boat, her unfettered laughter—and it was releasing a wash of melatonin over Jared's gray matter.

The memory had been buried so deep in his brain that it wasn't directly available to Jared; when Glio found it, flooding his host's basal ganglia with the calming enzyme, the side effect was to help Jared focus.

"I'd like to meet you in person to explain," Ethan answered.

"Hey, wait." Jared thought hard for a moment before realizing what it was he needed to ask. "How did you get this number? And how did you know the listing had been removed?"

"I got your number from Hannah Hinawi."

"The lobbyist? Are you a lobbyist? If so, you should call my number in Salem, and—"

"Hannah works for me. Or, to be more accurate, she works for someone who works for someone who works for someone who works for me."

That was a lot of someones for Jared's brain to process, but he got the point. "So what do you want from me?"

"I can help ease your suffering, and I can make sure your family is well provided for. I'd like to explain in person."

The wave of melatonin was fading; it was being replaced by a rush of adrenaline. Jared's heart was racing, and his mind was fogging up again. Not knowing what else to do, he said okay.

"Great. Where can we meet?"

Even in this less than fully lucid state, Jared knew the answer. It was public, comfortable, and one of his favorite spots in the world. "When?" he asked.

"Now."

***

When Jackie rubbed the sleep out of her eyes the next morning, Megan was gone. She grabbed her iPhone and saw that it was already eight forty-five. She was missing first period. Why hadn't anyone woken her up?

She was just about to go downstairs and find her parents when she noticed she had a new Facebook message.

Max

I am sorry I miss you. Yes, this was bad time because I am in school. LOL! Will you be online at school today? I will like also to talk to you. I will look for you.

Jackie loved how Max typed a broken version of English. She thought it made him seem even cuter than his photo. He had been teaching Jackie Russian a few words at a time. Her favorite was "nimnoshka," in English, "a little bit." She liked the way it sounded.

"As in 'I don't like school, not one nimnoshka'?" was Jackie's response when Max had taught her the word. Jackie wasn't playful like that with anyone other than her dad, but with Max being so far away it was easy. She got an LMAO from Max, and wondered if he knew what the acronym stood for.

Jackie pocketed her phone and went in search of her parents.

She wasn't two steps outside her door when she ran into her father.

She looked at her feet and mumbled, "Hi, Daddy."

Jared wrung his hands and cleared his throat. "Why don't you go downstairs, Snowflake. Your mom and I want to talk to you. I'll be there in a minute."

Jackie nodded. The walk from the second floor to the kitchen felt miles long. She found her mother at the kitchen table, staring blankly at the wall, a coffee cup clutched between her hands. The cup was empty save a few drops of brown liquid littered with black specks.

"Mom?"

Deirdre hadn't noticed Jackie come in, and she jumped at hearing her daughter.

"Oh, Jax! You scared me."

"Why didn't you wake me up?"

Deirdre didn't know how to respond. "I thought maybe you needed sleep," she said in a quiet voice.

"Because of Dad?"

"Because of Dad."

An entire conversation passed between mother and daughter unspoken: the knowledge that nothing about their lives would ever be the same again, and the helplessness in their complete, utter, and mutual inability to do anything about it.

Jared rounded the corner into the room, gave Jackie an awkward pat on the shoulder, and took a seat at the table. He struggled for words but came up empty. His shoulders sagged, he shook his head, and he finally said, "I'm so sorry."

Jackie didn't understand. *Why was he sorry?* Not knowing what else to say, she asked: "Is it all true?"

Jared nodded.

"Even the eBay stuff?"

Jared nodded again.

"Can't you stop it?" Jackie asked, trying to keep the hopefulness out of her voice.

"I wish I could, but the doctor said there's no cure. I'm going to die."

Jackie was referring to the eBay listing and wasn't prepared to confront the reality of her father's illness so directly. A lump formed in her throat, climbed up the wall of her esophagus, and tried to push itself all the way out of her mouth. She made a short, clipped noise of anguish.

Deirdre, realizing that Jared had misunderstood his daughter's question, jumped in and steered the conversation in a different direction. "Your father and I talked about the eBay listing. He knows how upset we all are. But it doesn't matter now. eBay took the listing down. Apparently we're not the only ones who think selling a human life is a bad idea." Deirdre's tone and glare at Jared left no room for misinterpretation; she was pissed off. Jackie was upset, too, but couldn't be mad at her father knowing what she now knew. She wanted to ask her father so many questions—Did the cancer hurt? Was he scared? How could he do this to her?—but it was all too raw, too new. She decided to change the subject.

"Where's Meg? Shouldn't she be part of this conversation, too?"

"We talked to her earlier this morning," her mother said.

"And?"

"Your sister, whatever faults she may have, is a strong girl." Her mother paused and looked at Jackie a long moment before continuing. "We're going to need you to be strong, too, Jax."

Jackie nodded but pushed the thought away. Everything about the world was off-kilter. Jackie felt like she was on a spinning ride at the amusement park and wanted to get off. "Is she still here?"

"Meg? No, I took her to school."

"Can I go, too?"

Deirdre and Jared looked at each other, and then looked at Jackie like she was a stranger.

"You *want* to go to school?" Jared asked.

"Kind of." Jackie put her head down, letting her bangs fall over her eyes.

Neither one of her parents answered right away. Jackie knew why they were surprised. Other than the day of the Kevin Memmott affair, no one in the Stone family could remember a single day in the entire history of their lives when Jackie actually wanted to go to school.

"Of course, honey," she said. "Your dad will drive you."

"Yeah, sure," Jared said, then shook his head like he was remembering something important. "Oh, wait. I have a meeting downtown. At least, I think I do."

"Okay, get dressed, Jax. I'll take you. And, Jare," Deirdre said, standing up, "don't do anything stupid."

Jackie wasn't sure what her mother meant, but she was glad to see her father smile and nod in agreement.

***

After Glio was done giving Baby Jackie a sponge bath, he stumbled onto something truly remarkable. There was a part of Jared's cerebral cortex that had never been consciously tapped. In fact, no human had ever consciously tapped this part of his or her cerebral cortex. It was part of that apocryphal 90 percent of the brain that a person never uses. Only it wasn't apocryphal, at least not to a high-grade glioblastoma multiforme.

As he dived deeper and deeper into the cortex, Glio swam through shimmering curtains of neurons flashing with bursts of fuchsia, indigo, and aquamarine, the light show a borealis of the mind. Eddies and jets of intelligence carried him through funnel-shaped clouds of thought ending in a Class V rapid, where Glio dropped without warning into a synaptic sea, entering the warm, enveloping waters with a pronounced splash.

He paddled through unchartered lakes and canals, devouring schools of thought that defied category or explanation, existing like the dark matter of the universe, heavier and with more gravity than could ever be seen, heard, smelled, tasted, touched, or realized. It was π to the 4,790,523rd digit, the complete understanding of the human genome, and the one true meaning of love. These were the thoughts, ideas, and truths that formed the background hum of humanity, the music all people heard without knowing it. It was the fuel of desire, ambition, and curiosity. And, cell by cell, Jared Stone was losing it all.

These neurons were a power boost to Glio, propelling him forward with greater speed and resolve.

With each bite Glio took of this previously inaccessible corner of the brain, Jared's eyes lost an iota of sparkle. It was as if he were the personification of a story where someone was removing all the adjectives, conjunctions, and adverbs, so the only things left were nouns and verbs.

Glio swam on. Or rather Glio swam.

***

Hazel Huck was talking to a newspaper reporter when she got the news about the auction.

"I'm looking now," the reporter was saying, "but I don't see the listing anymore."

The reporter wouldn't reveal the source that had confirmed Hazel's real-world identity, but Hazel figured it had to be a War Craft admin. They would be the only ones to know.

Once she had been outed, Hazel saw no reason not to cooperate. Perhaps by going public, she thought, the fund-raising effort could be defibrillated back to life.

Hazel knew this would mean the end of her online anonymity, and her guild friends would know she was just an awkward high school kid from the heart of Dixie. But some things, she thought, trump self-interest.

"Can you tell me the auction number so I can search again?" the reporter asked.

"Auction number?"

"Well, it's really called an item number. On the right side of the screen."

Hazel opened her laptop and maneuvered to eBay. And then she saw. The listing was gone. She had a message in her in-box that the auction had been removed by the administrator for a violation of eBay's service agreement.

"I'll have to call you back," Hazel said, and she hung up.

***

When Sherman Kingsborough saw that the auction had been delisted, he was caught between waves of relief and anger.

Like so many people of unchecked wealth, Sherman was a broken soul. He had spent his teen years in a drunken haze, his father—or really, his father's lawyers—always there to bail him out when he got into trouble, which was often. When the old man died, Sherman thought for a moment that perhaps he should grow up, assume a responsible position in society. But he had no frame of reference for doing so. In fact, it was just the opposite. With no parental or authoritative oversight, and with unlimited funds, Sherman could indulge his most perverse desires. He struggled against it at first, but it was no use; he gave in and let his id take over.

He argued with himself, made promises that each time—whether it was carnal relations with a fourteen-year-old Thai prostitute or bribing nature-preserve wardens to hunt Bengal tigers—would be the last. He would lead a better life, put his money to more constructive use, practice tai chi, eat well, and go to church. But as time passed, his internal exhortations grew more hollow. He had waded so often into the waters of depravity that he'd lost the ability to disgust himself.

Cold-blooded murder, though, was new and frightening ground. And while that excited Sherman, it also gave him pause. *Perhaps*, he thought, *this is one step too far, even for me.*

On the other hand, this Jared Stone was going to die, and Sherman could help him financially, so really, it was nothing more than an agreement between gentlemen. It wasn't as if Sherman were going to walk down the street and murder a vagrant just for the fun of it. No, this was reasonable, this was right.

His anger, as was inevitable, won out over his relief. He had been mentally preparing to kill another human being—psyching himself up, as it were—and now he was being denied that pleasure. *Not pleasure*, he thought, *opportunity.*

Posting the auction and then removing it—in his current state of mind it didn't matter to Sherman that it was eBay and not the user that had taken the listing down—was just wrong. *I should sue the bastard*, Sherman thought. *Or I should find this SOB and kill him anyway.*

Sherman blinked. Once. Twice.

Find him and kill him anyway. He paused to let the idea sink in.

Find him and kill him anyway.

Huh.

***

When news of Jared's auction being delisted reached Sister Benedict, she didn't have time for even one "Jesus, Mary, and Joseph," before she was on the phone to the Cardinal's office.

"This is the office of Cardinal Trippe, archbishop of the Northwest Province of the Holy Roman Catholic Church. May God bless the Pope and the United States of America. This is Father Todd, may I help you?"

"Yes, Father Todd. This is Sister Benedict Joan from the Sisters of the Perpetual Adoration. I need to speak to Cardinal Hippie—I mean Trippe—Cardinal Trippe. I need to speak to him right away." The Sister was so upset at her gaffe that she bit her knuckle hard enough to draw blood.

If Father Todd noticed, he didn't let on. "I'll see if he's available, Sister," he answered flatly.

The Sister waited an interminable amount of time as she listened to the hold music—first "Amazing Grace," then "Ave Maria," then "Battle Hymn of the Republic." It was an alphabetical tour of inspiring Christian hymns, and each new song made her want to scream. The Sister reminded herself that patience is a virtue, though at the moment she could not understand why.

"So, Sister, how goes our little project," the Cardinal offered as greeting when he finally came to the phone.

"It's not, Your Eminence. This is why I'm calling."

"Continue," he said.

The Sister relayed the news about the auction being removed. "We have to do something."

"I'm sorry, I don't think I understand," the Cardinal answered. "This man is no longer trying to sell his life? Wasn't that what we found objectionable?"

"I thought," Sister Benedict answered stiffly, "we found it objectionable that this man was going to die when we could preserve his life."

"Sister," the Cardinal said, a note of conciliatory kindness in his voice, "people die every minute of every day. If it is written in God's plan that this man should be called home to our Heavenly Father, then who are we to interfere? Let it go."

"But, Cardinal Trippe," she began, "we still have an opportunity to bring glory to this parish—"

"I'm sorry, Sister. This is the ending we wanted. I implore you to put Mr. Stone out of your mind. If anything, perhaps you should call on the family and see if you can provide comfort in their time of need." The Cardinal offered a blessing, bade her good-bye, and the line went dead.

The Sister slammed the phone down in anger, then crossed herself three times and said two Hail Marys to atone for her outburst.

All the steam went out of her. She hadn't realized she'd been standing, and she flopped down in her chair. *Perhaps,* she thought, *the Cardinal, fool that he is, is right.*

Sister Benedict Joan had no intention of visiting Mr. Stone and his family; he wasn't even a member of the parish. She did her best to forget about the whole sordid ordeal.

***

Jackie wasn't prepared for the reaction waiting for her at school. She and Megan had stayed in Jackie's room all night, so neither one had seen their mother and father on the evening news. But lots of other kids had seen the telecast, or at least knew about it.

For the most part, everyone avoided Jackie, which wasn't anything new. On a normal day Jackie would walk down the hall unnoticed, like she was a ghost. No one would make eye contact because they couldn't see her.

But today was different. Suddenly, everyone could see her, but no one wanted to look.

She arrived just in time for her morning free period and went straight to the computer lab. A few people looked up as she entered, all of them turning their attention back to their computer screens a little too quickly, like she was disfigured, like she'd been struck by lightning. Even the teacher avoided making eye contact.

Jackie found a free terminal, logged on to Facebook, and lit up when she saw the little green dot next to Max's name. He was online.

She started to type hello when his message popped up:

Max

Solnyshko!

This was the very first Russian word Max had taught Jackie. It was a term of endearment that meant "little sunshine." She loved it.

Jackie

Hi, Max

Max

For why were you looking me last night?

Jackie

It's "why were you looking for me last night," Max.

He insisted that Jackie correct his English at every opportunity.

Max

Yes, why were you looking for me? I am sorry I was not online.

Jackie

That's okay. It's just that I had some bad news, and I needed to talk to someone.

Max

What news is this?

This was the first time Jackie was confronted with talking about it to anyone other than her family. Even typing it was harder than she realized it would be.

Jackie

It's my dad.

Max

Your father, yes?

Jackie

Yes. He's dying.

The words lay there on the screen, flat and without emotion. Pixels without meaning. Only they held all the meaning in the world for Jackie.

Max
Is this some American catchphrase for which I do not know the meaning?

Jackie
He has a brain tumor.

There was a long pause before Max responded. Jackie filled the void with a million unpleasant thoughts.

Max
Solnyshko, I do not know what to say. I am, what is the word, condolences.

Jackie
Thanks, Max. I'm sorry to dump this on you.

Max
Nyet, this is what friends are for.

Jackie
I'm not sure that's something I would know anything about.

Jackie hated herself for sounding so pathetic, but she didn't know what else to do, how else to be. The reality of her father's condition was starting to settle in, to become inescapable, and Jackie started to cry.

It was silent weeping at first, followed by audible sobs, ending with near-hysterical wails of despair.

The teacher, a nice woman named Ms. Onorati, was at her side in an instant. With a gentle touch, she took Jackie's elbow, helped her to her feet, and guided her to the nurse's office, whispering platitudes all the way down the hall. The Facebook chat was left unresolved.

Max

Solnyshko?

Max

Jacquelyn?

***

Glio caught a whiff of something grotesque coming from the limbic region of Jared's brain and stopped dead in his tracks. *No*, he thought, *not grotesque, dangerous.*

He was interpreting electrical impulses that had been converted from nearly undetectable odors and rendered as unconscious thought. The undetectable odors were coded and relayed to Jared's brain by a vestigial organ, the vomeronasal organ, located between Jared's mouth and nose.

Ever since Homo sapiens had first organized into hunter-gatherer societies, the vomeronasal organ had been waiting around for something to do. Before that time, the small wad of sensory neurons tucked away in the human nose served as kind of olfactory radar. It told people when danger was near, when an animal or other human was afraid, and sent strong signals to the hypothalamus when someone in the neighborhood was horny.

But the vomeronasal organ wasn't vestigial as much as dormant; because Glio had been consuming Jared's neurons at an alarming rate, the organ, compensating for the reduction in its owner's brain power, was jarred to life. It grabbed every pheromone within a thirty-yard radius and flooded the olfactory bulb with information.

The smell filtering through to Jared's brain was so strong that Glio felt nauseous. Somewhere in the immediate vicinity was a predator. For the first time ever, Glio lost his appetite.

***

Jared didn't smell anything as he shook Ethan Overbee's hand. Unlike Glio, Jared's first impression of Ethan was, on balance, positive. Or at least he thought it was. He wasn't sure.

At five feet eleven inches, Ethan was about the same height as Jared, and carried with him a youthful gleam that gave him an air of both mischief and charm. He had hair the color of oak and eyes to match. His angular face looked like something a Renaissance sculptor might have used as a subject. Jared thought all these things in an instant, and none of them consciously. They were simply filed away for future access, and for future dining by his unwelcome guest.

Jared and Ethan were meeting in the café at Powell's City of Books. It was Jared's favorite spot in all of Portland, and when Ethan had suggested a public meeting, Jared knew this would be the place.

When the owner of Powell's tagged his store a "city" of books, he wasn't kidding. The massive space occupied an entire city block and boasted half a dozen rooms, each larger than the average bookstore and each devoted to a collection of related topics. Even seasoned customers would use the maps provided at the front of the store, taking any help they could get to find that one literary needle in the overwhelming haystacks of words.

It didn't take Jared long to spot Ethan when he entered. He was the only man in a twenty-block radius wearing a suit, tie, and matching handkerchief. With no body art, piercings, or conspicuously colored hair, Ethan would have stood out even without the Armani threads.

The two men exchanged pleasantries, ordered coffee, and got down to business.

"I'm sure you're wondering why I wanted to meet you, Jared. May I call you Jared?" Ethan began.

"I'm wondering about a lot of things these days. But if I recall, and I'm not entirely sure I do, you called about my eBay listing."

"Yes, the listing. I'm sorry the auction was removed."

"Yeah, damnedest thing," Jared answered.

"Actually, I have a confession to make."

Jared waited for Ethan to continue.

"I'm the reason the listing was taken down. I brought it to the attention of the eBay standards and practices team. I didn't even know they had such a thing, but they do."

"I'm sorry?" Jared was becoming more confused by the minute.

"I needed to eliminate the competition."

Jared didn't know what to think. Was this man telling the truth? Was Jared hearing him correctly? Was he even sitting in Powell's at that moment?

"Why?"

"Well," Ethan began, "I could say it was to control the price, and maybe that is partly true, but really, it's because you and I need each other."

"I need you?"

"Yes."

Jared sipped his latte and waited for Ethan to continue.

"I can guarantee that you will die with a minimum of pain and discomfort, and I can assure you that your family will be well cared for."

"I don't suppose you can help me not die."

"No, Jared, I'm sorry, I can't."

"You can't."

"No."

"And how can I help you?"

"I run a television studio, and I want to televise your death, in prime time."

"I'm sorry?"

"A reality series, *Jared's Brain* or something like that. We'll have cameras all over your house, filming twenty-four hours a day; we'll edit it down to an hour each night. We'd need your family's consent, of course. But they will be very well compensated."

"A reality show? My life?"

"I could lie to you, Jared, and tell you how your story will inspire people all over the world, how watching someone die with dignity and with the love of their family will help others deal with their own trauma, that it will have a healing, cathartic impact on humanity. Hell, all that might even be true. But really, you'll sell advertising. Lots of advertising."

This raw honesty was a key part of Ethan's charm. His ability to cut away the fat of an encounter, to leave only the essence of a thing, was what made him so successful.

When he was ten years old, Ethan had organized the other children of his neighborhood to compete in a kid Summer Olympics. When Neil Sullivan face-planted during the stunt bicycle competition and needed nine stitches and one thousand dollars' worth of dental work, it was Ethan who spoke to the boy's parents.

"Mr. and Mrs. Sullivan, I could tell you that none of us knew this was going to happen, that we didn't think anyone would get hurt, but I would be telling you a lie. All of us—me, Neil, all of us—did this because there *was* a danger that someone could get hurt. It was a thrill. But all of us, especially me, are really, really sorry."

Later that night, Mrs. Sullivan conveyed the story, with a lump in her throat, to Ethan's mother. Not only did Ethan escape any punishment, his parents bought him a new video game console just for being honest.

"How much will my family get?" Jared asked.

"I like that," Ethan answered. "A man who cuts to the chase."

"I don't exactly have a lot of time."

"Point taken. We'll pay your family five million dollars."

"Five million dollars," Jared repeated.

"Yes."

Jared let the idea sink in. It was more money than he could have hoped to get on eBay, and it sounded like his life wouldn't have such a terrible end, at least as far as such things go.

He couldn't see a reason not to agree, though he once again had a nagging feeling that he was forgetting something. Unfortunately, he couldn't remember what else he had recently forgotten.

"Okay," Jared said. "Let's do it." It never even occurred to him to negotiate.

***

"Please," Jackie said, pleading with the school nurse, "I'm fine. You don't need to call my parents." She'd managed to get her tears under control just after arriving at the nurse's office. All she wanted now was to go back to the computer lab to let Max know she was okay.

The nurse, a bureaucrat to her very soul, would have none of it. She got Jackie's mother on the phone.

"Jax?" her mother said.

As soon as Jackie heard her mom's voice, the waterworks started again. Deirdre was there fifteen minutes later.

Jackie cried all the way home, all the way up the front walk to her house, all the way up the stairs to her bedroom, and didn't stop crying, couldn't stop crying, as she checked Facebook, only to find Max gone. He had left her a message.

Max

Solnyshko, Jacquelyn, I am worried. Please send me message when you are once again online.

Jackie started to type a response, but it proved too hard. She was too upset. She threw herself on her bed, burying her face in her stuffed animals, the largest a three-foot-tall giraffe her father had won for her at a carnival and that she, for reasons she could no longer remember, had named Twiggy. She pounded her fists into the mattress and screamed into Twiggy's soft belly until all the fight drained out of her and she fell asleep.

***

Perhaps by coincidence, or perhaps through some larger inter-connectedness of all things in the universe, as Jackie slept off her breakdown at school and Jared slept off his encounter with Ethan Overbee, Glio was feasting on the memory of the day Jared had won Twiggy, the giant giraffe.

The entire family was at a festival at the local Greek church, the large parking lot replete with rides, games, and vendors selling exotic foods. Deirdre, her smile occasionally crossing the line to a giggle, was munching on a confection dripping with honey and rolled in chopped almonds. Glio was intoxicated by the smell of the thing and wanted to try it. Or, more to the point, he wanted Jared to try it. But Glio was only consuming memories; he couldn't affect their outcome. He felt a pang of frustration that he was limited to being only a theatergoer, a voyeur, but he shook it off.

The pleasing odor of the cookie mixed with the bright lights, ringing bells, and delighted screams of children scattered throughout the festival created a feeling of excitement and unmit-igated joy for Glio. If this was a carnival, he never wanted to leave.

Glio turned his attention back to his host. Jared was aiming a gun of some sort at the mouth of a frightening plastic clown head. In the framework of Glio's limited experience, the scene didn't make sense. He looked to his left and right and saw a row of children on either side all doing the same, some with the intensity and concentration of a chess grand master mid-match, some with the attention span of a gnat.

Glio looked down and saw four-year-old Jackie, all smiles and wonder, hugging Jared's leg. "Daddy wins, Daddy wins, Daddy wins!" she was saying over and over again.

Megan, sitting in a stroller, was clapping in time with Jackie's chant.

"Not yet, Jax, not yet," Jared said.

The booming voice of a mustached man, standing behind the counter on which the gun sat, caught everyone's attention. "Okay, folks, first one to make the balloon pop wins. Everyone ready?"

The children all screamed yes while Jared looked down at Jackie and winked.

"On your mark, get set"—here the man paused for dramatic effect—"GO!"

Jared's gun was aimed perfectly. Not a drop of water was missed or wasted as it arced into the mouth of the clown. As the clown drank, a balloon attached to its head filled with air and inflated.

Glio was taken with Jared's feeling of frenzy and amazed it didn't cause his hands to shake or his attention to wander. Jared's sense of self, his power of concentration, was simply wonderful.

In a matter of seconds, Jared's balloon popped, and he was declared the winner.

"You'd think he'd let one of the kids win," a disgruntled parent muttered loud enough for Glio to hear as she escorted her child away. The child, Glio noticed, didn't seem to care.

"Okay, sir, what'll it be?"

Jared picked Jackie up and sat her on the counter. She was so light. So fragile. So . . . perfect. "What do you say, Jax? How about that teddy bear?" Jared pointed to a giant, brown bear.

"No. I want the giraffe." Only she pronounced it "jraff." Jared leaned down and kissed her. Before he could pull away, Jackie threw her arms around her father's neck and whispered, "I love you, Daddy." Glio could feel the lump in Jared's throat.

"You heard the lady," Jared said. "We'll take the jraff." As the carnival worker retrieved the giant toy, smiling at the undeniable cuteness that was Jackie, Jared asked his daughter what she wanted to name it. Jackie was about to answer when Megan, bouncing in her stroller, said, "Twiggy, Twiggy, Twiggy!"

Jackie shrugged her shoulders; Twiggy it was. No one knew why, and no one questioned it. Glio could tell from the flavor of the memory that this was the first in a long string of incidents in which Megan would assert her dominance over Jackie. Glio knew this because Jared had superimposed twinges of confusion and regret on the memory after the fact.

But that didn't matter to Glio. All he knew was that the more complex the memory, the more intricate the emotional construct, the more delicious it was. He savored every last drop.

***

Back in his Portland hotel room, a luxury suite at one of the city's older, grander hotels, Ethan sat on the bed and laughed.

He had to admit, it was a strange day. He felt part exhilaration and part fear that he had just purchased a human life. Well, not technically, but Ethan was too much the pragmatist not to see and understand what had really happened. He had purchased a human life. And for five million dollars.

In the scheme of the great wide world, that's chump change, he thought. *Maybe because this poor schmuck really is a chump.* He laughed out loud at his own less-than-clever quip.

Ethan knew in his heart of hearts that this show, which he was toying with calling *Life and Death*, was going to be the biggest show in the history of television. Bigger than all the Super Bowls combined. Bigger than the final episodes of *M*A*S*H* and *Seinfeld*, bigger than the TV news on the morning of 9/11.

He got up, went to the full-length mirror on the inside door of the wardrobe, and looked deep into his own reflection.

"Ethan Overbee," he said aloud, "you are the shit."

***

Deirdre didn't say a word when Jared finished telling the family about the television show. The only sound in the room was that of Trebuchet licking his private parts.

"Guys?" Jared asked, confused. He seemed to think this was good news, like Deirdre should get up and give him a high five. "You'll never have to worry about money again," he added in a voice that was both unsure and timid. "It's really no big deal. Our lives will go on as normal, just with a few cameras in the house. And besides, they're mostly just interested in seeing me die."

That started Jackie crying again. Her blond ponytail bounced with heaving sobs that she tried but failed to hold back.

"Girls," Deirdre said to her daughters, "why don't you go upstairs? I want to talk to your father."

Neither Jackie nor Megan said a word. They simply got up and left the table. Megan put an arm around her older sister as they left the room, nuzzling her head into the nape of Jackie's neck. This in itself was astonishing to Deirdre. On most days, the girls weren't oil and water; they were gasoline and a lit match.

When they were toddlers, Jackie three and Megan one, Jackie protected and loved her baby sister. So much so that Deirdre constantly admonished her older daughter: "Get off your sister, Jackie" or "She hit you because she wants you to stop trying to hug her."

Even then, Megan seemed to have disdain for Jackie. She learned to say the names of everyone in her life—Mama, Dada, "Taybooshay" (for Trebuchet), even Danny and Lexi from daycare—before she figured out how to say Jackie.

When the two girls attended the same elementary school, Jackie looked after Megan. She walked her to class, made sure she had her lunch, and let her hang around her older friends, the few that there were.

At first, Megan accepted Jackie's help as the natural order of things. But as time wore on and she became enmeshed in her own social network, Megan wrote Jackie off. She went from being Susan Pevensie's little sister, Lucy, to Cinderella's wicked stepsister Drizella. At least that's how Jackie saw it, and on some days, Deirdre thought she was right.

It wasn't just that Megan no longer had time for Jackie, it was that she taunted her, belittled her, did everything she could to crush her spirit. Jackie was so caught off-guard by the sudden change that she just absorbed the abuse, never fighting back.

Once, when Megan was trying to impress a group of friends visiting the house after school, she locked Jackie in a closet until Jackie swore that she, Jackie, was a lesbian. Megan didn't really know what the word meant, and Jackie, two years older, didn't understand why Megan thought it was an insult. But the cruelty with which the taunt was administered left no room to question Megan's intentions. By the time Jackie caved to her sister's demands, screaming, "I'm a lesbian, I'm a lesbian!" she was hysterical. She didn't hear Megan unlock the closet door or leave the bedroom. Deirdre found Jackie asleep in the closet two hours later, when it was time for dinner. Jackie offered no explanation.

(While she didn't sell her sister out, Jackie did, later that night, when everyone was asleep, steal Megan's favorite lip gloss, Raspberry Sparkle. She managed to keep her laughter in check the next day as her sister frantically tore the bathroom apart looking for it. It was a small but significant act for Jackie. The lip gloss was a kind of trophy, proof that she shouldn't be trifled with, even though she was trifled with more often than not. Jackie still kept the lip gloss in the back of her underwear drawer, wrapped in a pair of socks.)

That now, in the wake of all that was happening with their father, they found solace in each other's arms, in each other's company, was a sign to Deirdre of how much life was changing in the Stone household.

But just because Jared was sick didn't mean the world had to turn completely upside down. Deirdre had had enough.

"Are you fucking kidding me? All of America watching our daughters watch their father die? This is supposed to be good news?"

"But, D," he began.

"But nothing. We can't go through with it."

"I already signed. We're committed."

"No, Jared, you're committed. We're outta here." Deirdre got up from the table and started to leave the room. She made it all the way to the door before Jared said, "It's five million dollars."

Deirdre stopped in her tracks.

"D, I'm going to die. No matter what we do, I'm going to die. Let's at least cash in."

Deirdre didn't turn around, but she didn't leave the room, either.

PART THREE

Lights, Camera, Action

Friday, September 25

The day the cameras moved into the Stone family house, it was raining. A cool, misting drizzle, more typical of January weather in Portland than late September, made the air thick with moisture and with anticipation.

A collection of men hauled large black chests from two vans parked on the street. Jackie and Megan watched from Jackie's bedroom window and thought that the men looked like roadies setting up for a concert.

Deirdre stood in the foyer as they passed and thought they looked like angels of death.

Trey wondered if they had kibble.

Jared didn't wonder anything; he was lying on the floor of his office, snoring.

As the television crew unpacked its equipment and began placing cameras and microphones all around the house, Glio found himself lying on a long flat table staring up at a bright light. A cloth strap held his head firmly in place. Without warning, the table began to slide into a tube of some sort. There were a few clicks and some whirring sounds, and the table slid back out.

A twenty-something woman with patrician features, a Texas accent, and pert breasts smiled at Glio. She told him that the radiologist would read the scan results and send them to his doctor in twenty-four to forty-eight hours.

The memory being consumed was Jared's first CT scan, and Glio delighted in the range of emotions he got to experience. There was awe at the technology, lust for the nurse, fear of the report, and, of course, fatigue and confusion. It was like a never-ending-memory bowl at Olive Garden, and Glio wasn't shy about going back for seconds. Or thirds.

***

Late that same night, after the crew had gone, jumbles of wires and cables now strewn everywhere, Jackie left her room and found her mother sitting on the couch. Deirdre was in her flannel pj's, her feet up on the coffee table, a MacBook on her lap. Jackie couldn't help but notice the lines around her mother's eyes and arching down from the corners of her mouth. The woman was tired, beaten down. Jackie had been so consumed by her own feelings that she hadn't really considered what this whole ordeal had been doing to her mom.

"Hey, Jax." Deirdre closed the computer and patted a spot on the couch.

Jackie sat down, but she didn't snuggle in as it seemed her mother hoped and expected she would. She stared at her hands for a long moment before letting out a big breath of air. "Mom, why are we doing this?" Jackie motioned to the cameras that had been installed in all four corners of the living room ceiling, each one seeming like a malevolent eye just waiting to wake up.

The interminable pause before her mother answered told Jackie most of what she needed to know. "The truth?" Deirdre asked. Jackie nodded. "Money." Her mother's voice was flat, devoid of life.

Jackie didn't know how to respond to that. She thought back to the day she learned the real value of money.

When she was eight and Megan was six, they set up a lemonade stand at the end of the driveway. Jackie could still remember the feeling of anticipation as she and her sister and mother squeezed lemon after lemon, mixing the juice and the rinds with water, ice, and sugar. The kitchen, to Jackie, smelled like summer.

Because she was between second and third grade and had mastered her writing skills, Jackie was tasked with creating the sign that read "Lemonade, Fifty Cents." The next line, "Keep Cool. Keep Fresh," was a slogan Jackie had devised on her own, and it made her swell with pride.

Her father set up a card table, along with a shoe box filled with quarters and dollar bills to make change, and they waited. Then, as Jackie believed with all her heart would happen, a car stopped. And then another. And then another. They kept on coming.

Some of the drivers refused to accept change, making the lemonade stand profits soar, and each looked like a happy, satisfied customer. Thinking back, Jackie realized that most of the "customers" were neighbors and family friends that Deirdre had probably called and asked to stop by. But on that July day, Jackie felt every bit the entrepreneur. When all was said and done, the girls had made ten dollars, five dollars each.

"What are you going to do with your money?" Deirdre asked.

"I'm going to buy a tiara!" Megan, only six, was already well along the path of the person she was destined to become.

"I'm not sure," Jackie said. "I think maybe I want to buy a book. But is five dollars enough to buy a book?"

"I'll tell you what," Jared answered. "Let's go tiara and book shopping and see what we can afford."

Twenty minutes later, the whole family was in the car, the girls each clutching a pocketbook filled with their newfound wealth.

"Can we go to the tiara store first?" Megan asked.

"Actually, Peanut, we're closer to the bookstore." Jackie knew her father would want to go to the bookstore first. The family seemed to find time almost every weekend to pay a visit to Powell's. Jackie loved it. Megan groaned.

After they parked, as they were about to go in the front door, Jared put a hand on Jackie's shoulder. "Hold up a sec." Deirdre, Jackie, and Megan followed his gaze and saw a man sitting a few feet down from the door. A sign that read "This is awkward for me, too . . ." was propped in front of him, and next to it sat a tattered basket lined with a smattering of loose change and dollar bills.

Jackie watched her mother's alarm as her father approached the man. Jared had recently won his first election and had been going out of his way to connect with the community. Jackie thought this must be part of his job. She followed her father, Megan and Deirdre staying a few feet behind.

"Hi," Jared said.

The man looked up and met Jared's eyes. He seemed confused. Jackie couldn't tell if he was confused that Jared was talking to him, or just confused in general. His clothes—a dirty pair of blue jeans; a black sweater with little holes in the shape of some nighttime constellation, which must have been warm in the summer heat; and boots with the soles worn thin—along with the sign and money, told Jackie that this man was homeless. She knew from television and from overhearing adults talk that there were homeless people in the world, but she wasn't sure she had ever seen one, and she definitely had not met one.

When the man didn't answer, Jared squatted down so they were eye level. He extended his hand and said, "Hi, I'm Jared Stone. I'm your state representative." The man paused a beat before he burst out laughing. Jackie thought the man was old at first, but on hearing him laugh she thought maybe he wasn't much older than her dad. His laugh was genuine and infectious. Her dad laughed, too, and it made Jackie smile.

"Yeah, I'm guessing you don't really care that I'm your representative. Maybe you've got bigger fish to fry."

"Mister," the man said, speaking for the first time, his voice gravelly but each word spoken clearly, "I wish to holy hell I had a fish to fry."

Jared smiled at this. "You know the city has shelters. You can get a good meal and a warm bed," he offered.

"I know. But you can only stay so many nights in a row."

"Do you work?" The man shook his head. He was about to say more, but he looked at Jackie and Megan and thought better of it. Jackie could tell the reason he couldn't work was some sort of dark secret that he thought might scare children. Even at eight, this touched Jackie; this man who had nothing still had concern for her.

"Well," Jared said, taking his wallet out of his jacket, "maybe this will help a little." Jared placed a twenty-dollar bill in the basket. The man stared at it in disbelief for a second, wondering if maybe there was some trick, but then he snatched it up in one fluid motion.

"It will help a lot," he said. "Thank you."

"Do you have a name?"

"Richard."

"Well, Richard, it's nice to meet you." Jared stuck out his hand again, and this time the man shook it. He smiled at Jared and nodded to Deirdre, Jackie, and Megan.

"C'mon, girls," Jared said, moving back toward the entrance to the bookstore.

"Wait." They all turned to look at Jackie. She opened her small pocketbook and took out the five one-dollar bills her mother had given her in exchange for the pile of quarters she'd earned at the lemonade stand. "Here," she said, crouching down and gently laying the money in the man's basket with great care.

The man met her eyes and sort of smiled; somehow that made him seem sadder. He nodded but couldn't find any words of thanks to offer. Jackie was confused and worried that maybe she'd done something wrong. When she looked up at her mother in alarm, Deirdre's smile told her everything she needed to know. She pulled her into a tight hug and kissed the top of her head.

"You take care now, Richard," Jared said, "and you put my daughter's money to good use." He steered his family into the bookstore.

It wasn't until years later that Jackie understood her father's final admonition to Richard, that he not use Jackie's money, the hard-won money of an eight-year-old girl, for drugs or alcohol. On that day, Jackie simply felt proud; she felt good. So very good.

Megan clutched her own pocketbook to her chest and, once they were in the store, proclaimed that she was not "giving my money to that dirty man." Jared shook his head and smiled, chalking it up to Megan's age. No one said a word as they fanned out and went book shopping.

Jared and Deirdre bought Jackie a book anyway—Judy Blume's *Otherwise Known as Sheila the Great*—as a reward for her selfless behavior. While they did stop at another store so Megan could buy a tiara (also with financial help from her parents), Jackie couldn't remember ever seeing her sister wear it.

Jackie thought about that day as she processed her mother's one-word answer to the question of why they'd signed on with the television network: *Money.*

The word in this context seemed filthy; it filled Jackie with a kind of dread. "Okay," she said, "but I hope we're going to do something good with it."

Deirdre looked at her daughter, sighed, and nodded. "C'mere," she said, and held out her arms. Jackie curled up, resting her head on Deirdre's lap. She fell asleep while her mother stroked her hair.

***

With the memory of his first CT scan—and the fear and apprehension that came with it—now gone from Jared's psyche, his thrice-weekly trips to the doctor didn't cause him nearly as much anxiety.

The radiation treatments—which Jared thought of as "microwaving my brain," though he could no longer remember why he thought that—were painless. But they were making him tired. He thought about stopping the treatments and asked the doctor about it.

"Really, Jared, it's up to you," she told him. "It's what we talked about when I first signed you up for the program." Jared tried to recall that conversation but couldn't seem to find a marker for it anywhere in his memory. "The treatments may buy you a little more time, but they may also make the time you have left less . . . less . . ."

"Alive?"

"Yes," the doctor answered, "less alive. You should talk this over with your family."

Deirdre was ready to support either decision, treatment or no treatment. She was like that, a partner and ally to the very end. She went with Jared to the cancer care center at the hospital, held his hand as he waited for the treatments, and kept the house running as he withered. It made Jared love her all the more. But as nice as Deirdre's support was, it wasn't especially helpful for making decisions. Jared needed someone to tell him what to do.

Ethan, the man from the television studio, seemed to think continuing the radiation was a good idea. "If I were in your shoes, I'd want every second I could have with my kids. But it's your choice, Jared."

Jared didn't know why Ethan was so interested in his health—he didn't even remember telling Ethan about his dilemma—but thought it was nice that the man cared. Besides, it was the only real advice Jared was getting, so he took it.

The treatments continued.

***

Glio was under assault. Searing, blinding streams of fire were slicing through him like Darth Vader's lightsaber through Luke

Skywalker's arm. *That's just what it feels like*, Glio thought, *like I'm being attacked with a lightsaber.*

With tendrils too numerous to count and stretching simultaneously into different parts of Jared's brain, Glio had grown large. The lightsaber was managing to cut off small pieces, each one shriveling and dying as it was severed from the central tumor.

The radiation was making the pathways through Jared's memories feel like an all-night rave gone wrong. Flashing strobes and thundering sounds restricted Glio's movements; he could hardly get from one neuron to the next without losing his way. And it wasn't just the focused blast of ionized electrons that were causing distress; Jared Stone's entire immune system was attempting to wage war against the invader, his corporeal being was at DEFCON 1.

Jared's brain, Glio realized, was fighting back.

Glio was stunned enough to pause, but only for a second. Jared's brain had made the classic mistake of bringing a knife to a gunfight.

Steeling his resolve, Glio bared his metaphorical fangs and tore through Jared's gray matter, unleashing a force more terrifying than hurricanes, earthquakes, or tornadoes, more terrifying than anything in heaven or on Earth. He didn't know or care that he made his host fall over. The only thing he could do was satisfy his appetite.

And so he did.

***

"A reality series?" Hazel asked the question into the headset tethered to her computer. She had asked for Bluetooth-enabled wireless headphones for her birthday, but her parents, looking for any possible way to discourage the hours Hazel spent playing online games, bought her a wristwatch instead. Hazel, after pretending to admire the delicate chrome braiding on the band, buried it in her sock drawer the minute she was alone in her bedroom, forgetting it was there a few days later.

"Yes, a reality show," the voice came back through her headphones. Hazel, or rather her character, Guinevere the Glad, was standing on the edge of a sparsely wooded forest deep in the heart of Azeroth. She was talking with a fellow guild member, Kirkadelic, a level fifty-two Night Elf Rogue. "It's called *Life and Death*, and it airs next week."

Despite her stomach-turning worry, the revelation of Hazel's true identity had turned out to be a nonevent in the World of Warcraft. Three other guild members even drew inspiration from Hazel and confessed their own true identities. In one fell swoop, a policeman became a retired schoolteacher, a sommelier became a sanitation worker, and a nineteen-year-old female college student studying meteorology became an unemployed thirty-seven-year-old man.

"So, what," Hazel asked, sounding more perturbed than she wanted to, "we sit at home and watch Jared die while we eat Doritos and drink Coca-Cola?"

"Hey, don't kill the messenger," Kirk answered, "but yeah, something like that. I'm sure that's who's sponsoring it. 'Enjoy a refreshing Coca-Cola as you watch a fellow human being succumb to the joy that is brain cancer.'"

"Ugh. I think I need to go lie down. I'm going to log off for a while."

"You mean people play this game sitting up?" Kirk asked the question just as Hazel clicked "quit" and whooshed out of the game. She took her headphones off and flopped down on her bed.

"No way am I going to watch that show," Hazel said with conviction to her ceiling fan. Both Hazel and the ceiling fan knew it was a lie. She was like a drug addict swearing off her next dose. It never worked. And for reasons she couldn't understand, Jared Stone had become Hazel's drug.

***

There was only one television at the Sisters of the Perpetual Adoration convent. It was the very same color set the original Mother Superior received as a premium when she opened the order's first checking account in the mid-1970s. It had a round dial for changing channels and a built-in antenna. The picture was fuzzy, but it picked up the few remaining broadcast channels.

The nuns and novitiates kept the television clean and dust-free, like they kept everything clean and dust-free; to them it was just another piece of furniture. As far as they knew, the set—which lived in a common room away from the dormitory—had never been turned on.

This was true. Except from eleven p.m. to midnight, Mondays through Fridays, and then only for Sister Benedict.

First it was the late news, which kept the Sister informed of all that was wrong with the world. (This was where she had watched Jared interviewed by the local Portland media.) After the news was the real allure of the television, *The Duke Hamblin Show*, the Sister's one and only guilty pleasure.

The newest entrant in the flooded market of late-night television hosts, Hamblin had a conservative agenda that expressed itself through stale political jokes, a feigned disdain for the "Hollywood elite" (even though movie-star interviews were his bread and butter), and enough God references to embarrass a camera-hungry professional baseball player.

Hamblin had just finished his monologue and was going to a commercial break when he read a network promo: "Don't forget to watch *Life and Death*, the most important reality series in the history of television. Beginning one week from tonight on ATN, you will follow the life of Jared Stone as an inoperable tumor slowly consumes his brain. Our cameras have complete access to his home, twenty-four hours a day. See how he and his family deal with terminal illness and death. This will be a truly unprecedented and transformative television event. We'll be right back."

The peanut-butter-slathered cracker that had been in Sister Benedict's hand fell facedown onto her habit, sticking there for a moment before sliding to the floor. She didn't even notice she had dropped it.

***

When Sherman Kingsborough saw the commercial for *Life and Death*, he was drunk. He had been sitting in one of the seventeen rooms of the eight-thousand-square-foot Palm Beach mansion bequeathed to him by his father, the young man's only company a bottle of Maker's Mark.

The week after Jared's auction had been delisted, Sherman slid into a terrible funk. He was frightened at the ease with which he was not only prepared, but eager to slay a fellow human being. And yet he couldn't get the idea out of his mind.

He had flown from his father's house in Aspen to his father's house in Provence to his father's house in Palm Beach, trying to outrun his own wicked thoughts, but it didn't work. Now he was trying to drink them out of his head.

He was drunk enough when he first saw the commercial that he wondered if it wasn't some sort of alcohol-induced hallucination. He was just sober enough to know it was real.

Sherman had only one thought: *This is a sign. I must kill Jared Stone.*

***

Before Jared got sick, a typical weekday in the Stone house would begin like a typical weekday in any middle-class home.

The first to wake up was Megan. When life is good, when you're popular, pretty, and filled with hope and ambition, you bound out of bed. She would spend an hour primping and prepping for school, leaving no detail untouched. Her assortment of makeup, accessories, and style magazines was more appropriate for a twenty-four-year-old fashionista than it was for an eighth grader.

Deirdre, almost a cliché of a suburban mom with a full-time job, would sprint through her morning routine: take a shower (she had it down to seven minutes), get dressed (each day's ensemble laid out the night before), check e-mail (always amazed at the two a.m. time stamp on messages from her boss), and cajole Jackie awake (never succeeding on the first try, never failing by the third).

Jackie, once roused, would spend a few extra minutes with her head on the pillow, staring at her phone. When life is bad, when you don't have close friends, when you shift between apathy and despair, you don't bound out of bed, you sort of roll out. Her finger would work its way through each of her social media sites, her brain, fresh from a good night's sleep, absorbing all the news and information it could. She would pick out the least flashy clothes she could find, take her backpack, and trudge down to the kitchen.

Jared, unless he had to be in Salem or at a client or constituent meeting, would stay in his pajamas—ratty flannel pj bottoms and a rattier Trail Blazers T-shirt, make lunches for all three Stone women, and then cook everyone breakfast. He took full responsibility for getting everyone ready for the day, and he loved it.

Megan would chatter through the pancakes, eggs, or Jared's specialty, Island French Toast, while Deirdre read the paper and Jackie read a book. Jared would walk all three to the door, kiss each good-bye, and, with Trebuchet at his side, watch them go. Then the two of them, Jared and Trey, would go for a walk around the block, come home, and retreat to Jared's office.

Jared would work on graphic design projects or legislative issues, and Trey would sleep, occasionally waking up and nudging Jared for another trip outside or a scratch behind the ear. If he had no pressing deadlines, Jared would play Tiger Woods Golf on the Wii console that the family had given him for Christmas.

If Norman Rockwell had painted in the early twenty-first century, the Stone family would have been his inspiration.

Jared's cancer changed everything. The *Life and Death* crew, having established a beachhead in the Stone house, changed it more. The people coming and going; the not so artfully hidden cameras, cables, lights, and microphones; the constant stream of phone calls from the media—and not just the media, but THE media—with the *Today* show and *Good Morning America* scheduling interviews with Jared and his family.

With all their expenses covered by the network, and with Jared's health in sharp decline, Deirdre took an indefinite leave of absence from work. She didn't trust the ATN employees alone in her house all day long and wanted to be there for her husband and daughters. Not sure how else to fill her time, she helped Jared with household chores, meaning she took them over completely.

Jared abandoned his few remaining projects and tried to devote what was left of his attention to the television show. He wound up sleeping most of the time instead.

The girls still went to school, but with their newfound celebrity, their days were anything but normal. Megan now spent *two* hours primping and preening each morning. Jackie, in response to the media attention foisted on her family, shied away from Twitter, *The Huffington Post*, and *The Daily Beast*. With the Internet—her one outlet to the world—more or less severed, she retreated further into her shell.

The Stones did their best to adapt to the new normal that had descended on them, trying to make it part of the landscape. But this was different from trips to the mall and family game nights. This was a twenty-four-seven spotlight on the end of their father's and husband's life with all the world watching. Their house was being transformed into a cruel kind of fishbowl, and all they could do was pucker and swim.

***

Ethan Overbee spent the week before the *Life and Death* premiere in Portland. Normally he left the work of producing a show to the hired hands—which is how he thought of the crew—but he was too personally and professionally invested in this particular show to leave anything to chance.

Moving between the control truck and the house with the confidence of a conquering general, Ethan used his considerable charm to win over everyone involved in the project. From the director to the camera people to the sound engineers, Ethan established himself as a benevolent leader, a man who would give their lives meaning and make their careers matter.

He even managed, to Jared's great relief, to get Deirdre and Megan to feel better about the program. He talked about how what they were doing was important, how it would ease the suffering of so many people who were facing their own battles with terminal illness. Ethan cast himself in the role of hero, and it worked—with two notable exceptions.

Every time Ethan entered a room, Trebuchet left. Though he was adept at fawning over them when he needed to, Ethan hated animals of all kinds, and that was not lost on Trey. Like all dogs, Trebuchet's vomeronasal organ was fully operational, and it told him to stay away from this human. He didn't growl at Ethan, but his tail would stop wagging and hang to the floor when the two were in the same room; invariably Trebuchet would find the nearest exit.

The other exception was, of course, Jackie. No matter how hard he tried, Ethan couldn't get the girl to warm up. She would sit politely and listen as he regaled them with stories of television, Hollywood, and glamour. Then, when attention was directed elsewhere, she would follow the dog out of the room. She just didn't trust the man. It was like he was selling something her family really didn't need.

For Jackie, it was all becoming too much to bear. First was the news of her father's inoperable cancer, then the eBay listing, and now television crews invading her house. Jackie was drifting upside down in the void of space. No direction, no propulsion, no air.

The kids at school had treated her like a leper after they found out her father had a brain tumor. On some level that hurt her; on another, she was happy for the privacy. But now that the Stone family was going to have its own television series, kids went from ignoring Jackie to making her the center of attention. The #LifeAndDeath hashtag and the two-minute trailer, now on YouTube, were trending in a way and manner that Jackie just couldn't understand. Why did all these people care? She couldn't get from one class to another without answering a question, overhearing gossip about her family, or deflecting some ill-formed taunt. Worst of all, a particularly vapid girl in the senior class had started a *Life and Death* Fan Club and was distributing T-shirts. A photo of the Stone family, taken from Jared's Flickr account and featuring a particularly surly Jackie, was emblazoned on the front of the shirt. How could anyone, Jackie wondered, be so thoughtless, so callous, as to join a fan club to watch her father die?

She begged her parents to let her stay home, but Deirdre insisted that they not give in to the glare of the television lights, that "everything should be as normal as we can manage." Jared didn't seem to grasp the gravity of his daughter's reaction, or he did grasp it but didn't trust that he *really* grasped it, and deferred to Deirdre.

The only peace Jackie found in her daily routine was chatting with Max during her computer lab. Turning a blind eye to the Facebook news feed, lest she stumble across a post about *Life and Death*, Jackie would move her mouse directly to the chat window and click on Max's name. Other than Trebuchet, he was the one thing in Jackie's life that was constant and unchanging. Mostly.

Max

Tell me, Solnyshko, what is this euthanasia?

This was Max's first question in their first chat after she had abandoned him the morning of her crying fit. She had sent him a private message, assuring him that everything was fine and that she just wanted him to forget about it and move on. Max took the request to heart and pretended like it had never happened. But that didn't stop him from trying to find other ways of getting Jackie to talk about her predicament.

Jackie

Why?

Max

Just something about which I was reading.

Jackie

"Just something I was reading about," Max.

Max

Yes, that.

Jackie

It's like when someone is sick and dying and you help them end their life.

Max was silent for a moment.

Max

You mean, you kill them?

Jackie

Well, yeah, but only because they are really sick.

Max

I am not sure this I understand.

Jackie

"I'm not sure I understand this," Max. Put the noun at the end.

Max

Yes, yes. But tell me, do people do this? Help each the other die?

Jackie

I don't know. I guess so. But only when they're so sick they're going to die anyway.

Max

As with cancer.

Jackie

Yes.

This was hitting close to home, but Jackie, for some reason, didn't mind. For one thing, it was Max. He was a million miles away. For another, it was good to finally talk about it without really talking about it.

> **Max**
> This does not to me seem right. Oops. This does not seem right to me.
>
> **Jackie**
> ☺
>
> **Max**
> Smiley face because it does not seem right?
>
> **Jackie**
> No, Max, smiley face because the way you talk is cute.

I cannot believe I just typed that, Jackie thought to herself.

> **Max**
> This I like the sound of!
>
> **Jackie**
> LOL!
>
> **Max**
> What?
>
> **Jackie**
> Nothing, Max, don't worry. But tell me why you think it's wrong?
>
> **Max**
> To help a person die?
>
> **Jackie**
> Yes.

Max

Because life is . . . what is the word? Please wait while I
look it up.

There was a long pause while Max consulted his Russian–
English dictionary.

Max

Because life is sacred.

Jackie

Yeah, it is. So then why make a person suffer before he
dies if he's going to die anyway?

There was another long pause, and this time Jackie wanted
to change the subject. Her own feelings on euthanasia were
starting to crystallize, but she didn't want to get all weird and
eggheady on Max.

She was saved by the bell for the next period.

Jackie

'Bye, Max, I have to go to my next class. Next time let's talk
about something fun. ☺

Max

Anything for you, Solnyshko.

Jackie left the computer lab and went to her locker. Someone
had taped a news article there.

Quest for Stone

(AP) Huntsville, Alabama—When seventeen-year-old Hazel Huck stumbled on the eBay listing for terminally ill Oregonian Jared Stone, something touched a nerve.

"I don't know," said the teenager in a phone interview. "It just didn't seem right that this guy was reduced to selling his life."

Stone, a graphic designer and a member of the Oregon state legislature, was diagnosed with a high-grade glioblastoma multiforme, a usually fatal brain tumor. He claimed to have less than six months to live, and he was selling his life on eBay to the highest bidder.

Huck, a senior at the Florence Nightingale School for Young Women, turned to her friends in cyberspace to raise money to bid on Stone's listing. An avid participant of role-playing games like World of Warcraft and Dark Age of Camelot, Huck invited her cyber friends to join her on a quest. Her goal was to win the auction, and to allow Stone to die with his family and his dignity intact.

"It was amazing how fast people responded," the modest girl said. "We all sort of got Jared fever."

Using her World of Warcraft character, a level sixty-five druid called Guinevere the Glad, Huck created a viral campaign inside the fantasy world.

"It just took off. Everyone thought it was so cool that we could do something tangible together. You know, instead of just role playing."

Unfortunately for Huck, her efforts, impressive though they were, would fall short. Mr. Stone's reserve—the minimum bid needed to win the auction—was $1 million, $700,000 more than the cyber group was able to raise. And a week later, the auction was delisted for violating eBay terms of use.

"It's sad that we didn't get to help," Huck said, "but I'm glad we tried, and glad we came together."

Someone had scrawled "Your father's a freak!" across the top in red marker. Jackie took the clipping down and put it in her bag, taking care not to rip it. She thought for a minute about finding somewhere to hide from her classmates for the rest of the day, but she just didn't have the energy. Jackie slumped her shoulders and shuffled off to biology. The thought of dissecting a frog, once revolting, no longer seemed so bad.

***

Life and Death was scheduled to run from nine to ten p.m., seven nights a week for as long as Jared was alive. Each episode would feature an edited collage of scenes from the Stone household, shot during the previous twenty-four hours, mixed with interviews with Jared and his family. Ethan's plan was to use the first few episodes to get viewers comfortable with the show's premise, then introduce viewer interactivity along with celebrity drop-ins.

The pitch to potential advertisers was simple: If the television network gave people permission to watch another person die, they would tune in, in droves. It wasn't a hard sell. Car companies, laundry detergents, feature films, and fast-food establishments all bought time, and all created custom spots to run during the program. Each one tried to out-condole the other, with the coup de grâce being a McDonald's ad that ran thirty seconds of icy blackness with small gray McDonald's arches in the bottom corner. In the last ten seconds, off-white letters fade in, telling the audience that "No matter what, we all have to eat. McDonald's, the official meal of *Life and Death*."

The premiere episode ran on a Thursday night, and the Nielsen numbers were through the roof. Nearly 80 million households watched the opening scene of Jared and Deirdre sitting on their front porch, looking happy, healthy, and normal. It was an edited interview conducted by an unseen producer as they answered unheard questions. The cut from answer to answer was intentionally rough, jarring the viewer ever so slightly. Deirdre did most of the talking.

Deirdre: We've been married for twenty years.

Jared: We met in college [jump cut] NYU.

Deirdre: It was a physics lab. We were both fulfilling a science requirement, and we both hated it.

Jared: We skipped one day and went for coffee. We've been together ever since.

Deirdre: I'm originally from here [jump cut] Portland. So we settled here. We wanted to be near my mom. It was great when the girls were young. They got to know their grandmother well, before she passed away. [jump cut] Cancer of the bile duct.

Jared: We have two kids. Jackie is fifteen, and Megan is thirteen.

The camera zoomed in and froze on Jared's face, the pain and confusion in his eyes unmistakable.

Jared: Or at least I think that's how old they are.

The title credits ran, and the show was off and running.

***

Ethan watched the first episode of *Life and Death* alone in his palatial Malibu living room. The network brass, having bought into the notion that Ethan had stumbled onto the next wave of reality TV, wanted to have a party to celebrate the premiere and the unprecedented amount of advertising dollars it generated. But Ethan declined. He thought that now was the moment to appear introspective, aloof, to start to create the legend of Ethan Overbee in the minds of his peers. *Just like Steve Jobs,* he thought.

He watched the show on a custom-made, eighty-inch, Bluetooth-enabled plasma television embedded with video-conferencing capabilities and surround sound. He sat in an armchair made of burnished leather and held in his hand a tumbler of Beefeater gin, with a lime and a splash of tonic for good measure.

Ethan simply could not believe how well the first show had gone. In a week, all of America would be watching the plight of poor Jared Stone. Hell, even he wanted to see what happened next. It was compelling, heart-wrenching, beautiful television, even if it was a bit morose.

Melancholy was nothing new to television. Every news department in America feasted on tragedy. When a hurricane hit, they were the first ones in (and the first ones out). When terrorists blew up a domestic target, they provided round-the-clock coverage. When a lone gunman opened fire in a post office, they interviewed every family member of every victim, every relative of the shooter, and every talking head with an opinion or theory, no matter how stupid. Jared Stone was no different. There was even an internal discussion at ATN to run the show out of the news department, but Ethan wasn't about to let his baby go.

As he watched the final credits roll beneath a teaser for tomorrow night's episode, Ethan was so emotional he wept.

***

During the airing of the premiere episode of *Life and Death*, Glio was feasting on Jared's memory of his first date with Deirdre. Maybe it was because he and Deirdre had told that story to the *Life and Death* cameras. Or maybe it was the other way around, and Jared told the story knowing on some subconscious level that the memory would soon be lost forever.

Glio found himself blowing across a latte to cool it, looking at Deirdre. She had green eyes, a button nose, and dirty blond hair pulled tight in a ponytail. Her long, slender fingers massaged her coffee—which was black, unaltered—in a manner that was something between seductive and provocative. Glio was so nervous as he relived this moment from Jared's life that he heard little of what Deirdre was saying. The mantra playing over and over again was "She's out of my league. She's out of my league."

After coffee, Glio and Deirdre walked through Washington Square Park, south into Soho and west into the heart of Greenwich Village. As the day wore on, Glio felt his confidence grow. His inhibitions dropped as he fell in love. His heart skipped a beat every time he paused to look at Deirdre; then he would dive back into the conversation and lose himself in the bubble that was growing around them.

When the date came to a close, four hours later, they were standing outside the entrance to Deirdre's dorm. Glio mustered the courage to kiss her good-bye. He was surprised that when their lips met a snippet of the memory of Jared's first kiss, consumed earlier, was inserted into the timeline he was watching, was living. Jared, Glio realized, compared every first kiss to that very first kiss.

He watched Deirdre retreat into the lobby of her dorm, and then he floated away, both in the memory and in Jared's brain.

***

Sherman Kingsborough didn't like the man sitting next to him. He had little patience for the hackneyed rhetoric spewing from the guy's crooked mouth.

The two of them were parked in the cell phone lot at the Portland International Airport, the radio in Sherman's Mercedes playing N.W.A's "Fuck tha Police." The classic gangsta rap song was Sherman's half-baked attempt to project an image that he was tough. It wasn't really working.

"It's going to cost you," the man in the passenger seat was saying. He was dressed in jeans, a brown leather bomber jacket, and very dirty work boots. His name was Bobby—"Just Bobby," he had told Sherman—and he looked so much like central casting's idea of a petty criminal that you had to figure him to be anything but.

"I told you, money isn't an object. I just need to get into that house."

After watching the first episode of *Life and Death*, Sherman began to formulate a plan. He would break into Jared's house in the middle of the night, when not very much was happening and not many people were stirring, neutralize any bystanders, and then kill Jared, making sure the deed was captured by one of the television cameras that seemed to be stationed in every room. When it was done, Sherman would remove his mask, revealing his identity. Then he would begin his flight from justice.

For Sherman, there were precious few ways to push the envelope of existence. Murder and flight were not only new experiences, they were exciting. And the worst-case scenario—capture—only meant that Sherman would get more new experiences: trial and prison. He had become the living embodiment of the cliché that idle hands make the devil's work. Sherman and Satan were forming quite the partnership.

The way he lived his life, Sherman had consorted with no shortage of shady characters. Bobby was just another cog to Sherman, a piece to be used and discarded. Still, he thought the guy was so unsubtle that he was kind of funny.

"There's a fuckload of security on that house," Bobby told him.

"Yes, I know. If there was no security, I would just ring the doorbell."

"Okay, okay, Richie Rich, don't get your panties all twisted up." Bobby laughed at his own inane joke.

"Can you help me?" Sherman asked, ignoring the nickname.

"Yeah," Bobby said. "Me and my buddies can make sure no one will be awake to stop you from going into the house, and we can make sure the house goes dark."

"I don't need the house to go dark. I just want to get inside unseen, and then be able to get away quickly."

"Fine, the house won't go dark. We'll make sure no one sees you come in or out. What are you doing in there, anyway? Is this some sort of heist?"

Heist? Sherman thought. *People really say "heist"?* "No questions," he said.

"Fine. Going to cost you, though."

"For Christ's sake, I told you—"

"Relax, relax, I'm just fucking with ya. Fifty thousand dollars." Bobby had a shit-eating grin, thinking he was about to take Sherman to the cleaners and back. It took all of Sherman's resolve not to laugh in Bobby's face.

***

The second episode of *Life and Death* was a master class in editing. As serious as Jared's decline was, as uncertain as he was about himself, it seemed so much worse on television.

In real life, Deirdre would ask Jared a simple question—"Does the dog need to go out?"—and Jared would be a beat late in answering. On the show, Deirdre would ask the question, and the editors would cut back and forth between Jared and Deirdre five or six times. The cuts were artificial, and the bewildered and pained facial expressions on both husband and wife were culled from other scenes, reactions to questions or comments that had nothing to do with walking the dog. But television was television. If it was on the screen, it was true. This was particularly difficult for Jared. When he watched the episode back at night, he just assumed he was every bit as confused as the show made him seem. He would shake his head and grunt as he replayed the scene in his own head.

Jackie Stone wasn't confused at all; she knew spin when she saw it. The whole thing made her blood boil, and something in her snapped. All of Jackie's darker impulses bubbled to the surface, and she took action.

At five a.m. the day after the second episode aired, Jackie quietly barricaded the front and rear doors of the house with small pieces of furniture stacked one on top of the other. Once she believed the doors were secure, she started going through the house with black nail polish, painting the lenses on each of the tiny button cameras hidden in every crevice and corner. It took the crew most of the day to undo the damage Jackie caused. She waited silently in her room all afternoon and evening for a scolding from her parents, or at least a talking-to from the director, but it never came.

Jackie's punishment came that night when episode three aired. Her attempted coup was, of course, captured on tape. It was cut together with footage of Jared lying on his office floor, of Megan talking on the phone to her friends, and of Jackie sulking. They showed every inch of Jackie's bedroom—including a smiling unicorn holding a rainbow in its teeth; the ceramic trinket, a remnant from an earlier phase of Jackie's life—while the voice-over painted her as a troubled loner with few friends who was having difficulty accepting her father's condition. Jackie saw it as a secret message from the producer: straighten up and fly right, or else.

The next Monday at school, where she was alternately cheered and jeered, was the longest of her life.

Jackie wanted nothing more than to talk to her father, but she knew the conversation would only wind up on television. So she retreated to her room, turned out the lights, and lay on her bed. *Let's see if this makes for good viewing,* she thought to herself. The producers didn't care. Jackie, from their perspective, had been neutralized.

Where are all the good people in the world? she wondered as she lay there in the dark. Then she remembered the news story that had been taped to her locker.

Jackie turned on the light, retrieved her book bag, and pulled out the article about Hazel Huck and her efforts to raise money to save Jared. She read it again and again, trying to drown out the reality of the world around her. She wanted to lose herself in that article, in that world.

***

Dappled sunlight fell on Sherman Kingsborough's face as he walked through the Portland Japanese Garden. He was disappointed that it didn't have a more lyrical name, like the Morikami Japanese Gardens near his father's mansion in Palm Beach, but he had to admit, the place was pretty damn nice.

Sherman had once dated a Buddhist girl who spent her time schooling him in the ways of The Middle Way. He did everything to woo her, including a spontaneous trip to Japan and a tour of Buddhist temples. Of course, none of it made any difference to Sherman. He cared as much for Buddha as he cared for God, which is to say not at all. *The things I've done just to get me some strange*, he thought to himself.

The only lasting impact of his search for enlightenment—or rather sleeping with a woman in search of enlightenment—was a penchant for Japanese architecture and Japanese gardens. He found them oddly soothing.

So it was not surprising that Sherman found himself admiring a Japanese maple, a soft carpet of its burgundy leaves on the ground beneath his feet, just hours before he was scheduled to embark on his mission to kill Jared Stone.

The girl he'd dated had taught him a few relaxation techniques—he liked to think of them as tricks rather than techniques—and he tried to employ them as he wandered the garden, but it was no use. His adrenal gland was working overtime, flooding his system with narcotic levels of stimulant. His mind was focused as if all his thoughts were being filtered through a magnifying glass, and his muscles were straining not to burst out of his skin.

He was ready.

***

Jared was spending an increasing amount of time lying on his office floor with the lights out. The few times he did engage with the outside world, other than his daily interviews with the *Life and*

Death producers and his visits to the doctor, were almost entirely with the right-to-die lobby. He had become their poster child, and something of a cause célèbre in the world of euthanasia advocacy.

Given his situation, Jared wanted to do as much for the lobby as he could. When he had the strength, he scheduled phone interviews with area newspapers and radio stations, and he had been working on an editorial for the *Oregonian*, but he couldn't seem to finish it:

Death with Dignity: An Insider's Perspective
by Jared Stone

As most readers know, I have a brain tumor. It's an inoperable high-grade glioblastoma multiforme, and it is killing me. This is unequivocally true; as much as anything can be unequivocally true when you no longer know what "true" means. There are no drugs; there is no surgery; there is no miracle in my future. Within four months, probably less, I will be dead.

I have decisions to make. Do I allow my family to watch me suffer and wither away? Or do I end my suffering and leave them earlier than I might otherwise?

Whether I choose to exercise my right to assisted suicide is a choice for me, for my family, and for my health-care providers. There is no reason, no logical reason, the state should involve itself in my personal affairs.

And that's as far as he could get. He knew what he wanted to say, or at least he thought he did, but couldn't figure out how to get it down on paper. He wasn't even sure what the first word of the next sentence might be.

A friend in the legislature, a coauthor of the expansion to the Death with Dignity Act, offered to finish the editorial for Jared, but that somehow didn't seem right. Jared just needed a bit more time with his mind sharp; if he could have more time he could put the editorial to bed. Unfortunately, the moments of true clarity were coming in shorter and less frequent bursts.

Jared gave up on the editorial and lay back down on the floor. His mind kept making more interesting and unusual anagrams. His favorite was "life and death"—*inflated head*—something poetic that he hoped to remember to tell the producer for the next day's interview segment of the show.

He knew he should be turning his attention to more serious matters—his family, his future, his legacy—but he couldn't seem to muster the interest. His brain was growing so devoid of memories that it was lacking context. For example, he knew his daughter Jackie was upset, but he wasn't sure he knew what that really meant. He wasn't even sure what he was supposed to feel.

Jared lay for a long moment thinking about Jackie, when he had what he thought was an epiphany, if that was the right word. He propped himself up on one elbow and spoke to the dog in the dark. "Hey, Trey. I think I really fucked up."

Jared put his head back down, closed his eyes, and slept. The memory of that moment would be gone before he woke.

***

Bobby the Hood had done his job. Sherman Kingsborough was

utterly alone as he skulked around the rosebushes outside the Stone house. His entire body, other than his eyes, was clothed in black Lycra. His $6,300 digital watch—which was good to water depths of one hundred meters, showed all twenty-four time zones, and responded to a voice command with its own preprogrammed, New Zealand–accented woman telling you the correct time—was flashing 3:33 a.m., the same time it had been displaying for at least ten minutes. In a pique of frustration, Sherman took the watch off and ground it into the sod outside Jared's kitchen. A muffled and lilting 3:33 a.m. seeped from the grass.

Sherman crept on until he found the back door, the one that matched the entrance on the map Bobby provided. As promised, it was unlocked and unguarded.

The house was completely dark. The only light came from a clock on the kitchen stove, which was, correctly, displaying the time as 3:51. Sherman took out his waterproof, plastic map of the house's interior and studied it under the glow of his red penlight. The drawing had been done by a member of the *Life and Death* security staff, who was—at that very moment— en route back home to Juárez, Mexico, the $10,000 he had been paid tucked neatly into a money belt he wore beneath his new leather jacket. The same person provided Bobby with the information that Jared almost always spent the night in his office, which was circled on the map.

Sherman moved forward on his belly, slithering out of the kitchen and up the stairs like a snake. He had practiced this so many times on his own stairs he could now move as if he had no bones in his body. When he reached the top, he checked the map again and realized he was right in front of the door to Jared's office. He was so close his forehead almost touched the wood.

He removed a twelve-inch hunting knife from the sheath that hung from his belt. Sherman clutched the knife in his hands and thought of the hours he practiced plunging the blade into the life-size dummy he had purchased. The dummy was meant for training guard dogs, but it had served his purpose. Sherman had done everything he could to mentally and physically prepare for this moment. The entirety of his brief life, he believed, had led to this place and time, had put him on the precipice of the ultimate human experience: the act of playing God.

And then he paused.

Who am I, he thought, *to decide who should live or die?* He lay there for a long moment, unable to move forward or move back. For a while, Sherman thought he might just stay there until the sun came up, letting the Stone family find him. *Maybe*, he thought, *they can help me*. But the feeling passed.

"Who am I to decide who should live or die?" he asked again, this time whispering it aloud. "I am Sherman mother-fucking Kingsborough, bi-otch, that's who." Proving once and for all that absolute power corrupts absolutely.

With all the stealth he could muster, Sherman reached up and turned the knob of the door, nudging it open gently. His constant attention to his physical being, his trials on Everest and in sailboats and on hang gliders and bungee cords, and his hours of practice specifically for this night had paid off. Sherman Kingsborough entered Jared Stone's private lair as if he were a ghost. He closed the door behind him. His moment had come.

***

As Jared slept, Glio was in the midst of consuming what Jared once described as a transcendental memory. He was at Big Sky Resort, sitting on a log in front of the BBQ shack at the top of the quad lift that served the gentler of the resort's two mountains.

Snowflakes were drifting lazily by, sticking to his gloves, hat, and eyelashes as he sipped hot chocolate and listened to Marshall Tucker sing "Can't You See," the music blaring through speakers outside the shack. It was one of the few times in Jared's life that he was completely and utterly in the moment. Nothing existed before that time and nothing after it. Jared, and now Glio, was perfectly centered. *This*, Glio thought, *is what it means to be alive.*

Jared had traveled to Montana with two guy friends during a college break. Deirdre, who he had been dating for almost a year, hadn't come along on the trip. It was the thought of Deirdre that pulled him out of his reverie. And that's when he knew he was no longer complete without her. He—Jared, Glio, both of them—was going to propose to Deirdre as soon as he got back to New York. Thinking that, knowing that, was one of the happiest moments of his life.

It was just at that instant, at the very zenith of his emotional contentment, when an eardrum-shattering scream exploded in Glio's head, or would have if Glio had had a head.

***

While Sherman Kingsborough was slithering into Jared Stone's home office in Portland, Hazel Huck, two hours later in Central time, was just waking up to get ready for school. Like much of America, she had been watching *Life and Death*. And like much of America, she'd been transfixed.

Having spent so much energy trying to raise money to help Jared, Hazel found it jarring to actually see the man and his family. He wasn't what she had expected, but then she wasn't really sure what that was.

Hazel liked Jared, Deirdre, Jackie, Megan, and Trebuchet. They were a nice family. She especially liked Jackie's act of defiance, painting the camera lenses. She knew she would have done exactly the same thing, because, if she was being honest, something about the show left a bad taste in her mouth. Jared Stone looked like he had comfort, and she presumed he would have wealth, but it seemed to her that he'd sold out, that there had to be a better way to die.

As she watched the Stone family, she couldn't shake the feeling that she'd failed them. That she was supposed to save them. But it didn't matter. It was all beyond her control.

Hazel stepped out of her pajama bottoms and trudged into the bathroom, trying to put the Stone family out of her mind, at least until eight p.m. that night.

***

While the door to Jared's office was clicking shut, Sister Benedict was lying in bed, unable to sleep. In three short hours, her forces would mobilize. With the Cardinal's blessing, the Sister had organized a small army of the righteous to surround the

Stone household in protest of the grotesque television show being filmed there.

In addition to the Sisters of the Perpetual Adoration, Sister Benedict had pledges of support from three other area convents—the Sisters of Holy Mercy, the Order of His Holy Brides of Repentance, and the plainly named Sisters of the Crucifixion—as well as from dozens of parishioners. If she played her cards right, and if the good Lord blessed her with media coverage, Sister Benedict knew that her effort would take on a life of its own, attracting good and devout Catholics from throughout the region.

Sister Benedict didn't need sleep. She was infused with the power of God.

***

A thousand miles south, Ethan Overbee sat on his Malibu terrace, staring at the white foam of the dark waves crashing on the beach. He was swirling a glass of translucent Hierbas in his hand. Ethan rarely slept more than three or four hours a night, and he knew that on this night, sleep would be elusive, if it came at all. He was happy to sit in the chill air and think.

In ten short hours, the ATN board was scheduled to meet. Ethan planned to use the political capital provided to him by the early success of *Life and Death* to begin his assassination of Thaddeus St. Claire. He would start slow, using this first meeting to call attention to Thad's skepticism about airing the show. Over the coming months he would paint Thad as being out of touch, a relic of the days of sitcoms and dramedies, someone deserving of a gold watch, a severance package, and maybe a cruise.

Ethan dozed there on his chair, his dreams of power and avarice blending with the repetitive tones of the ocean, lulling him into a sleeplike trance. He could hear his name over and over again in the folding waves.

"Ethan . . . Ethan . . . Ethan . . ."

***

Unaware of an intruder in their house, Deirdre, Jackie, and Megan all slept.

***

Sherman Kingsborough lay on the floor of Jared's office, the knife in his hand. The room was pitch-black, and Sherman was sorry he hadn't brought a pair of night-vision goggles. He waited for his eyes to adjust, but the darkness was nearly absolute.

Then he heard breathing.

Jared Stone.

Sherman crawled slowly toward the sound, a siren song leading him to his destiny. The anticipation and excitement of the moment were everything he'd hoped they would be. This was Everest all over again.

He stopped just short of the body; close enough to feel the breath on his forehead. Jared must have been sleeping on his back with his head turned to the side. *His breath*, Sherman thought, *is foul*.

Careful not to touch Jared and wake him up—now that he was this close, he realized he didn't want a struggle—Sherman raised the knife above his head, estimating where Jared's chest would be, paused one more time to check his resolve, and brought the blade down with all the strength his muscles could manage.

The knife found its victim, the flesh and bone giving more resistance than Sherman expected. But Sherman's well-toned, twenty-three-year-old arms, amped up on speed, had pushed with enough force that the knife went all the way to the floor.

In that instant, the moment the blade stopped its forward motion and caused Sherman's arms to recoil, two haunting sounds stunned him into immobility. First was a tremendous, inhuman howl of agony, hurt, surprise, and death. Sherman wasn't ready for that. Every fiber of his being now rebelled, wanting only to pull the knife out and turn back time. *Surely*, he thought, *I can turn back time. I'm Sherman motherfucking Kingsborough, bi-otch.* But the "motherfucking" and the "bi-otch" had lost all their edge. His brain even added an "Aren't I?"

The second sound was a very confused "What the fuck?"

***

Nineteen-year-old James Wynn was the first person to reach Jared's office in the wake of Sherman's attack. He was a production assistant, which he had quickly learned meant "any freaking job we want you to do," and had been in the truck with the third-shift director, watching as Sherman Kingsborough slithered into the pitch-black room.

"Who the hell is that?" said the director, a twenty-five-year-old recent graduate of UCLA who had landed the job through the good graces of an uncle at the network. He was pointing at a monitor showing the view from a camera equipped with a night-vision filter.

"Does he have a knife?" James asked the question to no one in particular as he peered closer to the screen.

"Holy shit!" the director screamed. "Get in there!" He grabbed his cell phone and dialed 911. James, who stood five feet seven inches tall and weighed all of 125 pounds, fully clothed and soaking wet, bolted from the control truck without stopping to think about what he might be running into. He was across the lawn, in the front door, and halfway up the flight of stairs when he heard the howl. His blood ran cold, but he still managed to push himself faster. He reached the office door a step ahead of Deirdre and Megan.

James paused for a second, sucked a breath deep into his chest, and pushed the door open. He reached in and flipped the light switch just inside the room.

It took him a minute to process the scene, his comprehension quickly aided by Deirdre's scream, and then Megan's. He could hear Mrs. Stone usher her daughter away.

There, in the middle of the office, sitting on the floor were Sherman Kingsborough and Jared Stone, both shielding their eyes from the sudden introduction of light. Just to Sherman's left, lying in a pool of blood, was Trebuchet, panting his final breaths.

"What the fuck?" Jared said again. He grabbed his temples and rolled onto his side.

James, like Sherman, was speechless.

Trebuchet gave one more whimper and gave up on life. That's when they heard the sirens.

PART FOUR

House (of Stone) Arrest

Tuesday, October 13

Maxim Andreevich Vasilcinov liked Jackie Stone. He liked her a lot. In fact, she was his only friend.

Max was the plump, pimply only child of a single mother. The photo he used for his Facebook profile was the result of an Internet search for "cute teen boy." He didn't have a girlfriend, he had never even held another girl's hand, and he wasn't particularly good at sports; nothing about the persona he presented to Jackie Stone was real.

When Max first heard about the social media exchange program, he was crestfallen. *Now*, he thought, *I can be reviled by children on two continents.* When he told his mother that he didn't want to participate, she lifted his chin and stared deep into his eyes. "Solnyshko," she said, "maybe this is a good thing. Maybe this is a chance to wipe the slate clean, to be the person you wish you could be."

Hearing that was like clouds parting over Max's ever so slightly misshapen head. He took the advice to heart.

He bought a special notebook and wrote pages and pages about the new Maxim Vasilcinov. In his fantasy, he had two parents; his father was a bureaucrat with the ministry of education, and his mother stayed at home to take care of him and his younger sister, Sasha. He had many friends at school, and he was a very fast runner. He was learning to play guitar on an old, used electric that his father had purchased from a secondhand shop. His favorite songs to play were by Green Day and Nirvana. And, so far, he had kissed three different girls.

Not one word of it was true.

The deeper Max delved into his imaginary world, the more engrossed he became. He started, on some level, to believe that the fantasy Max was real. The other students at his school didn't notice that, since the invention of this new Max, the old Max was walking a little taller, with a little more swagger. To them, he would always be "malo mudak," the little ass. But he didn't care, or at least he didn't care as much as he used to.

When the day finally came that he would meet his new Facebook friend, he was ready. Max had memorized his new life, had practiced different phrases; he would be bold and daring and all the things real life had beaten out of him. His teacher, a Polish immigrant named Miss Loskywitz, didn't say anything when she saw that Max was using a picture other than his own for his profile. She thought he was a nice boy who needed a break.

Max presumed Jackie was a boy when they first met. (Jackie's profile picture was of Trebuchet.) When he realized Jackie was a girl, his heart sank. Not only was his fiction designed specifically for an American boy, he didn't know how to even begin to talk to girls.

But it didn't matter. Jackie made it easy. She made everything easy.

Before long, Max was telling her about his fondness for movies, how he had studied all the great filmmakers, going as far back as Russia's own Eisenstein and his film *Battleship Potemkin*, and right up to and including the films of David Fincher. His mother even bought him a cheap video camera for his fourteenth birthday, and Max, using a pirated copy of Avid editing software, spent most nights cutting together snippets and vignettes cribbed from video-upload sites. More than anything in the world, Max wanted to emigrate to Los Angeles, New York, or London and make movies. Having a connection to an American teenager seemed like a good first step, especially one as nice as Jackie.

It was clear to Max that Jackie was as unhappy in her life as he was in his. He almost came clean, telling her the truth about himself, but couldn't do it. He was too invested in the new Max. And besides, he thought maybe Jackie needed someone like the new Max in her life. She deserved better than the real Max.

He wasn't ready to admit it to himself, but Max was falling for his new pen pal . . . falling hard.

***

Jackie was having a dream about Max when Megan's scream woke her up. She leaped out of bed and went for the door on pure instinct, but something deep in her gut stopped her. She stood there, hand on the doorknob, panting and afraid.

No more, Jackie's brain was telling her, *no more*.

She could hear the commotion down the hall, near her father's office. People were talking loudly and they sounded hysterical.

No more.

She sat back down on the edge of her bed, her hands folded in her lap. The trouble, she knew, would eventually come to her.

Jackie, who was one and a half years older than Trebuchet, thought of herself as the dog's older sister. Her very first memories were of petting Trebuchet, her fingers plunging deep into his fur and grabbing his skin, the dog staying still and letting her explore, never complaining, never barking, never nipping.

The two grew up together, forming one of the special bonds that can only be forged between man—or in this case, little girl—and dog. As soon as she was old enough, Jackie joined Jared and Trebuchet on their daily walks, her father letting her hold the leash, the dog knowing when to moderate the force of his pull.

There was a soft knock on the door.

Jackie muttered a barely audible, "It's open," and Megan poked her head in. Jackie looked at her sister, seeing immediately the fear in her eyes, but didn't say a word.

Megan came all the way into the room, closed the door behind her, and sat down next to Jackie. Where Jackie's hands were motionless, Megan's couldn't stop moving.

For her part, Megan had always felt something between jealousy and relief that Jackie and Trebuchet shared such a special relationship. Jealousy because the dog hadn't chosen her, and relief because she didn't think she could handle the responsibility of that kind of devotion.

"Weird," she would say when she saw the dog sitting outside Jackie's door in the morning, waiting patiently for her to wake up. Megan understood enough about Jackie and Trebuchet's relationship to want to shield her sister from the scene in her father's office. But there was no way around the truth.

"Someone—broke into the house," Megan stammered, looking for the right words. She looked confused; all the color was gone from her face.

"What happened?" Jackie's voice was flat, defeated. She took a long breath before asking, "Is it Daddy?"

"It's Trey," Megan said.

***

After Trebuchet had been taken away, after Sherman Kingsborough had been carted off to jail, after all the other people had finally left Jared's office, he and Deirdre were alone.

"What the hell just happened?" he asked her, truly confused.

"You don't remember?" Deirdre asked, alarmed.

"No, D, I remember, but what I'm remembering can't be real."

"It's real, Jare."

"Sherman Kingsborough, the boy billionaire, broke into our house to kill our dog?"

"No, honey, Sherman Kingsborough, the boy billionaire, broke into our house to kill you. He missed."

Jared didn't know what to say.

"The police say he was the guy on eBay who sent you that message, the one wanting to know how fit you were," she added.

"Huh," was the best Jared could muster.

"How's your head?"

"It's got a brain tumor."

Deirdre looked at him sideways.

"I'm kidding. Sorry. It feels better now that everyone is gone. The doctor says stress makes it worse."

Deirdre took Jared's hand. "That's the first time I've heard you make a joke in weeks."

"Really?"

"Really."

"So what now?" he asked.

"I don't know. The director said they're going to take the show off the air for a couple of days."

"Where are the girls?"

"In Jackie's room."

"Did they see any of this?"

"Megan did."

Jared nodded. He stood up but lost his balance and immediately fell over.

"Whoa," Deirdre said, catching him and helping him onto the futon. "Jare?"

"I'm okay. I think I just need to rest." He lay back on the futon, letting his head sink into the cushion, his eyes closing.

Deirdre turned to go.

"D?" he said, his eyes still closed.

"Yeah?"

"I'm sorry."

"For what?"

"For everything."

***

As a general rule, Hazel Huck kept to herself at school. Her closest friends, from the math club, the chess club, and Advanced Placement European History, could be more accurately described as friendly acquaintances. She *went* to school. She *went* to class. But she lived in Azeroth.

"I'm sorry, Hazel, about that man." Paula Lake was a nice girl with bad acne, bad breath, and no social graces. She more or less vomited the words at Hazel as they passed in the hall between sixth and seventh periods.

Hazel didn't know what she was talking about, but since Paula was so often the butt of someone else's joke, Hazel simply nodded politely and smiled.

"I know how hard you tried to raise money to save his life. I play a level twenty mage, and I saw the 'Save Jared' T-shirts all over the place. Once I heard it was you, I wanted to talk to you."

This has something to do with Jared Stone? Hazel thought. "Thanks," she said. "We did our best, but it probably turned out okay. The television network has a lot of money. I'm sure they'll take care of him."

"Don't you know?" Paula asked.

"Know what?"

"Oh, wow." Paula snorted. She then recounted the events of the preceding night, talking so fast that Hazel could barely keep up.

It took Hazel a beat to process it all. The news hit her like a slap in the face. Given her love of dogs, the part about Trebuchet was particularly hard to hear. She thanked Paula, closed her locker, and left school. Thirty minutes later, she was logging in to Azeroth.

***

Sister Benedict was up with the sun. She went through her normal morning routine, using the toilet, brushing her teeth, combing her hair, dressing. She had taken a bath the night before and now felt clean, scrubbed, and ready for battle.

Her novices, sensing from the Sister the importance of the day's events, were assembled in the convent's central courtyard early, shifting nervously; some of the younger women whispering and giggling. They were mostly under twenty-three years old, and given that they had eschewed the trappings of larger society, they were, as a group, socially younger than their years. They resembled a gaggle of conservatively dressed Catholic high school girls as much as they did pious Sisters of the Perpetual Adoration.

Sister Benedict strode into the morning sun like Patton, her posture so perfectly perpendicular to the ground that she seemed to glide more than walk.

It's a beautiful day, she thought to herself, and she was right. In typical Portland fashion, the weather did exactly what it wasn't predicted to do. The forecast had called for a cool rain, but the system had blown through without producing any precipitation, leaving a deep blue sky with cottony clouds and a light wind.

"All right, girls," she called in her most authoritative voice. "What are we going to do today?"

"Save a life," they answered in unison, their enthusiasm and sincerity barely evident.

"Come now," Sister Benedict answered. "What are we going to do today?"

"Save a life," the novices answered again, this time with more gusto.

"Right. Now line up."

The dutiful girls fell into a single line organized by height, shortest in front, tallest in back, as if they were the Von Trapp children meeting Maria for the first time. The young nuns stood with ramrod-straight posture, trying to emulate their leader's bearing. And then they waited.

Sister Benedict looked at her watch, a heavy, ugly, utilitarian thing that made her wrist look more masculine than normal, which is to say, very masculine. The bus she had arranged to transport them to the Stones' house was running late. This made her seethe.

"Timeliness, girls," she said, addressing those closest to her, "is next to cleanliness, and we know what that's next to, don't we?"

"Godliness," a few of them answered halfheartedly. Sister Benedict shook her head and walked off. The morning wasn't unraveling in the glorious way she had imagined.

She went back into the convent to call the bus driver, a devout man who owned his own limo company and often provided the sisters with pro bono transportation.

"Mr. Jenkins," Sister Benedict practically spat into the phone, "while I understand that your willingness to provide the bus is an act of charity and generosity, it does not excuse your being more than fifteen minutes late."

"Oh, Sister," Mr. Jenkins responded. "I'm sorry, I thought you knew."

"Knew what?"

"Mr. Stone, his entire street is cordoned off."

"I'm sorry?"

"It's all over the news. Someone broke into Mr. Stone's house and killed his dog. His television show is suspended indefinitely."

***

On hearing the news of Trebuchet's murder, Jackie was motionless. Megan told her everything she saw and heard, but it was too much for Jackie to process.

"Are you okay?" Megan's voice was so timid, it was barely audible. She had expected her big sister to cry or scream, to do something. Instead, Jackie sat there, still as a tree on a windless night. More than anything, this frightened Megan.

"I don't know" was the only answer Jackie could find.

"I'm scared, Jax."

Jackie looked up and saw her sister for what she was: a thirteen-year-old girl whose life was coming apart just as quickly as her own. It triggered a protective response in Jackie that harkened back to their preschool days.

"I know, Meg, I am, too."

"What's going to happen now? And what's going to happen to Daddy?" Jackie knew that she and Megan would turn back into their submissive and dominant selves in the morning, but for now she needed to be there for her little sister.

"I'm sorry, Meg," Jackie answered, taking Megan's hand and looking her in the eye, "but Daddy is . . . Daddy is . . ."

Megan nodded. "I know," she whispered, "but how soon?"

"I don't know." Jackie paused for a long moment. She thought about how much her father had changed. Not just the forgetfulness, but his physical appearance, too. He had lost so much weight, and his skin had an almost gray quality to it. He was starting to look like a ghost. "Soon, I think."

The sisters stayed there for a long time talking about everything that had happened and was happening in their lives until they both fell asleep in Jackie's bed.

Jackie had strange dreams of medieval warriors killing dragons, with the dragons transforming into black Labs, their chests pierced by glowing, flaming swords. When she woke up, light was sneaking through the slits in the venetian blinds, making a television test pattern across her comforter.

Megan was gone. Probably downstairs with her parents. Jackie knew she should go to them, to see how her father was, to find out what was going on, but she wasn't ready.

She reached for her phone and opened Facebook. She was immediately confronted by an image of Trebuchet lying in a pool of blood in her father's office, with Jared out of focus behind the dog, palms pressed against his temples. The photo was posted by one of the entertainment blogs Jackie followed.

She screamed and dropped the phone.

"Jax?" her father asked a moment later from the other side of the door. "Are you okay? Can I come in?"

Jackie wasn't ready to see her dad. She cleared her throat, ready to make an excuse, but it was too late; Jared opened the door and let himself in.

"Hi, Snowflake," he said. "Are you okay?"

Jackie loved that her father still called her Snowflake. The nickname had started on a family ski trip in the Cascades when she was six years old.

"But I'll fall and get hurt," she had told her parents as her mother strapped on the big, clunky boots. She was terrified of getting on skis.

"Who's going to get hurt more, you or the snowflakes, Snowflake?" her father had answered. Jackie giggled, so Jared said it again, and she giggled some more. She still didn't want to get on the skis, but her father kept calling her Snowflake, wearing down her resistance until eventually she threw in the towel and gave the skis a try.

"Daddy," Jackie said now, the morning after what had happened with Trebuchet, "we shouldn't." She motioned to the cameras.

Jared looked at his hands, like he was studying the intricate lines on his palms, like he was waiting for them to say something.

The silence underscored a tension that had been building between father and daughter, the first in the entire history of Jackie's life. She wanted to collapse in his arms, bury her head in his chest, and tell him everything. She wanted to tell him how much she hated the television show and Ethan Overbee; tell him about Max and about how she and Megan had actually talked all night; tell him how sorry she was about Trebuchet. Most of all, she wanted to tell him how sad she was that he had cancer, and how scared that made her feel.

But she couldn't. She wouldn't. Not with them watching.

"Just because there are cameras here, honey," her father said as if reading her mind, "doesn't mean that we can't talk." Jackie wanted to believe him, more than anything she wanted to believe him. "The TV show and the, the . . ."

Jackie wasn't sure if her father couldn't bring himself to say the word, or if he couldn't remember it. "Cancer," she finished. "The cancer."

"Yes, the cancer. Those things don't mean that we're still not Snowflake and Daddy-Man—"

"Ready to save the universe," Jackie said in sync with Jared. It was another private joke between the two.

Her father smiled at her, and that was all it took. Jackie melted into his arms and hugged him like she would never let go. In her mind's eye, she saw herself clutching her father. Then her brain framed it in a television screen. She let go. The presence of the cameras was overpowering.

"I'm sorry, Daddy, about everything. But I don't want them watching us." She kept her eyes on her father.

He seemed confused for a minute before letting out a big breath of air. "Yeah, you're right." Jared looked up at the camera in Jackie's bedroom and patted her knee. "Come down whenever you're ready. I'll make you breakfast." Jackie grabbed her father's arm and kissed him on the cheek.

***

Glio watched as Jared and six-year-old Jackie played superheroes. He could see in the construction of the memory some small sense of regret that Jared and Deirdre were raising only female children, and a small sense of guilt that Jared, in his desire for a son, had made Jackie something of a tomboy. But the feeling was fleeting, ephemeral, like the barest hint of piano buried deep in the mix of some overproduced pop song.

Jared and Jackie had taken all the pillows and cushions off the living room sofa, a two-piece sectional with chocolate-colored suede, and built a fort. Jared had used blankets to create a roof and was squirming on his belly in and out of the makeshift structure, following Jackie's lead.

Glio could hear Megan in the other room; she was talking to an imaginary friend, a princess of some sort. The sound triggered a secondary and different pang of guilt in Jared, that he wasn't paying enough attention to his younger daughter. Glio was amazed as he watched his host file the feeling away for future reference, as if he were putting a folder in a drawer, knowing that he should revisit it later but not giving it enough importance to remember to do so.

"What do we do now, Snowflake?" Jared asked.

"We have to stop the bad guys," Jackie whispered. "They're right outside the fort. They goed away but came back when we came in here."

"They went away," Jared corrected.

"They went away but came back!" Glio saw how awestruck Jared was at the complexity and fervor of his daughter's imagination. It was his first real hint at the enormity of the loss the Stone family was facing. But as Jared had filed away his own guilt, so, too, did Glio.

"So we're superheroes?" Jared asked, fully engrossed in the game.

"Yeah, we're superheroes!" Jackie whispered with gusto.

"What are our names?"

"You're, you're, you're Daddy-Man!" Glio was infused with a rush of oxytocin. It was a wonderful feeling that made him want more.

"I love it," Jared whispered. "But who are you? Jackie-Girl?"

"No, silly," she answered. "I'm Snowflake! S-N-O-W-F-L-A-K-E." Jackie had just learned to spell the word, and for the past two days had been doing so every time she said it aloud. For Glio, another massive hit of oxytocin.

Glio understood that this was one of Jared's most treasured memories. Each time his host recalled it, the memory would fill his host with feelings of joy, warmth, and stability. Glio felt almost guilty as he absorbed every frame of it into his growing mass.

***

Ethan Overbee stared in disbelief as the chairman of the ATN board of directors dressed him down. Thaddeus St. Claire sat to the chairman's left, shaking his bowed head in sorrow, feeling the pain of his protégé's failure.

The goddam fraud, Ethan thought to himself. *We're supposed to believe he had nothing to do with this?*

ATN was getting roughed up by the media in the wake of the public relations debacle that was the murder of Jared Stone's dog, and the board was taking it out on Ethan.

"We put our neck out there on this one, Overbee," the chairman said, "and the jackals are sharpening their fangs. How the hell did that man get into Mr. Stone's house? Where was security?"

"That wasn't just any man, Roger." Ethan was the only employee at the network to call the chairman by his first name. Everyone else called him Mr. Stern, or just "sir." Ethan felt it was important to establish himself as an equal early on in their relationship, and Roger Stern, fifty-seven, ulcer-prone, overweight, and perpetually dour (known to most of his underlings as Jabba the Stern), had tolerated it. "It was Sherman Kingsborough. Think of the publicity."

"Think of the publicity?" The chairman was incredulous.

"When we go back on the air tomorrow night, every person in America will tune in. *Life and Death* will be the highest rated show in the history of—"

"We're not going to be on the air tomorrow night, Ethan." Thad St. Claire's voice was gentle but firm, decisive.

"I'm sorry, what?"

"Thad's right," Stern added. "We need to take a few days, let the family grieve the loss of their dog, let America catch its breath. I heard from three different CEOs today that they don't want their spots aired until the furor dies down."

Ethan breathed a silent sigh of relief. For a moment he had been afraid that the board was going to cancel the show.

"Okay, Roger," Ethan began again, careful to talk directly to the chairman and not to Thad. "I understand. But at least let us conduct some interviews with the family. We need to get some footage in the can about the incident, for when we go back live."

Stern looked at Thad, who nodded his approval. That more than anything stung Ethan. He was no longer in control, if he ever had been.

"And Ethan," Stern said, leaning in close.

"Yes, Roger?" Even Ethan withered a little under the tycoon's glare.

"Don't let another fuckup like this happen again."

Ethan nodded, making a mental note that truly powerful people didn't need to include an "or else." At that level the threat was de facto implied.

***

After her father left, Jackie opened her phone again, this time ignoring the Facebook news feed and going straight to the chat. Max was already there.

Max

Solnyshko, I am so sorry. I do not know what to say.

Max already knew what had happened. Jackie wasn't surprised.

Jackie

How did you find out?

Max

It is all on the Internet.

Jackie

Of course it is. Why shouldn't it be?

Max

Solnyshko, do I say something wrong?

Until that moment, Jackie had been feeling worn out, beaten. But now anger was starting to creep in around the edges of her resignation.

Jackie

No, Max, it's not you. It's me.

Max

For how long will your show be off the air?

Jackie

What?

Off the air? This was news to Jackie.

Max

The Internet is saying that *Life and Death* will be on hiatus. I have to look this word up.

Jackie

Max, I haven't left my bedroom since it happened. You know more than I do. What else did it say?

Max

You wish to know?

Jackie

Yes.

Max

The man who does this to your dog, he is very wealthy man. Billionaire. Sherman Kingsborough. I have heard name.

Jackie had heard the name, too, though she didn't know much about him. Something about climbing Mount Everest and getting in trouble with police in some Asian country.

Jackie

I am so sick of this whole thing, this whole stupid television show. I wish it would just go away.

There was another long moment of silence. Jackie, who was thinking about Trebuchet, just watched the screen, hoping Max would say something to make her feel better.

Max

Tell me, Solnyshko, you do not like being on television?

Jackie

No.

Max

But doesn't everyone in America want to be on television?

Jackie

Not everyone, Max. But that's not the point. It's the show. It's awful. They edit it to make my dad look more confused than he is, and . . . and it's so hard at school now. I wish I was dead.

Max

No, Solnyshko, you must never ever say this.

Jackie felt bad. She wanted Max to like her, but she was doing everything she could to make herself thoroughly unlikable.

Jackie

You're right. I'm sorry.

Max

No. You must promise me you will never say this again.

"Max, I promise you I will never say this again."

Jackie

Okay, Max, I promise.

Max

Good. This is good.

Jackie

But it doesn't help me. I'm still stuck here.

Max

If you do not like their television show, make your own.

Jackie

What do you mean?

Max hadn't meant to type that, but now that he had, an idea was starting to take shape, a devilish idea that would help Jackie and would bring the two of them closer together.

Jackie could sense his fingers, eight thousand miles away, working across the keyboard like a tsunami. She could feel his excitement building, and that got her excited, too.

By the time they were done chatting, Jackie, in a completely unexpected twist of fate, actually found herself smiling.

***

Sherman Kingsborough woke up in jail, disoriented. He was the only tenant of a small cell with a cot, a sink, and a toilet. He couldn't remember where he was or how he had come to be there. This was not an uncommon feeling for the young billionaire. The only thing he knew with certainty was that his bladder was about to burst.

After relieving himself and splashing some water on his face, Sherman sat down and reconstructed the events of the previous evening. Every time he pictured that poor dog—he could still hear the sound of its death wail—his stomach and throat filled with bile. Sherman liked dogs. He liked them a lot.

In one sense, he was relieved that he hadn't killed Stone. And he was relieved that he was incarcerated. The weeks' long nightmare of his murder quest had finally come to an end. He likened the experience to what athletes called "roid rage," a stupefied, mindless sort of aggression brought on by an overuse of steroids. Only Sherman hadn't used steroids. He wasn't sure what to make of the whole thing, but at least it was over.

He had a vague memory of meeting with both a district attorney and a defense lawyer before being dumped in the jail cell. He knew he was being charged with attempted murder in the first degree, breaking and entering, criminal trespass, and cruelty to animals. He also knew the DA was requesting that Sherman be held without bail, and that the defense lawyer thought it likely the judge would go along. The combination of his money and the depravity of his actions made him too great a flight risk.

But rich people, he believed, had a way of staying out of trouble.

Right on cue, the guard approached his cell.

"C'mon, dog killer," the guard said.

"Is my lawyer here?"

The guard snorted. "Lawyer? Way I hear it even the public defender don't want your case, and he ain't got a choice. No, we're moving you to a more secure location on account of the death threats."

"Death threats?"

The guard snorted again as he opened the door. "You're not what the world would call a popular man, Sherm," he said.

And with that, Sherman Kingsborough was removed from his Portland jail cell and from the life of the family Stone forever.

***

Jared was in a stupor as he munched his Cheerios. His mind, overwhelmed by the events of the past few hours, had more or less shut down. What was left of Jared's brain ceased conscious activity. Still seated at the table, Jared's chin dropped down to his chest, and his breathing became even and regular.

For Glio, this was like a sunny Sunday morning sitting on the front porch with a good book and a mug full of oolong tea. He loved nothing more than watching and experiencing his host's dreams.

As is often true of unconscious thought, the dream seemed like a broken reproduction of the real world. It reminded Glio of a Picasso painting he had once consumed as part of an afternoon Jared and Deirdre spent at the Museum of Modern Art in New York City. All the pieces were there, but they were jumbled, placed out of order, and then reassembled in a grotesque hodgepodge that seemed to mock reality.

In the dream, Jared was telling his family that he had cancer.

In real life—in the memories already imbibed by Glio—Jared and Deirdre had two separate conversations: one with

Jackie, one with Megan. Where Jackie had been stoic, quiet, and shell-shocked, Megan had been dramatic and full of questions. "What does cancer feel like? Can the doctor see it? Can't they just operate and take it out of you? What will happen to me? Will Mommy remarry?" That last one made Jared laugh and Deirdre cry.

Glio had marveled at these twin memories, at how he could feel not only Jared's tension and anxiety but that of his family as well. It was as if some kind of alpha waves were emanating from his wife and daughters, allowing them to convey emotion without verbal communication. It was fascinating.

But that was reality.

The dream took those two scenes, combined them, and turned them on their head. In it, Jared didn't have cancer, Jackie did. She sat calmly, smiling, her face lit as if by an Oscar-winning cinematographer. "So the doctor told me that I have four months to live. But don't worry, everything will be fine, don't ya think?" Jared felt a pounding in his chest he was sure everyone could hear. He looked in terror at Deirdre and Megan, but both sat mute. As he watched, their faces—first their mouths, then their noses and eyes—faded from view.

"I'm dying, Daddy, how does that make you feel?" Jackie was sneering at her father. Jared's pounding heart became so loud that he was only picking up every third word. "Isn't . . . hilarious . . . dying? . . . It's . . . Won't . . . be . . . without . . . ?" Then Jackie laughed. Deirdre and Megan kept fading while Jackie laughed. Dream Jared screamed real Jared awake. He was panting, and he was crying, his cereal and milk spilled all over the table.

Glio stopped eating. His appetite just wasn't there. The emotion had overwhelmed the hunger.

***

Ethan Overbee was on the next plane to Portland. He seethed in his first-class seat as he thought about what had happened. Everything he'd ever wanted was in his grasp, and this lunatic, this Kingsborough, had taken it away.

No, he thought, *that's not right. Kingsborough didn't take it away. My staff did. My goddam staff did! How the hell did this happen?*

When Ethan arrived on the set of *Life and Death*, the entire crew was lined up and waiting for him. What he couldn't understand was why, to a person, they were all smiling.

In the center of the gathering stood the third-shift director, who'd called the police, and James, the PA, who was first on the scene when they saw Sherman Kingsborough outside Jared's office door. The rest were gathered around them like a proud extended family at a high school graduation.

Holy fuck, Ethan thought. *Do they think I'm here to give them some sort of medal?*

"Holy fuck," he said, looking around the room, making eye contact with as many of his hired hands as he could muster. "Do you guys think I'm here to give you some sort of medal?" He could feel the air go out of their collective sails.

He spent the next thirty minutes taking them to task, talking about the unprecedented lapse in security, the lack of attention to detail. He talked about the trauma to the Stone family, how America was counting on *Life and Death* to help heal wounds, and how they, the crew, let America down, how they let the network down, how they let him down.

By the end of it, at least two staff members were openly sobbing. Not because their feelings were hurt, but because they had let Ethan Overbee, deputy executive in charge of programming for the American Television Network, down. He was that good.

When he was done with the crew, Ethan asked the Stone family to assemble in the living room. He had thought about how to handle this conversation all the way up on the flight from LA. He needed them to buy into what would come next.

"Deirdre. Jared. Jackie. Megan." He said each name slowly, looking at each one in turn, burning a hole in their souls with the intensity of his gaze. "I am so sorry about Trebuchet. Everyone at the network is just sick over this. Roger Stern has asked me to personally convey his deepest condolences."

The Stone family was the breathing embodiment of its motionless, wordless name. Somewhere nearby a cricket chirped. Ethan pressed on.

"Of course, we're going to pull the show off the air for a couple of days. Give everyone a chance to catch their breath and regroup. Allow you to grieve in private. We'll do a few interviews with the four of you during the downtime, but the schedule will be very light."

"Ethan?"

"Yes, Deirdre?"

"What if we don't want to continue the show?"

Ethan had worried about this and planned for it. He didn't miss a beat. "If that's what you really want, we can talk about it. But think about it, Deirdre, imagine if your family was on the other side of that TV, if you and your girls were viewers of *Life and Death*. Wouldn't you want them, wouldn't you *need* them, to have some closure, some resolution after this episode?"

Deirdre didn't answer. She just stared at Ethan. Jackie stared at her hands, and Jared stared out the window, his attention drifting. It was Megan who whispered "yes." It was sotto voce, but emphatic.

Ethan smiled. Not the smile of a victor, but the smile of a paternalistic older brother. Deirdre managed a small nod, indicating that her question had been withdrawn.

"I also want to assure you," Ethan continued, knowing that he was just getting to the tricky part, "that we will never let anything like this happen again." He waited a beat before he continued, like he'd rehearsed in the back of the town car on the way from the airport. "We're going to tighten security."

Jared and Megan each breathed a sigh of relief, literally exhaling the tension from their bodies.

"That's great, Ethan," Jared offered. "Thanks."

Deirdre sat still. She blinked a few times. She looked lost.

"What do you mean by security?" Jackie asked.

No one expected Jackie to talk, so everyone turned to face her. This made her cheeks flush and her brow furrow. "I mean, I'm just wondering is all."

"No, no, Jackie," Ethan continued. "It's a great question. All the cast and crew will be searched each day before entering the house."

"But aren't we the cast?" Jackie asked, her voice cautious and tentative.

"Yes, yes, you are. We need to make sure nothing harmful to the show, to your family, gets slipped into a backpack or purse. This is as much for your protection as anyone else's."

"But the man who broke in, Kingsborough, he wasn't a member of the cast or crew," Deirdre offered.

"Good observation, Deirdre. Yes, to protect against another Mr. Kingsborough"—here Ethan made quote signs with his hands—"we're building a perimeter around the house."

"Perimeter?" Deirdre asked.

"Yes, a seven-foot fence completely surrounding the property. Without proper identification, no one will be able to get in."

"Or out," Jackie muttered, her head down, her chin practically touching her chest.

"I'm sorry, what was that?" Ethan asked.

"A seven-foot fence?" Deirdre interjected, hoping to stave off a confrontation between Jackie and Ethan. "That seems kind of extreme, doesn't it?"

"It's not as bad as it sounds," Ethan answered. "We'll plant hedges on either side so it won't be an eyesore."

"Still . . ."

"Just think about poor Trebuchet," Ethan said, playing what he hoped would be his trump card.

At the mention of Trebuchet, Jackie got up and left the room. No one stopped her, and Ethan thought this was a good thing. The girl had been trouble from the start, and she wasn't adding anything positive to this conversation. He was holding back from playing his actual trump card; the contract Jared signed allowed the network to pretty much do as it pleased. If the show stayed on the air, Ethan Overbee was the master of this domain. But as it turned out, he didn't need to play that card.

"I guess," Deirdre offered, like a reluctant friend being dragged to a movie she really didn't want to see. "I guess it's for the best."

Jared patted her hand and said, "I need to go lie down."

And just like that, without any vote of cloture, debate ended.

Later that afternoon, construction started on what everyone involved would come to think of as "The Wall." Ethan was regaining control.

***

Max's plan was simple. He and Jackie would create a shadow version of *Life and Death* and post it on YouTube. She would shoot video with her iPhone and send it to Max. He would edit it into a finished product and upload it. They would do it "down below the radar" as Max suggested, for as long as they could.

Jackie
It's "under the radar," Max. And why would we need to do that? Do you think people will really want to see our video?

Max
Solnyshko, do you not know that you are television star?

Jackie didn't know how to respond. While she knew in her heart of hearts that Max was right, she didn't want to admit it. But it was getting harder and harder to deny.

The week after the premiere aired, Jackie received a stack of mail that was more than fifty times the sum total of all the mail she'd received in her life.

"Fan mail," the show's producer had said when she dropped the stack on Jackie's bed. It was heavy enough that it caused the comforter to wrinkle and bunch around it.

"For me?" Jackie asked wide-eyed.

"Of course it's for you," she answered.

Jackie moved the pile of mail, along with the five that followed it, to the floor of her bedroom closet, unopened, untouched. Now she wondered if she should read them.

When she was four, with her mother's help, Jackie wrote a fan letter to Steve, the easygoing host of *Blue's Clues*. She nearly fell over when she got not only a letter in response but an autographed photo of Steve, Blue, Tickety, and Side Table Drawer. Now that she was older, she realized that Steve hadn't actually written the response; it, along with the photo, was a form letter. But it didn't matter; for that one day in her four-year-old life, the world was perfect.

Jackie made a mental note to start going through the stacks of letters. Besides, she knew it would bore the director to tears to watch her open mail, and that meant Jackie would be largely out of the next episode.

She turned her attention back to Max.

Jackie

Do you think they'll let me film them?

Max

Tell them it is for class project.

Jackie

Oooh. Good idea!

Jackie had never felt so conspiratorial, and she found herself enjoying it.

Jackie

What are we going to call our show?

Max

I was thinking on this. I think we call it "The Real Stone Family of Portland, Oregon"? It is joke on terrible show we see in Russia called "Real Housewives of Orange County." I hope this is not too, what is word, unsensitive?

Jackie

LOL. The word is insensitive, Max, and it's not. I love it. But can we change it to Family Stone instead of Stone Family?

Max

Yes, of course. Is this how American families are called?

Jackie

No, but my grandfather used to listen to a band called Sly and the Family Stone, and it became a kind of joke in our house.

Max

Da. It is settled. "The Real Family Stone of Portland, Oregon." We go into production right away.

***

Jared barely made it to his office futon after the meeting with Ethan. Once there, he drifted quickly off to sleep. With fewer and fewer memories for his brain to access, the fewest possible neurons were firing; only those needed to control his most basic bodily functions were active. Jared's sleep was as peaceful and deep as Crater Lake.

It was in this moment that Glio reached the nadir of his existence, the consumption of Jared's seminal memory. All people have such a memory, the one moment in time that, more than any other, defines who they are and who they are to become. For most, it's something that happens in the fourth or fifth year of life, after the brain has developed enough intellectual capacity to begin to comprehend the world, but not enough emotional capacity to process the new thoughts streaming along its synaptic pathways. For a few people, those able to overcome the circumstances of an unfortunate existence, it happens later in life.

Jared's seminal moment happened just after his fourth birthday.

The sky was the color of the Caribbean Sea, a few clouds billowing through the ether like punctuation—ellipses and commas, not periods or exclamation points. The sun warmed Jared's skin as he sat in the grass moving a toy cement mixer back and forth. His father, engrossed in a book, sat in a lawn chair a few feet away.

All of a sudden, little Jared began to blubber. Quick as a wink, his father was kneeling beside him—though in Jared's memory, his father moved in slow motion, taking an entire age of man to cross the stone patio to his distraught son.

"What is it, Jared?" his father asked, his concern real but measured.

"Bug!" Jared shouted, and pointed at a grasshopper that had landed on his truck. "Bug!"

"Oh, well, we can fix that," his father said. Glio expected to see the father shoo the grasshopper away, but he didn't. He was astonished to see Jared's father pick up the grasshopper and hold it out for his son to examine, the creature immobile in the gentle grasp of the man's forefinger and thumb.

"You see, Jared," his father told him, "whatever you're afraid of is probably way more scared of you."

Jared was just old enough to grasp this concept, and he let it rattle around in his brain.

"Really?" he asked.

"Really," his father told him. "Just look at this grasshopper. You're ten times his size."

Jared smiled.

"No, wait, you're a hundred times his size." Jared's smile crept into a laugh. His father went through a thousand, ten thousand, a hundred thousand, and a million until little Jared was doubled over in laughter.

He was scared of many things after that but never so completely frightened that he was paralyzed. That moment helped Jared see the world the way he was sure it was meant to be seen. The lesson followed him unconsciously through the rest of his life, giving shape to the character that would come to define who he was.

When Glio finished the memory, he swam through a sea of psychoses, largely calm waters dulled by the pain-relieving drugs Jared had been prescribed in the wake of the radiation.

From there, he climbed mountains of regret, reaching their craggy summits with ease. On the other side was a kind of Shangri-la of mirth: memories of joy and abandon.

But through it all, Glio knew something was wrong. There was a foul aftertaste on the wind, the stench of disease. And Glio knew. He knew that he, or rather the corporeal he, the physical body, was dying.

Now that he had an identity and memories, Glio very much wanted to live. He also knew that death, unlike the grasshopper, wasn't afraid of him, that it couldn't be. But still, the memory of that day with Jared's father gave comfort to Glio in a way he didn't think was possible.

Glio was becoming Jared Stone. But he also now knew that Jared Stone was going to die. Glio didn't know how, but he needed to stop that from happening.

In the meantime, he would continue his feast.

***

Two days before *Life and Death* was scheduled to return to the air, Jackie started collecting little snippets of video. Max told her to keep them short, under twenty seconds each.

"Excuse me," she would say, interrupting a crew member, "I'm doing a school project on the show. Can I film you while you work?"

The entire crew was suffering from a mélange of guilt and posttraumatic stress over the murder of Trebuchet and would have done just about anything for the Stone family. Each one tripped over the next to help Jackie get some behind-the-scenes footage. They showed her how to light a set, taught her about the 180-degree rule for framing a shot, and gave her tips on when to use a close-up versus an extreme close-up.

At first, they mugged for the camera, smiling at Jackie, offering a small quip or bit of wisdom. But as that day and the next wore on, they started to forget Jackie was there. The irony of this—that the crew should have the same reaction to being filmed as the cast of *Life and Death* or *Big Brother* or *Survivor* or any other reality show, that they completely tuned out the existence of the cameras—wasn't lost on Jackie. The project made her feel subversive, rebellious, and so very alive.

***

Jared read the bathroom scale in disbelief. He'd lost thirty-five pounds in the last month. He looked up and saw his reflection: the skin under his eyes was a dark brown—any darker and he would look like a scrawny baseball player using a grease pencil to stop the glare of the sun—his cheeks were starting to sink back into his face, and his hair was thinning. He *looked* like he was dying.

The doctor told Jared to expect some side effects from the radiation therapy he'd been receiving since his diagnosis, and he wondered if this was part of it.

The treatments were kind of weird. The radiation technician had him lie flat on a table—the table reminded Jared of an operating table, or maybe a table in a morgue—and fixed a mesh mask over his head and face. The idea was to make sure his head was in the exact same position for each treatment.

"If I zap you a little too far to the left," the technician told Jared when he was first being fitted for the mask, "I'll fry your ability to blink your eyes. A little to the right and I can make you act like a chicken."

Jared thought that maybe this was supposed to be funny, so he laughed politely.

"I'm just kidding," she said, confirming his suspicion that a joke had been told, "but we do need to make sure that tumor stays where we want it."

"I'd prefer it not be in my head," Jared said, trying a joke of his own.

Once the mask was on, the treatments were almost peaceful. He would lie still and try to clear his mind. It was forty minutes of uninterrupted lack of interruptions three times a week. He could have done without the side effects, however.

The nausea hit hard after his third treatment. He tried all manner of remedies to settle his stomach: Pepto-Bismol, silver nitrates, opiates prescribed by his doctors, even blackberry brandy and ginger ale. The only thing that seemed to make him feel better was vomiting. Eventually, though, the severity of the nausea settled down, or maybe he just got used to it.

Now, standing in the bathroom, all of it seemed like a blur.

Maybe it's more than side effects, he thought. *Maybe dying, without the radiation, looks like this, too.* He tried to remember friends, relatives, and colleagues he'd lost to cancer over the years, but no one was coming to mind. That didn't seem right. There must be someone.

The only thing Jared knew for sure was that he was tired. So incredibly tired.

***

The return episode of *Life and Death* aired exactly one week after the Sherman Kingsborough fiasco. It opened with this warning in bold white letters on an all-black background:

> **The first five minutes of tonight's episode of *Life and Death* include scenes of graphic violence that are not suitable for young viewers. Parents are encouraged to escort children from the room.**

The warning was on the screen for a full twenty seconds before the voice-over started.

It was Jackie's voice. It had been taken from an interview she'd done with one of the producers the day after Trebuchet died. The producer, a young, attractive woman with the unfortunate name of Andersona (the same person who had delivered the fan mail), sat with Jackie on Jackie's bed. It was an old fashioned girl-to-girl heart-to-heart. But the video of the interview wasn't on the screen when the voice-over started.

This is what viewers saw and heard:

JACKIE: Of course I loved him. He was my best friend. [Her voice chokes.]

FADE from warning about graphic violence to a grainy image of Trebuchet's bloody body on Jared's office floor.

JACKIE: That man, Mr. Kingsborough, he wanted to hurt my father.

DISSOLVE TO a stupefied Sherman Kingsborough being escorted from the Stone house in handcuffs.

JACKIE: I don't know why anyone would want to hurt us. I just don't understand.

DISSOLVE TO Jared lying on the office floor, clutching his temples in obvious agony. Next to him is the blood-soaked rug where Trebuchet had been stabbed.

JACKIE: Yes, I think he's in heaven. With my grandma.

DISSOLVE TO Jared, Deirdre, Jackie, and Megan burying Trebuchet in a hole in the backyard. It's clearly been filmed without their knowledge by a camera hidden in a nearby tree.

SOMBER MUSIC starts softly and begins to swell.

JUMP CUT TO JACKIE and PRODUCER on Jackie's bed. Jackie is crying hysterically.

JACKIE: Please, can we stop? I need to stop. [Jackie buries her face in her hands. The sound of her heaving sobs fades slowly out and mixes with the music.]

FADE TO BLACK. ROLL OPENING CREDITS.

***

Late the following morning, Deirdre was sitting on the futon in Jared's office reading a book. Jared was lying on the floor, eyes closed. In the days before the cancer, before the cameras, this was unheard of.

Deirdre knew that Jared hated the term "man cave," but Jared's office, to her mind, was just that. It was his space, his kingdom, and she was careful not to intrude.

But now, now that she knew his time was limited, she wanted to spend every possible minute with her husband. Part of her wanted to be nearby in case he needed help, but mostly she just wanted them to be together. Spending time with Jared, even passive time, was the only cure for the overwhelming sadness that had settled in the marrow of her bones.

Raised voices were coming from downstairs. It wasn't unusual. There were often arguments between members of the crew—usually about something small like the placement of a light or the angle of a camera—and she had learned to tune it out. But this was different.

"How did they even get past the gate?" she heard someone ask.

"Everything okay?" Jared, his eyes now open, had heard it, too. "What's that ruckus?"

"'Can you describe the ruckus, sir?'" This was a line from one of Deirdre and Jared's favorite guilty-pleasure movies, *The Breakfast Club*; they used it with each other often when the girls were younger and more boisterous. Now Deirdre saw no flicker of recognition in her husband's eyes.

"The ruckus downstairs," he said.

"I'll go check," she answered, a new drop of despair added to the lake growing inside her. *Cancer*, she thought, *is like being nibbled to death by ducks.* She got up to go.

"Me too." Jared started to stand.

"No, sweetie, I've got this."

"Really, D, I have nothing else to do."

She looked at him and nodded.

When they got to the landing on the bottom of the stairs, they saw one of the new ATN security guards, a burly man in a black T-shirt that didn't quite fit, talking to someone at the door.

"This is private property, and you're trespassing. You have to leave now. If you don't, we will forcibly remove you." The guard said this in a flat monotone, but his sheer girth left no room to question his intentions.

"What's going on?" Deirdre asked.

"Oh, Mr. and Mrs. Stone," the guard said, seeming flustered. "I'm sorry to have disturbed you. The construction crew hasn't completed work on The Wall, and someone managed to get to the front door. Would you like us to call the police?"

Deirdre was about to answer, but Jared put a hand on her arm. "That depends," he said. "Who is it?" Deirdre turned to her husband and saw that the politician in him had found its way back to the surface. It was the most fervent sign of life she'd seen in Jared since they'd made love on Jared's office floor. She allowed herself a rare smile and hooked arms with him.

"Yes, who is it? We do have neighbors, you know."

"They say they're from the Portland Area Hospice Foundation."

Deirdre and Jared looked at each other before Jared said, "Let them in, please."

"But we're under orders from Mr. Overbee—"

"When Mr. Overbee starts paying the mortgage on this house, he can decide who does and does not get through the front door."

The guard, like the rest of the crew, was on pins and needles after the Sherman Kingsborough incident. While he did have strict instructions to let no unauthorized outsiders on the property, it was also made clear that he should make any and all accommodations for the Stone family. Had he known that ATN had assumed the responsibility for the mortgage on the house as part of Jared's contract, he might have acted differently. But he didn't know that, and Jared, largely because he didn't remember that detail, didn't offer it. The guard let the intruder pass.

The guest was a tall, slender woman steeped in middle age. She had curly, unkempt hair that was gray enough to obscure its original color; she wore a black pantsuit with a cream-colored shirt, a peacoat draped over one arm. The only word to describe her shoes was sensible.

"Mr. and Mrs. Stone," she said, extending her hand, "I'm Joanne Stark. I'm the director of the Portland Area Hospice Foundation. May I have a few minutes of your time?"

Deirdre and Jared each shook her hand in turn, then invited her into the living room. Deirdre watched the woman marvel at the television equipment strewn about.

"You don't see all this on TV, do you?" she asked.

"No," Deirdre agreed. "It would ruin the illusion of reality. Can I offer you a cup of coffee or tea?"

"No, thank you. I don't want to be an imposition."

"It's not an imposition at all. As you might imagine, we don't have many visitors these days." She could feel a silent understanding pass between her and Joanne.

"Really, I'm fine. I don't want to take up much of your time. I just want to talk with you about your options regarding Mr. Stone's condition."

As the three of them sat on the couch, Deirdre could see the wind go out of Jared's sails. His brief burst of energy had cost him. The spark that had been in his eyes just a moment ago was fading quickly.

"Please," Deirdre said, "call us Jared and Deirdre."

"Thank you. I'm wondering how much you know about hospice?"

"Quite a lot, actually," Deirdre answered. "My mother had hospice care during her last days."

"And how did you find that experience?"

Deirdre liked Joanne. As was the case with the hospice workers she had come to know during her mother's long, painful exit from the world, this woman had a mixture of directness and compassion. She was unafraid to confront difficult truths but not blind to the anguish they caused.

"It was a very positive experience, but as you can see, this situation is somewhat different."

"Is it? Do you have nursing care? Do you have—"

"Please," Deirdre interrupted. "I appreciate what you're doing. I believe in the hospice movement, and I hope your visit to our little circus turns out to be a good platform to promote it." Joanne, realizing she'd been outed, looked at Deirdre with something between resignation and admiration.

"But our situation," Deirdre continued, "is, in many ways, out of our control. Besides, all of this"—she swept her arm across the room, her motion taking in the television cameras and all that they represented—"has allowed me to stop working and care for Jared full-time. I can be here for him."

"Well," Joanne said, starting to rise, her coat still on her arm, "I do appreciate your time, and—"

"What does the hospice foundation think about the Death with Dignity Act?" Both women were surprised at Jared's sudden question. He asked it softly, staring at his hands, like he was trying to remember the words to say.

"We're opposed to it," Joanne answered matter-of-factly as she sat back down.

"Why?"

"Do you know, Jared, the number one reason cited for ending a life prematurely?" Deirdre watched her husband. She could see him searching for the answer. It was an answer he almost certainly knew at one point but had now forgotten. She wanted to cry when he shook his head no.

"People don't want to be a burden to the ones they love."

"Jared isn't a burden to us," Deirdre was quick to interject.

"Of course not, and that's exactly the point. You don't think it's a burden, but he does. Isn't that right, Mr. Stone?"

For his part, Jared didn't know if it was right or not. The feelings in his head were both more complex and more amorphous than that. Whether it was a result of the tumor or something else, he didn't know.

"It is called the Death with Dignity Act," he said, with an emphasis on dignity. "Isn't dignity a personal thing? Isn't it for me to decide what is dignified and what is not?"

Deirdre looked at her husband and sensed that something had changed, or was changing, and it made her scared. "Thank you, Joanne, for coming to see us," she said, standing up. Deirdre looked at Joanne, trying to plead with her eyes to just let the rest of the conversation go. Joanne got the message and stood up as well.

"Thank you both. And on behalf of the foundation, we really do wish you and your daughters well." With that, she left.

Later that night, after Ethan had fired the security guard and additional workers were brought in to complete The Wall, the conversation about the Death with Dignity Act was featured as the centerpiece on *Life and Death*. Missing was the confrontation at the door, Deirdre's tacit critique of the television equipment, and Jared's flash of lucidity. All that was left was a confused-looking Jared and a tense-looking Deirdre debating the merits of euthanasia with a hospice worker.

America was none the wiser.

***

The premiere episode of *The Real Family Stone of Portland, Oregon* aired two nights after *Life and Death* returned from its hiatus. In its brief nine minutes and thirty seconds, the YouTube video attempted to show the secret underbelly of *Life and Death*.

It opened with a clip of Jared reading aloud from one of his favorite books as Deirdre lay with her head on his lap. This was not the debilitated, confused Jared that the network presented in prime time. He looked thin, he looked older, but he looked alive. There were short scenes of the crew servicing the miles of cable and dozens of cameras that lay over the Stone house like an infestation of silverfish. The viewer could now plainly see that the house was less an environment in which people lived, and more a set in which actors played parts. Jackie had even managed to capture the crew in the truck—"Sure, sweetie, come on in," they had told her—reviewing the dailies. "If we jump from here to here, the director said, "it will make him seem more confused." Max, with his editing software, zoomed in to show that the clips they were manipulating featured Jared.

The Real Family Stone of Portland, Oregon revealed Max's crude but skilled editorial eye. It was exactly what he and Jackie had hoped it would be: a chronicle of the truth.

After the video was uploaded, they both sat and waited. Twenty-four hours later, they were still waiting. There had only been seventeen views, sixteen of them their own clicks. Jackie was crestfallen. Not Max.

Jackie

I told you, Max, no one cares.

Max

Nyet, Solnyshko, nyet. It is not that no one cares. It is that no one knows. Many people will care.

Jackie

Like who?

Max

The many people who watch you on television.

Jackie

But how are we supposed to know who they are?

And then it dawned on Jackie.

Jackie

Wait. I think I can answer my own question.

Max

?

Jackie

Don't go away, I'll be right back.

Two minutes later, Jackie sent Max a photo of the stacks of her fan mail.

***

Sister Benedict Joan's press conference was scheduled to begin at eleven a.m. sharp. Most of the reporters who had promised to come had not yet arrived—par for the course in their profession, she thought—but it didn't matter, a schedule was a schedule. The Sister was about to step to the podium when she felt a light touch on her shoulder. The Sister whirled around and was confronted by the impish smile of Cardinal Trippe.

"Why don't we give this a few more minutes," he said gently.

"Timeliness is next to cleanliness, Your Eminence," the Sister stammered, "and you know what . . ."

"Yes, yes, Sister. But wouldn't our larger goal be better served by more, not less, media?"

The Sister gritted her teeth and tensed her neck in frustration but nodded a curt assent.

"And you're sure you're okay to do this?" The Cardinal nodded toward the podium. This was the third time the Cardinal had asked this question, each time his smile broad and blindingly white. The Sister was growing to hate that smile.

"I'm sure His Holy Eminence is merely teasing me," she answered, making it clear that Sisters of the Perpetual Adoration did not enjoy being teased.

"Not teasing at all, Sister. It's just that the pressure of speaking publicly can be paralyzing if you haven't done it before."

"I am only here to introduce Your Grace. Nothing more."

Three more reporters had filed in, and Sister Benedict tapped her watch.

Cardinal Trippe grinned, shook his head, and gently plucked the stack of index cards from the Sister's hands. "Please, Sister, go ahead." The Sister let out a breath of air and stepped to the podium.

"Ladies and gentlemen," she began, her voice gruff and unrefined. The sound of it through the microphone caught her off guard. She was, as the Cardinal had predicted, frozen. *The damnable fool got inside my head,* she thought in a panic. The Sister looked to the Cardinal, who nodded his encouragement for her to continue. For the first time, she found his presence oddly soothing, almost beatific. It gave her an unexpected jolt of confidence.

"Please welcome Cardinal Matthew John Trippe." Her mouth was too close to the microphone, and it caused a momentary ring of feedback. She stepped down from the podium, forcing herself to keep her head high. The Cardinal took her place.

"Friends," he began, making eye contact with each of the reporters before him. The Sister marveled at the ease with which the man worked the room. *Maybe,* she thought, *he's not so useless after all.* "We are here today to call attention to an affront to the dignity of human life that is taking place in our community. Of course, I refer to the television show *Life and Death.*"

For the next thirty minutes, Cardinal Trippe read through the index cards prepared for him by Sister Benedict, each one more inflammatory than the one that came before. They threw every epithet under the sun at *Life and Death* and the American Television Network. Two of the cards were so filled with bile and hate that the Cardinal, much to the Sister's chagrin, simply ignored them.

No matter. The Sister, having recovered from her poor performance at the microphone, was ebullient. She finally felt like they were doing something, and what's more, she knew in her heart of hearts it was only the beginning. Sister Benedict Joan was certain that her part in the Stone affair was not yet over.

***

Ethan Overbee was sitting at his eight-foot-by-four-foot solid oak desk in Los Angeles when his phone chimed with two alerts, one from Twitter, one a text message. The desk, which was really the size of a conference table, vibrated with each notice.

Ethan had two Twitter accounts, one for the industry at large, and a second private account that only a few people knew about. It was this second account—he had programmed it to send alerts—that was now trying to get his attention.

A private message from @spandau1965, Heloise Spandau, one of his lieutenants in the programming department at ATN, appeared on the screen. She was a no-nonsense, nose-to-the-grindstone employee who didn't suffer fools gladly. Once, at a full department meeting, Spandau called a junior employee "stupid" and told him that the "air you're breathing could be put to better use." It's not that she was wrong—the junior employee was stupid, he was wasting someone else's valuable air—but Ethan still had to talk to Heloise after the incident, trying to impress upon her how you can catch more flies with honey. That was six months ago; the junior employee was no longer with the company, Spandau was still Ethan's lieutenant.

"Catholic Cardinal Blasts Life and Death"
http://bit.ly/1OLEziq

Ethan clicked through the link and saw excerpted highlights from Cardinal Trippe's press conference. He had to smile to himself. *Don't these people ever learn? The more they protest, the more viewers I get.*

The second alert was a text message from Roger Stern.

"What the fuck is this?"

There was a link to YouTube and the first episode of *The Real Family Stone of Portland, Oregon.*

Ethan, who knew nothing of Jackie's Russian accomplice, was quick to notice that he was only the twentieth person to click on the link. Roger, he knew, was overreacting. Plus, it was mostly harmless stuff.

Ethan added a reminder to his Evernote to speak with Jackie about the propriety and decorum with which she needed to approach any behind-the-scenes footage.

And then he promptly forgot about it.

***

Deirdre could see that Jared was slipping. After the encounter with Joanne from hospice, he retreated to his office and slept for four hours. The brief exchange was that taxing.

Deirdre was sitting in the kitchen when he woke up and came downstairs. She went to the counter and made him a latte without asking.

"Thanks, D," Jared mumbled. She did her best to smile and gave his shoulder a gentle squeeze as she passed. Her heart sank, feeling all bone and no muscle. "We need to talk about my will," he blurted out. Deirdre nodded and sat down.

"Where do you want to start?" she asked.

"Well, first, um, do I already have a will?" Questions like this from Jared were becoming increasingly commonplace.

"No, sweetie. It's something we keep meaning to do but haven't gotten around to."

"Well," he said, "there's no time like the present." He paused a bit and then said, "Keep limits on net ether."

"I'm sorry?"

"It's an anagram for 'no time like the present.' *Keep limits on net ether*." Alarm bells were going off in Deirdre's head. "Is that something I do, make anagrams? Because I've been making a lot of them lately."

Deirdre couldn't find the words to answer, so she just shook her head.

"I didn't think so. I half wonder if the brain tumor is trying to talk to me through the anagrams."

"I don't really know how to respond to that, Jare. How long has this been going on?"

"I don't really know."

"Have you told your doctors?"

Jared hung his head and mumbled at the table. "I don't really know that, either."

"Oh, sweetie."

"O, thee wise."

"Huh?"

"Another anagram."

"That's actually kind of amazing."

Jared paused, then looked up at the television camera not so carefully hidden in the kitchen cabinets. "I guess it'll make for good viewing tonight." (Jared was right. The clip of him riffing anagrams with Deirdre had more views than any other clip on the official *Life and Death* website that day. ATN was able to sell a sponsorship to a dictionary publisher.)

"What were we talking about?" Jared asked.

"Your will."

"Oh, I see."

Deirdre wasn't sure what that response meant and wondered if it was another anagram, but she figured it, like everything else in this conversation, wasn't good. There was no doubt about it; they were entering some sort of end game. Deirdre started to imagine how it might play out. Would Jared simply just die? Would he wither like this for months, or longer? The one thing she knew for certain was that Jared had passed the point of no return. She had seen it with her mother.

Her mind kept jumping to the conversation with Joanne from hospice, and how Jared had introduced the topic of euthanasia. Deirdre hadn't yet let her thoughts go down that road, but now she wondered if Jared had been thinking about it. She wanted to ask him, but she couldn't do it with the cameras here. Maybe she could find a time on one of their visits to the doctor.

When she looked up from her reverie, Jared had nodded off.

She contained her emotion, got up, gently woke him, and helped him back to his office.

***

Jackie and Max planned to unveil the second episode of *The Real Family Stone of Portland, Oregon* one week after Jackie put "Operation Answer Fan Mail" into action.

Working with Max, Jackie had created a promotional sheet for their show: a pixilated black-and-white photo of Jared, Deirdre, Jackie, and Megan sitting on a couch and watching television. The scene depicted what the vast majority of middle-class American families did every single night, and was remarkable for how unremarkable it was. Across the top of the sheet, in thirty-six-point Calibri, were the words: "*The Real Family Stone of Portland, Oregon*: The Truth Behind the Most Popular Show on Television, Now on YouTube."

Jackie printed out 342 copies (one for each piece of fan mail she planned to answer) and included a typed, personal message:

Thank you so much for writing to me! If you want to see what life is really like in our house, watch the video series I'm posting on YouTube. This sheet explains it all. The next episode will be live one week from today!

And then she dated it and signed it in ink.

Jackie folded the sheets, stuffed and stamped the envelopes, and mailed them.

In addition to the 342 letters to adoring fans, Jackie also sent a copy of the promo sheet to Hazel Huck. Her address was easy enough to find—there were only four Huck families listed in Huntsville, and with a bit of Googling, she was able to determine which was the right one. To Hazel, Jackie added this handwritten note:

Hi, Hazel!

We don't know each other, but I wanted to thank you for what you tried to do for my dad. I read about it in a newspaper. I'm glad there are still nice people in the world. I also thought you would like to see my new video series. Tell all your friends.

Sincerely,
Jackie Stone

Andersona, the ATN producer who had, under orders from Ethan, been trying to develop a relationship with Jackie, was thrilled that her charge was answering her fan mail. She sent

Ethan a note to report that "the Stone girl is finally getting on board with the program."

Andersona provided Jackie with the envelopes and stamps and offered to take her to the post office. She even let Jackie interview her for her "school video project." She was starting to feel a really strong bond with the girl.

For Jackie and Max, everything was going according to plan.

***

The lead director of *Life and Death*, a veteran of reality TV by the name of Nigel, was growing concerned. Jackie and Deirdre were keeping to themselves, and while Megan had her friends over, they expended so much energy mugging for the camera that the footage wasn't really usable. Worst of all, Jared spent more and more time sleeping. None of it was making for very good television. Nigel spoke to the producers, who spoke to Ethan, who arranged for the first celebrity drop-in.

While viewership for *Life and Death* remained high, the incident with Sherman Kingsborough and Trebuchet left a bad taste in the collective mouth of America, so none of ATN's franchise stars were willing to be connected to the show. The best the network could offer was a character actor from a sitcom called *Oh, Charlie*. It was a family-based, formulaic show about a teenager named Charlie who always seemed to be getting into trouble and then posting his exploits online. It was like a pale imitation of *iCarly* for boys. The actress who played Charlie's aunt Kelley—Jo Garvin—was tasked with doing the drop-in.

The producers prepped the family at their daily morning briefing. They encouraged Jared to get lots of rest as they

wanted him at the "top of his game" when their guest arrived; the girls were asked to dress in their finest clothes and "smile, a lot"; and Deirdre was asked to serve dinner. Everyone agreed with varying degrees of enthusiasm: Jackie rolled her eyes, Deirdre shrugged, and Jared simply said okay. Only Megan, thrilled at the chance to meet a real TV star—not realizing that she had more star power than Jo Garvin by a factor of ten—had a grin that stretched around her entire head.

When their dinner guest arrived, the entire Stone family, even Jackie, was on its best behavior. Deirdre and Jared greeted Jo warmly at the door, invited her to sit down for hors d'oeuvres, and then into the dining room for a home-cooked meal. Dinner consisted of Shake 'N Bake chicken, Kraft Stove Top stuffing, Green Giant green beans, Wonder brand bread, and Entenmann's crumb cake for dessert. Everyone drank Coke, and everyone, other than the kids, had Folgers coffee with their dessert. The entire meal netted ATN nearly a million dollars in advertising placement fees.

The conversation was mundane. Jared and Deirdre talked about their home life, their struggle with Jared's cancer, and Jared's time in the legislature. Megan talked about school and boys and her favorite television shows, including *Oh, Charlie*, which, of course, gave Jo an opportunity to promote the next episode. She had even managed to bring a thirty-second clip, which the family awkwardly interrupted dinner to watch. Jackie was mostly silent.

When the meal was over, everyone escorted Jo to the door to say good night. Jo, who wanted the girls to now call her "Aunt Jo," even kissed Megan on the head before she left.

Of course, the next night, when the episode aired, America saw a decidedly different version of events. Thanks to the magic of editing, every member of the Stone family, even Jackie, hung on Jo's every word. Only Jared—who had been a polite if somewhat withdrawn host—didn't seem to be part of the conversation. The editors succeeded in making Jared look befuddled. They had captured a series of grimaces he made in normal response to conversation and used those to project the image of a man in dire pain.

When Jo was interviewed by Andersona after dinner, in a temporary studio built on the front lawn of the house, she was able to make herself cry when talking about how moved she was by Jared and his family and how cancer was such a truly awful thing.

"Honey," Andersona said when the cameras stopped rolling, "you're going to win an Emmy for this."

Jo hugged Andersona and then winked at Jackie, who, at Andersona's invitation, had been sitting in the corner, recording the entire scene with her iPhone.

**

At first, Hazel Huck figured the letter from Jackie was some sort of prank. But there it was on YouTube, the premiere episode of *The Real Family Stone of Portland, Oregon*. It was more of a home movie than it was a television show, but it was still captivating to actually see Jared Stone and his family behind the scenes.

She sat down and wrote a quick note back to Jackie, thanking her for the letter and telling her how much she admired what she was doing. She included her e-mail address.

Ten minutes later, Hazel was logging in to Azeroth, sharing the *The Real Family Stone of Portland, Oregon* link with all two hundred of her guild members.

***

The day after Jo Garvin came to dinner, Jared slipped into an uneasy sleep on his office futon. Glio, who was becoming less brain tumor and more Jared every day, continued the unstoppable assault on his host.

Having dined on the vast catalog of memories from Jared's early life, and bored with the more recent offerings, Glio turned his attention away from memories and focused instead on other parts of the brain. Glio swam from the hippocampus to the cerebellum, which controlled some of Jared's more basic motor skills and bodily functions.

First he feasted on the neurons that regulated control over Jared's bowels and bladder; then it was the grouping of cells that moved Jared's blood in that narrow band of acceptable pressure; and finally he sampled a small piece of the complex pattern of neurons that controlled Jared's balance.

It was interesting to Glio, but not satisfying. He swam back to the hippocampus and munched on memories of Jared's favorite movies like they were popcorn slathered in butter and salt.

***

When Jared woke from his nap, he found that he had soiled himself. It was the first time it had happened, and it was, he knew, a sign of how far his disease had progressed. He stood up to go to the bathroom and clean himself off and immediately fell back to the ground with a thud.

"What the fuck," he was able to mutter.

He gathered his wits as best he could and pushed himself up on his hands and knees; he crawled to the bathroom, where he more or less collapsed. Jared knew he should probably call for Deirdre, but he was too embarrassed.

"Cancer," he said aloud, "is a bitch."

The cool tile of the bathroom floor on his cheek gave Jared confidence; he propped himself upright and steadied himself with the sink. After a miserable fifteen minutes spent struggling out of his clothes, rinsing them off, and then getting into the shower, he was clean and felt a little refreshed. He was still dizzy, and he could feel his heart race every time he stood up, but the worst of it was behind him.

With a Herculean effort, he made it to the bedroom, where, after shoving his wet clothes under the bed, he collapsed face-first onto the pillow and fell asleep.

Jared's secret stayed intact for exactly five hours, until *Life and Death* aired that night. The cameras had caught everything, including the "Cancer is a bitch" line, right up until he closed the bathroom door. It all ran before the opening credits.

After the first commercial break, Deirdre's face filled the screen. You could hear Andersona off-camera. "So what did you think when you saw Jared crawl to the bathroom?"

Deirdre's eyes welled up. "I'm not going to do this." She stood up, took off her lapel mic, and left.

As they watched the episode that night on the couch together, Deirdre wouldn't make eye contact with her husband. She did reach out for his hand, keeping her stoic eyes on the television screen. When he felt her touch, Jared realized Deirdre was passing him a note.

They watched the rest of the episode in silence. When it was over, Deirdre kissed his cheek and went to bed. Jared took the note to the only safe room in the house—the bathroom—and read it.

"Jare, don't ever keep something like that from me again. We should go see your doctor. And don't ever forget that they're always watching. The more boring we seem, the sooner they'll go away."

But Jared knew that wasn't true. He knew there was only one way the American Television Network was leaving the Stone house, and that was over his dead body.

***

The second episode of *The Real Family Stone of Portland, Oregon* was far more sophisticated than the first. In editing Jackie's new footage—of the crew, of the Stone family, of the house—Max did a masterful job mimicking the format of *Life and Death*. He cut disparate snippets of dialogue together to make them appear as if they were from one conversation; he used a narration Jackie had recorded, superimposing it over a variety of scenes that led the viewer to believe she was trapped in a strange kind of nightmare. The crowning achievement was the interview with Jo Garvin. Max did a split screen comparing the footage that aired (Jo crying) with Jackie's footage (Jo winking in delight at the thought of her Emmy). The truth of the situation was unmistakable: viewers of *Life and Death*, at least in that one interview, had been hoodwinked. This was documentary filmmaking at its very best.

The episode aired two days after America watched Jared crawl on all fours to the bathroom. Thanks to Jackie's letter-writing campaign, thanks to social media, and thanks to Hazel spreading the word through Azeroth, *The Real Family Stone of Portland, Oregon* had one thousand viewers in the first hour, twelve thousand by the following morning, and one hundred fifty thousand by nightfall that same day.

It had gone viral.

***

By sheer coincidence, Ethan Overbee was already in Portland when the second episode of *The Real Family Stone of Portland, Oregon* made its debut. While America was lamenting the steepening decline of Jared's health, Ethan was thinking two steps ahead. He knew that the star and centerpiece of his show, the most viewed show in the history of television, was on a collision course with a hospital, and once Jared was out of the house, all bets would be off.

Ethan also knew that denying Jared medical care would be tantamount to murder, and while that would make for good television, it wouldn't resonate with the sponsors. If he couldn't let Jared go to the hospital, he would have to bring the hospital to Jared. It was during his research into Portland area medical facilities that Ethan had his moment of inspiration.

The only religion to which Ethan subscribed was the adoration and worship of power. The common misconception was that people like Ethan were in it—whatever their particular "it" might be—for the money. They weren't. They wanted control. If you had control, money came naturally. The vast sea of the American middle class was certain it worked the other way. Get money, get power. It's why they had "get rich quick" schemes and "dreams of avarice" for their most aspirational thoughts.

They should have been called "get powerful quick" schemes, and "dreams of control." *Rubes*, Ethan thought about Middle America, when he bothered to think about them at all.

Ethan presumed that Cardinal Trippe, who was playing host to Ethan in the parish's modest office, would understand this perfectly. It didn't matter what kind of organization a person was in, Ethan believed, you didn't get to the top without some amount of clawing and scratching. Power was power no matter where you were. What Ethan didn't understand was why this combative and entirely unlikable nun was in the room, too.

"Mr. Overbee," Sister Benedict was saying, "your show is an affront to the very dignity of human life. It—"

"Please, Sister," the Cardinal interjected. "I'm sure Mr. Overbee saw our press conference."

"In fact, Your Eminence"—Monique had briefed Ethan on the proper thing to call a Catholic Cardinal—"it's why I'm here today. I think we can help one another."

"Your Grace," the Sister began, continuing to push her agenda. But the Cardinal, with a gentle, paternal touch, patted the nun's wrist, and she backed down. *Yes*, Ethan thought, *power*.

"Mr. Stone is, as you know," Ethan said, "gravely ill. He's coming to the point soon where he will need to be hospitalized."

"And that would be bad for your television show," the Cardinal added.

"Exactly. With Mr. Stone out of the house, we won't have much of a show at all. So I was thinking, what if we brought the hospital into the house? I've done some research, and by all accounts, Saint Ignatius is the best medical facility in the city, and if I understand correctly, it is governed by the Church."

"Interesting. But tell me, Mr. Overbee, given our public stance on your show, why would we want to help you?"

"Yes, why?" Sister Benedict couldn't help but add her voice to the conversation.

"First, it will put the fate of this man's soul in your care." Ethan had written that line down and memorized it. "Second, you will be able to preserve his life for as long as your doctors are able. And third"—here Ethan put his hands on the desk and leaned in—"the publicity for your parish will be unprecedented."

The Cardinal shook his head. "Mr. Overbee, I appreciate why you're here. You need to sell advertising dollars, and you concocted this scheme to both neutralize our criticism and help your show at the same time. Right?" Ethan, who was normally impervious to such things, was caught under the Cardinal's spell.

"Yes, Your Eminence, something like that."

"While we cherish all life, we don't have any desire to interfere with God's plan for Mr. Stone. If it is his time to be called home to our heavenly Father, then it is not for our Church or your television station to interfere." Ethan noticed the nun visibly bristle at this. "Nor do we care," the Cardinal added, "for the kind of publicity your show is generating." Ethan was starting to think he'd miscalculated and had run into a dead end.

"However," the Cardinal continued, "I am willing to arrange for medical care to be provided to Mr. Stone in his house, to keep him comfortable and ease his suffering as he exits this world, but I have conditions."

Ethan felt the ground grow solid beneath him. He was back in familiar territory. "Not to be crass, Cardinal Trippe, but how much?"

The Cardinal's eyebrows arched in such surprise that they nearly left his forehead, and then he laughed. "No, no, Mr. Overbee, you misunderstand me. We don't want your money. We want your show to pay heed to Mr. Stone's spiritual as well as his physical well-being."

"You don't want money?" Ethan was so flummoxed that he didn't quite know how to react.

"We want your viewers to see Mr. Stone's soul prepared for its journey into the hereafter. We want religion injected into the narrative."

Ethan wanted to laugh. He wanted to hug this foolish priest and his troll-like nun and thank them for restoring his faith in all the things that he, Ethan, found holy. "Of course, Your Eminence. We can feature a short segment each night where a priest tends to Mr. Stone's—how did you put it? Spiritual well-being?"

"Very good," the Cardinal answered. "Only, I wasn't thinking of a priest." At this, Ethan followed as the Cardinal turned his gaze to Sister Benedict. The nun, for her part, looked for a moment like she'd been slapped, then she looked like she'd won the lottery.

Ethan sized her up. She reminded him of the alien in *E.T.* He knew instantly that her approval ratings would be in the sewer, but that was okay. America liked to have someone to revile. *Yes,* he thought, *this could work.* "Welcome, Sister," he said with a smile like a jackal, "to the cast of *Life and Death.*"

One problem down, Ethan thought, *one to go.*

***

The knock on Jackie's bedroom door woke her up. She was pretty sure she knew who was on the other side.

Three hours earlier Jackie was in the kitchen being accosted by Andersona. The *Life and Death* producer exorcised no small number of personal demons through the verbal lashing she gave Jackie. The rant was loud enough and long enough that Andersona had to be restrained by another member of the crew. "How could you post that shit online?" she was shouting as she was pulled away. "I let you be my friend, you fucking bitch!"

"Bet they won't show that on TV," Jackie muttered to herself as she retreated to the safety of her room and stayed there. Her parents were out visiting her father's doctor, and Megan wasn't home, so Jackie was, for all intents and purposes, trapped.

When she found Max online, he was bubbling over.

Max

Solnyshko! Have you see how much people watch our video?

Jackie

Hi, Max. I did. It's pretty good.

Max

Pretty good? More than 100,000 people, and she says
pretty good!

Jackie

I'm sorry, you're right. It's great. You did such a good job
on it.

Max

Nyet, Jacquelyn, WE did good job, together. Are you not
excited?

Jackie

Well, Andersona was pretty mad. I feel kind of bad about it.

Max

No, Solnyshko, Andersona is enemy. She is one who make
your father look bad. She spins web of lies.

Jackie

Are we any better?

Max

Yes, we show truth. Pravda!

Max was right, Jackie knew, and it was making her feel
better. Still, she was certain there would be repercussions, and
not knowing what they were was hard. She said as much to Max.

Max

What is repercussions?

Jackie

It means consequences. That I will be punished.

Max

Your parents will punish you?

Jackie

No, the network.

Max was quiet while he processed that. Jackie had shot some footage that morning (though she hadn't been able to capture Andersona's outburst), and she tethered her phone to download it.

She and Max spent a few more minutes chatting, talking mostly about the shots he wanted her to get for the next episode of their YouTube show, and then bid each other good-bye. It was the middle of the night in Russia, and Max needed sleep. Not knowing what else to do, Jackie lay down on her bed, where she dozed off.

Then came the knock on the door.

She propped herself up on her elbows. "Who is it?" she said.

Ethan opened the door and peeked around its edge. "May I come in?"

Jackie shrugged.

Ethan entered the room and sat down on the lone chair. He looked around, taking in his surroundings. He nodded at the *Mean Girls* poster.

"Great movie," Ethan said.

"I know why you're here, Mr. Overbee," Jackie answered.

"I don't think you do." He locked his eyes on Jackie's face, making her squirm.

"You're not here to yell at me? About *The Real Family Stone of Portland, Oregon*?"

"Would it do any good?"

Jackie didn't answer. She wasn't really sure where this was going, and there was something in Ethan's demeanor that made her even more uneasy than usual.

"Maybe my parents should be here," Jackie said.

"Maybe, but they're not home, are they."

Again, Jackie didn't answer.

"You know," Ethan began, "you've probably ruined Jo Garvin's career. She's got two kids. Did you know that?"

Jackie didn't know that, but she thought that if Jo really loved her kids, she might have at least mentioned them during dinner.

"There never was any school project for your videos, was there?"

Jackie stared at her hands.

"Want to play it quiet? Okay, we can do that, too. What I don't understand, though, is how you managed to so successfully shield the identity of your YouTube account."

He didn't know about Max. Jackie felt a jolt of adrenaline; she controlled a piece of information that this man, who seemed to know everything, didn't have.

"No matter," Ethan said, standing up. "YouTube account or not, you can't make movies without this."

Ethan reached onto her desk, unplugged her iPhone, and pocketed it.

"Hey!" Jackie yelled, alarmed.

"Sorry, kiddo, you lost the privilege."

"That's my phone."

"It was your phone, Jackie," Ethan said, opening the door, "but now, everything in this house, everything on this set, belongs to me. And, Jackie?" He waited a beat to make sure he had her full attention. "One more episode of your show goes live, and I'll do a lot worse than take away your phone."

With that, he turned and exited.

***

Later that night, Jackie told Deirdre what had happened. Her mother went through the roof. She screamed at the director until he agreed to get Ethan on the phone.

"Now, now, Deirdre," Ethan said, trying to stop her from shouting, "Jackie is overreacting. It's true, I did take her phone away, but I'm sure you understand why the network can't have any more unauthorized behind-the-scenes escapades. It would be good for you, her mother, to remind her of that."

"Mr. Overbee," Deirdre began, her bear claws fully extended and ready to protect the interests of her cub, "I assure you—"

"And, Deirdre," Ethan interrupted as if he hadn't heard her at all, "one more thing."

Deirdre had a sick feeling in her stomach.

"Beginning tomorrow, the American Television Network, pursuant to the terms of your husband's contract and in coordination with the Saint Ignatius Hospital of Portland, will assume the responsibility for Jared's medical care."

"What? You can't—"

"Good night, Deirdre. I'll be on the set this week if you want to talk about it further."

The line went dead.

***

Sister Benedict Joan entered the Stone house as if she had lived there all her life. She was amazed to see how much of the space had been converted to a television set. The images projected on-screen made it seem like any other house, but such was the lie of the medium. Over the years, the Sister had caught glimpses of other reality shows—usually clips from *Real World*, or *Big Brother*, or *The Amazing Race*, shown by guests on *The Duke Hamblin Show*—and now she wondered if anything on television was real.

"Who are you?"

The Sister turned around and saw an angelic teenage girl staring at her, rosy cheeks, strawberry-blond pigtails, and the widest, bluest eyes she had ever seen. Having watched every episode of *Life and Death*, the Sister knew this to be Megan Stone.

"I am Sister Benedict Joan, young lady, but you may call me Sister."

"Okay, Sister, what are you doing in my house?"

Sister Benedict had hoped the Stone family would have been briefed. "Is your mother or father at home?"

"No, they went to see a lawyer. Something about Daddy's doctors."

"Ah, I see. Well, Megan, I am here to help take care of your father, and while I'm at it, I will help take care of you and your sister. You can think of me as your friend." Sister Benedict smiled.

The Cardinal had asked the Sister to be accommodating to the family, and to do everything she could to care for the well-being of the Stone girls. "They are going through a horrible ordeal, Sister. They need our love and support."

While she was an adequate teacher and a tough disciplinarian at the Annunciation School, Sister Benedict was not well suited to making nice with children. Her smile was creepy.

"Now," she continued, "is Jacquelyn at home?"

"No, *Jackie*"—Megan emphasized her sister's preferred name—"stayed late at school to work in the computer lab."

"Very good. It's important that young women learn modern skills."

A group of workers came in behind the Sister carrying a hospital bed and other hospital equipment. "Where to, Sister?" asked a burly man who trailed the group carrying a clipboard.

"Megan," the Sister asked, "can you show these gentlemen to your father's office?"

"Yeah, this way."

"Young ladies do not say 'yeah,' Miss Stone. They say 'yes.'"

I can see, the Sister thought to herself, *that I have a lot of work to do here.*

For her part, Megan just shrugged and led the men upstairs.

***

Glio leaped a metaphorical chasm. Until this point in his short life, he had been singularly occupied with the internal destruction of Jared's brain. Of course, Glio didn't think of it as destruction. He was merely fulfilling his preordained purpose in the world. He had no more choice in the matter than does the tide in the ocean. Had Glio stopped to consider the arguments for and against free will, he would have come down heavily on the side of determinism.

But things were changing. Having exhausted the most interesting of Jared's memories, having sampled and moved on from Jared's motor skills, having pulled back the curtain hiding the deepest darkest secrets of Jared Stone's brain, Glio needed something different. He needed to see the world beyond.

His first foray came largely by accident. While Jared and Deirdre sat in the offices of Morrison, Murphy, and O'Connor, a well-heeled Portland law firm, Glio, reaching out and exploring the places he'd never been, ambled his way from Jared's frontal lobe, to his parietal lobe, to the temporal lobe, down the auditory nerve, winding a long tendril around the cochlea, and all the way to Jared's eardrum. Glio was surprised to find himself actively listening to conversations in real time. It was fascinating.

"I'm sorry, Deirdre," an older male voice was saying, "this contract you signed is airtight. And even if we do challenge it, the network attorneys will use a scorched-earth approach to push us back."

"I'm sorry, Dan, I don't know what that means." It was a woman's voice that Glio immediately recognized as Deirdre's.

How strange, he thought, *to hear memories as they are being made.* Glio was glad for Deirdre's question as he didn't know what the lawyer meant by "scorched-earth," either. He wondered, if Deirdre hadn't asked, could he have asked? Could Glio have found a way to talk to this lawyer? Would it have been any different from Jared talking to the lawyer?

"It means they'll force you to spend so much money that you'll be bankrupt before you even get to settlement talks."

"What if we go rogue?"

"I'm sorry?"

"What if we just leave the house and don't come back?"

"I can't advise that, Deirdre. You won't get any money, and they'll sue you into oblivion. I'm also not sure Jared can handle that."

Glio sensed that everyone in the room was looking at him, or rather looking at Jared, though he was no longer sure he could tell the difference between the two. Feeling self-conscious, another entirely new experience, Glio retreated from Jared's ear and made his way back to safer ground.

Emboldened and excited by the experience, he planned his next foray into the world outside. He wanted to *see*.

***

Jackie

I have to go soon, Max, my parents are going to be here any minute.

Max

Ok, Solnyshko, you will use new phone for more footage tonight?

Jackie

Definitely.

Deirdre had promised to buy Jackie a new iPhone before picking her up from school and to help her sneak it into the house.

Max

This is good. Do zavtra . . .

Jackie

And to you, Max.

When Jackie exited the school, her parents were already waiting for her in the parking lot.

"How'd it go at the lawyers?" she asked as she slid into the backseat.

"Not so good, honey," Deirdre said. "I'm afraid we're stuck with this for now."

Jackie just nodded.

"But here." Her mother handed her a bag from the Apple Store.

"Is it all set up?"

"Yep!"

Jackie leaned into the front seat and kissed each of her parents on the cheek.

Jared, who had been both silent and still until this point said, "Oh, hey, Jax," seeming to realize for the first time that his daughter was in the car. He took her hand and squeezed it. Jackie couldn't help but notice how skeletal her father's fingers and wrist had become. She could feel every bone in his hand.

"You just keep right on making those movies, Jackie," Deirdre said. "They're wonderful."

"Thanks, Mom, but I had a lot of help."

"From who?"

"Um . . . it's a secret." Deirdre smiled, and Jackie knew what she was thinking. "I do not have a boyfriend, Mom."

"Okay, okay . . . whoever it is, though, keep working with them. You guys are doing a great job."

When they arrived at the house, a security guard opened a gate in The Wall. The seven-foot barrier separating the Stone family from the rest of the world was, despite assurances to the contrary from Ethan Overbee, very much an eyesore. When Jackie had first envisioned the wall, her mind had conjured the image of a giant white picket fence, something protective but neighborly. Instead, she was now looking at a chain-link fence with barbed wire on top. And while the network did stay true to its word to plant hedges, they measured only five feet. The sight of the fence rising up out of the bush was even more ominous than if the hedges hadn't been there; it was like something out of an apocalyptic science-fiction movie.

Jackie hid the Apple bag under her seat and tucked the phone into her hiking boot as the car pulled into the driveway.

Deirdre stopped short of the garage, control of which had been ceded to the crew, and the three of them stepped out onto the front lawn. A security table had been set up just inside the front door. As two security guards, one man and one woman, were going through Deirdre's purse and Jackie's backpack, Ethan stepped into the foyer from the living room.

"Hi, everyone," he said. "Janet," he said to the female guard, "please remove Jackie's shoes. Gunther, take Deirdre's and Jared's cell phones."

"What?" Deirdre shrieked.

"Don't worry, Deirdre," Ethan said, his voice dripping with sweetness, "you can have them back when you leave the house."

Not sure what to do, Jackie surrendered her boots and Jared tried to hand his phone to Ethan. "Thanks, Jared, Gunther will take that," Ethan said, gently pushing Jared's hand to the security guard. Jackie noticed that neither Gunther nor Janet could or would make eye contact with her, her mother, or her father.

"Ethan, this is too much."

"I'm sorry, Deirdre. This television show is a very important asset for the network, and we need to protect it."

"Asset? This is our home!"

"Mr. Overbee?" Jackie interrupted quietly.

"Yes, Jackie?"

"How did you know that phone was in my shoe?"

When Ethan smiled, Jackie knew the answer. From the look on her mother's face, she could tell that Deirdre knew, too. "You have a camera in our car, don't you?" she asked.

Ethan's smile widened, but he didn't answer. "Come with me. I have a surprise for you."

The three of them followed Ethan up the stairs to Jared's office in a trancelike stupor. When he opened the door, they saw that the small space had been converted to a fully functioning hospital room, replete with bed, IV drips, and a series of complex-looking machines with blinking lights and digital readouts. Standing next to the bed was not a doctor or a nurse, but a nun.

Looking at the woman, Jackie was immediately reminded of Dr. Seuss's description of the title character from her favorite childhood book, *The Lorax*: "Shortish, oldish, brownish, and mossy."

Before anyone could say anything, Jared let out a big sigh of relief, stumbled across the room, and crawled into the bed, giving the pillow a full-body hug.

"There, there, Mr. Stone, you rest. The Sisters of the Perpetual Adoration will care for you now."

Jackie turned and ran to her bedroom.

***

The opening scene on that night's episode of *Life and Death* was of Jared crawling into bed and Sister Benedict tending to him. There were interviews with the Sister, with Cardinal Trippe, and with the medical team from Saint Ignatius Hospital.

Missing from the episode were the daily interviews with the Stone family. The director and editor repurposed footage from an earlier episode and were able to cobble together some semblance of family reaction, but for the most part, other than Jared in the hospital bed, the Stones were absent.

After Ethan had confiscated all their phones and introduced Jared, Deirdre, and Jackie to Sister Benedict, Deirdre called a family meeting in the upstairs bathroom. It was the only room believed to be completely free of video and audio devices. It was possible Ethan had crossed that boundary, too, but Deirdre didn't have any other choice.

"Listen," she told her daughters, "from this day forward, we're not to help the producers or crew in any way. We'll fulfill the obligations of our contract but only the bare minimum. When they ask us questions, we use one-word answers. When a celebrity stops by, we excuse ourselves. When we're not busy, we read books, watch television, or use the bathroom. Do you girls understand?"

Jackie was on board before Deirdre had finished her first sentence. Not Megan.

"But, Mom, we're on TV!" Megan protested, as if the notion were so patently obvious it needed no further explanation. Deirdre was not to be persuaded, but Megan still put up a fight; she stomped, punched the shower curtain, and whined until Deirdre lost her cool.

"Enough, Megan," she snapped. "This is how it has to be. Do you understand?"

Megan held her head low, like a vulture, offering only the slightest nod of agreement.

This quasi act of civil disobedience from the Stone women was a new problem for Ethan. He could deal with naked aggression, cold-blooded capitalism, but not this. The show, if it didn't get more interesting soon, would start to lose viewers, and that would be, he knew, the end of his career. He had to find some way to motivate his cast to work.

***

Jared knew to expect the hair loss, but like so many cancer patients, he wasn't ready for it. All the other crap the tumor was throwing at him—the headaches, the confusion, the missing memories; the nausea, the fatigue, even the weight loss—were somehow internal. It was almost like if he just tried hard enough, he could find a way to beat them.

The hair loss was different. It was tangible proof to the rest of the world that Jared wasn't just sick, that he was really, really sick. Jared, of course, already knew this. But now that it was irrefutably obvious to anyone who looked at him—though if Jared was honest with himself, the hair loss was only the crowning achievement of his body's complete and utter deterioration—it made the whole thing seem somehow inescapable.

Not normally a vain man—Jared thought of his own fashion aesthetic, when he bothered to think of it at all, as "homespun"—his first instinct was to get a toupee. Ethan talked him out of it.

"Trust me, Jared, you don't want one of those things."

"Why?"

"Because everyone will know it's fake. And you know how they say the camera adds ten pounds?"

Jared looked down at his withering body and answered, "I hope so."

"Yes," Ethan hesitated, not sure how to react to the gallows humor, "well, it's even worse with toupees. If they look at all suspect in the real world, they'll look like misplaced pieces of carpet on TV."

Jared thought about this for a moment. He was about to shrug his shoulders and move on, but then he remembered something. "One of your producers told me that there are plenty of actors with natural hair loss, and that professional makeup artists can work magic so no one will be able to tell the difference. Isn't John Travolta really bald?"

"Ah," Ethan responded. Jared didn't know what that was supposed to mean, but he thought he detected a hint of annoyance. "I see. Well, unfortunately, Jared, the terms of our agreement forbid the network from doing anything more than medically necessary to aid you."

"Oh."

"But, hey," Ethan added, "you're free to get a toupee on your own. I just don't think you'd be happy with it."

Like she had done with the radiation therapy, Deirdre vowed to support whatever decision Jared made with regard to his hair. Which again wasn't much help.

Not sure what to do, or even what to think, Jared opted for the path of least resistance. America watched him lose his hair.

The *Life and Death* blog on the *People* website noted that Jared "went from looking sick to looking terminal."

Luckily for Jared, he didn't read *People*.

***

Jackie's phone was gone, but she still had her laptop, so she logged on to look for Max. She knew it was a long shot; it was already the middle of the night in Russia, and predictably, Max wasn't there.

Looking for some other way to occupy her time, Jackie sat down to read the latest onslaught of fan mail. Most of it was very nice, but some of it was creepy. One man, an old man, at least thirty, sent a naked picture of himself. He was fat and hairy, like an ape. Jackie knew she should tell someone, but she worried they would start screening her mail, and outside of school, it was her only connection to the real world. She felt like a bird with an injured wing, unable to fly, too tired to walk.

She read through letter after letter, each offering its "love," or "support," or "friendship," until they started to blur together. Jackie was just starting to nod off when she saw Hazel Huck's name on the return address of an envelope.

Dear Jackie,

Thanks so much for writing me. I absolutely loved THE REAL FAMILY STONE OF PORTLAND, OREGON. I think it's terrible that ATN is using the show to hurt your family. I can't even imagine having no privacy like that, especially at such a hard time. (Though I'd be lying if I said I wasn't watching.) Keep those videos coming.

If you want to write back, it's better to send e-mail to
guineverthegladd@gmail.com.

Your friend,

Hazel Huck

Jackie went immediately to her computer.

From: jaxouttathebox@gmail.com

To: guineverthegald@gmail.com

Subject: Trapped!

Hi, Hazel—Thanks for writing me back! I was so happy to
see your letter. The producer from ATN—a pretty big
jerkface named Ethan—took away my phone yesterday
so I can't shoot any more videos. My mom bought me a
new one, which I tried to hide in my shoe and sneak into
my house, but he took that one away, too. My mom says
we're on strike now, and we're not to give them anything
interesting to film. Anyway, I'm telling you because,
really, I don't know who else to tell. Thanks for listening.
YOUR friend, Jackie Stone

Two minutes after Jackie sent the message, she received a
Facebook friend request from GuinevertheGlad. As soon as she
clicked the "accept" button, an instant message popped up.

Hazel

Jackie?

Jackie

Hazel?

Hazel

Lol. Yes.

Jackie

How did you find me?

Hazel

Your e-mail address is a pretty unique handle.

Jackie noticed that Hazel had over four hundred friends. It made her feel silly for having only twenty, and most of those were really just acquaintances who more than likely felt sorry for her.

Hazel

Listen, I have an idea for how to help you.

Jackie

How?!?!?

Hazel

Have you ever played World of Warcraft?

PART FIVE

Rebellion

Saturday, October 24

Megan Stone liked being popular. She liked it a lot.

Okay, sure, it was horrible that Daddy was so sick, but if her family had to endure the unfairness of his disease, then at least they could do it on TV, where they would be famous, and rich, and powerful. How many other kids' dads get cancer? Lots. But none of them, Megan was sure, ever get to be on television.

And now her mother was ruining it.

Right there in Megan's house were the biggest, fanciest television cameras in the world, the most important producers, and the wealthiest sponsors, and all they wanted to do was film her, Megan Stone. Okay, maybe not her specifically, but still. And now she wasn't allowed to talk to them? It was so unfair. Megan knew it had to be because of Jackie and her stupid YouTube thing.

She couldn't understand her sister. If Jackie would just let her hair down and try a little makeup, she'd be pretty. And wasn't that better than being smart? What was so good about being a brainiac? Weren't those kids the ones who got picked on? Wasn't their life kind of miserable? It's not that Megan wanted to do badly in school—and she didn't—it's that she knew there were more important things.

If Megan wasn't allowed to talk to the producers, if she didn't talk on camera, she wouldn't be on the show. What would the kids at school think if Megan wasn't on TV anymore? They would think she was a loser, that's what. She would become a nobody. And to a girl like Megan Stone, there was nothing worse.

Just before she went to bed later that night, the same day her mom had laid down the law about the family doing nothing to cooperate with the *Life and Death* producers, she did something she hadn't done in ages. She got on her knees and prayed.

"Dear God, please help my mom understand how wrong she is. Daddy wanted us to be on this television show, and we owe it to him to see it through. Please send me a sign so I'll know what's right."

When Megan stepped out of school the following Monday and saw the limousine waiting for her—when all her friends saw the limousine waiting for her—Megan knew her prayers had been answered.

***

The meeting in Azeroth, a war council called by the all-powerful Guinevere the Glad, stretched over three days. It took place in a stone castle on a windswept virtual plain. The building was an impressive structure surrounded by a moat filled with unspeakable pixilated terrors. Looming above it all were twin spires, each flying pennants. It looked like a cross between Churchill Downs and Westminster Abbey. The grandeur of the location underscored the gravity of the meeting inside.

News of the war council spread to every corner of the realm, and everyone wanted in. Character upon character converged on the palace, creating an impromptu fair on the field beyond its walls. There were merchants selling goods, heroes fighting the monsters that the game insisted on spawning, and, of course, player after player after player dueling one another. It was a kind of Dark Ages Bonnaroo without the bands.

Only those with an invitation were let beyond the moat. Players who lived in Portland or had a connection to technology, television, and/or medicine were recruited. In an unprecedented move for a Warcraft guild, invitees were required to give their real life names, occupations, and places of residence. Two senior guild members were tasked with screening and reviewing all applicants, turning away far more than were allowed to pass.

It had taken Jackie no small effort to get there. She had "borrowed" her mother's credit card, and then spent more than five hours downloading the Warcraft software along with a never-ending stream of updates. She'd found the one spot in her room blind to the ATN cameras—in a corner on the floor, next to her closet—and sat there, huddled over her computer.

After a while, one of the producers poked her head into the bedroom, wondering how Jackie had vanished. When she saw Jackie sitting cross-legged on the floor, her MacBook in her lap, the producer shook her head and left. Twenty minutes later, and just a few minutes before Jackie finally arrived in Azeroth, a technician came in and affixed a new camera to the ceiling, aiming it directly at Jackie's corner. His face was riddled with guilt, and he muttered "sorry" before he left the room. It didn't matter to Jackie; they still couldn't see her computer screen.

Jackie's character was a male dwarf warrior called Gerald the Generous, the name a nod to Hazel's character. When she— or rather Gerald—first arrived in Azeroth, he was standing in a small outdoor plaza, surrounded by walking, running, and leaping avatars. The theme was medieval, or maybe more aptly, computer-generated medieval fantasy.

An enormous, green-skinned female elf was standing in front of Jackie's dwarf, its arms gesticulating wildly. When

Jackie moved her mouse over the character, she saw that it was Guinevere the Glad—Hazel. Jackie had no idea what to do. The two of them stood there like that for a couple of minutes.

Jackie was just about to give up when she noticed a small chat box on the World of Warcraft dashboard.

Hazel

Can you hear me?

GtGen

Hear you?

Hazel

Yeah, do you have your headset plugged in?

GtGen

I don't have a headset. Besides, anything I say out loud will just wind up on TV.

Hazel

Right, of course. Okay, we'll do this the old-fashioned way. We'll type.

For the next hour, Gerald the Generous followed Guinevere the Glad from one virtual glade to the next. Jackie learned how to manipulate her character, how to fight monsters, how to talk to people, how to pick up and drop materials, how to attach herself to a group, and so much more. She found the game mind-numbingly fun.

When she and Hazel arrived at the palace, they crossed a drawbridge and found two guards arguing with a muscular, human male warrior just outside the colossal stone door. Hazel could hear the conversation; Jackie could not.

"I am invited," the male warrior was saying.

"Sorry, newb," the guard answered. "This is a private guild meeting. No one under level fifty allowed."

"What's going on, Farsifal?" Guinevere asked.

"This newb is lost," he answered. "We're trying to help him understand."

"Nyet!" the warrior insisted. "Jackie invite me."

"What's going on?" Jackie typed into her chat box.

"Some kid who says he knows you," Guinevere responded. "I think he's Russian."

"Max?" Jackie typed.

"Solnyshko! Please tell them I am good."

"Jackie, did you invite someone?" Guinevere asked. "I'm not sure that was such a good idea."

"It's okay. He needs to be here. You can trust him."

Ten minutes later, Guinevere the Glad was banging the butt of her sword on the stone table, calling the council to order. The myriad side conversations died down.

Jackie waited as the first part of the conversation took place by voice. Hazel had warned her that this would be the case.

"This guild has done more good in the land of Azeroth than any in the realm," Hazel began.

There were murmurs of assent.

"We have slain mighty foes." The murmurs grew louder. "We have recovered plentiful bounty!" Louder still. "And we have helped those in need."

The assembled interrupted with "woots" and "huzzahs."

Jackie's Facebook IM flashed.

Max

Solnyshko, what manner of talking is this?

Jackie

I can't actually hear them, Max, but don't worry about it.
This is a role-playing game, so it might sound funny. Just
follow along the best you can.

Max

I will do my hardest.

Jackie

"I will try my hardest," Max, or "I will do my best." I think you
got them mixed up.

"We all know why we're here today," Hazel said. "Jackie Stone, daughter of Jared Stone, needs our help. Jackie will now tell us her tale."

Hazel had prepared Jackie for this—that she would need to tell her story to the guild. She had even written an introduction for her. Jackie copied and pasted it.

"Good people of Azeroth, members of the guild, I come to you with a heavy heart and ask that you hear my song." After that, Jackie just started typing in her own manner of speech, and pretty soon, everyone else reverted to the idiom of the early twenty-first century. She told them about her father and his disease, thanking them for the money they had raised for the eBay listing. She told them about life on the set of the television show. She introduced them to Max and explained how the two of them had made *The Real Family Stone of Portland, Oregon.* And she told them about Ethan Overbee, and how he had turned her home into a prison and had confiscated her phone, and how he and his minions were watching Jackie and her family twenty-four hours a day.

"What we need is a rescue," someone said. Others agreed.

"No," Hazel answered. "Jackie's request is simple. We need to get her a camera."

For the next hour, and spilling into the next two nights, the guild discussed various plans to get Jackie a camera. In the end, they settled on the simplest plan of all. Throw her one over The Wall.

No one was more surprised than Jackie to learn that the knight chosen for the task was her awkward, pimply-faced classmate, Jason Sanderson—the boy who had told her she looked nice in her Easter dress all those years ago.

It made perfect sense to Jackie that Jason lived in this world. When the real world treats you like garbage, why not find a better world, one without prejudice, judgment, and cruelty? She was only sad that she hadn't discovered this world for herself years earlier.

Jason was known in Azeroth simply as G. Ranger, and was now known to the guild as a hero among men.

***

Ethan knew the younger Stone girl would be easy prey. Hell, most of America would have known. In her interviews with the producer, the short segments that aired each night, Megan tried too hard. She fawned for the camera, used her hand to brush her hair back a little too often, and used the producer's name too emphatically. It played well enough with America because she was so young—Megan was cute, and she knew it—but overnight polling, which peeled away all nuance and stripped things down to their bare essence, said that her unfavorable numbers were on the rise; America was starting to see Megan as a stuck-up and self-absorbed brat.

Of course, those poll numbers were never shared with the family lest it affect their performance. But Ethan had seen them. In fact, Ethan was counting on them.

"Hello, Megan," he said as she climbed into the limousine. Megan, overwhelmed by the opulence, muttered hello in response. "Would you like something to drink?" Ethan motioned to the bar stacked with soda, juice, and milk. "We have Nantucket Nectars. You know, that's Jo Garvin's favorite." Ethan had no idea what Jo Garvin liked to drink, nor did he care. But he had seen how Megan adored Jo, and he was all too happy to exploit it.

"Oh, yes, please, Mr. Overbee. I would simply *love* a Nantucket Nectar."

Even here, Ethan thought, *the kid can't dial it down.*

"It's a shame about Jo," he said, passing her a bottle.

"Why? What happened?" Megan's concern was, Ethan could tell, genuine. His face betrayed no hint of the delight he was feeling inside.

"Your sister's video, Megan. It probably ended Jo's career."

Megan sighed. Written in that lone syllable of exhalation was a lifetime of frustration with Jackie, exasperation at why her sister had to be so weird. "End her career?" Megan asked.

"Yes. Jackie's video made Jo look like a fool, and America doesn't suffer fools gladly." Ethan didn't really think either statement was true. Jo would rebound, the tenacious ones always do, and America, he believed, was populated by cud-chewing cave trolls.

Megan felt bad for Jo—she was a star after all—but she wasn't sure what any of this had to do with her. "Didn't you take Jackie's phone away?"

"We did. But Jackie's video is only half the problem."

"What do you mean?"

"I can tell that your mom is upset with the show, upset with me." Ethan leaned in and dropped the volume of his voice, turning Megan into a coconspirator. Megan had used this same trick on Jackie countless times but didn't immediately recognize it on the receiving end. She nodded and leaned in, too, completely unaware that she was being played.

"I think," Ethan said, leaning in closer, "maybe she asked you and Jackie to stop cooperating?" Megan was silent. She felt uncomfortable at the line of questioning. More than anything she wanted to be back on the show, but she didn't want to get her mother in trouble with the network.

It never occurred to Megan to ask how Ethan knew what her mom had told her and Jackie. Not that he would have told her about the cameras in each of the house's two bathrooms. Ethan had strict instructions that the director was to never use or even watch footage from those cameras. It was the most ignored rule on set; male members of the crew would routinely watch Deirdre—and her teenage daughters—shower.

"I know how hard it is to defy your mother," Ethan offered, seeming to read Megan's mind. "I went through something similar when I was your age."

"You did?"

"It was in eighth grade. Is that the grade you're in now?" Of course, Ethan knew the answer to his own question. Megan nodded. "Right, so you'll understand. My mother and father didn't like the group of friends I hung around with. If you can believe this, my parents thought they were too square."

"Square?"

"They were nice kids, but a bit goofy. One of them loved movies so much that all he wanted was for us, our whole group of friends, to make our own movies. He had a Betamax recorder—"

"What's that?"

"Well, this was back in the 1980s, before there was all this digital technology. It was a great big camera that used video-tapes. To us, it was the coolest. Anyway, he used his Betamax to make movies. We all starred in them and had fun doing it. We would charge other kids in the neighborhood money to see them. My parents hated it. They thought I should have been hanging around boys who played sports, that sort of thing."

"Most of my guy friends play sports," Megan offered meekly.

"And that's a good thing. But my friends back then, we were like a team, a fraternity. You know what a fraternity is?"

Megan nodded again.

"So anyway, I decided to ignore my parents and hang out

with them. And this was doubly hard because my father was a colonel in the air force, and a pretty scary guy."

"So what happened?" Megan asked.

"To tell the truth, those guys are the reason I went into television. I wouldn't be who I am today if I had listened to my parents and hung out with different kids."

None of Ethan's story was true. His father was a mid-level manager at a regional bank, never in his life had he touched a Betamax recorder, and, like Megan, he only ever hung around with the popular kids. He wouldn't have been caught dead with the AV Club nerds. But the story, culled from a spec script that had crossed his desk, served its purpose. The girl was wide-eyed. Ethan almost felt a pang of guilt as he realized just how young thirteen actually is. Almost.

"So, Megan, are you willing to do what's right, even if it means going against your parents' wishes?"

"I-I think so," she stammered.

"Good," he said, patting her knee. Megan recoiled on instinct, but Ethan didn't notice. "Here's what I'd like you to do."

***

Sister Benedict settled into the ebb and flow of the Stone household with relative ease.

Her singular mission was to extend Jared's life as long as medicine and technology would allow. Where the caregivers and the church failed with Terri Schiavo, Sister Benedict would succeed with Jared Stone. The doctors warned the Sister that a brain tumor was a decidedly different matter than Mrs. Schiavo, whose brain had been severely damaged when it was starved of oxygen due to a massive cardiac event. But the Sister, who knew precious little about medicine, put her faith in God. He would not have brought her all this way, would not have granted her entry to this house, if He did not have a plan.

Besides, Cardinal Trippe had made it clear to the medical team that Sister Benedict was his emissary on the set, and that she spoke for him. The Sister knew that she was not exactly following the Cardinal's wishes when she instructed the doctors to do everything in their power to keep the man alive, but she was able to rationalize it. *The ends,* the Sister thought, *sometimes do indeed justify the means.*

Beyond the care of her patient, the Sister tried her best to avoid any connection to the television show. Of course, one did not set up camp in the Stone household without becoming a willing or unwilling participant.

Obeying the Cardinal's direction, Sister Benedict succumbed to the daily interview with the producer, and to being filmed almost continuously by the many "hidden" cameras. The first time she saw herself on TV, on the episode of *Life and Death* that aired the night she arrived in the house, she was mortified.

When did I grow so old? she thought, reaching for the lines on her face. *Is this what I've become?*

She dwelled on that thought for a moment and then shook her head to clear it. She recalled something her first Mother Superior used to say: "The ability to compartmentalize is a necessary fabric in the thread of any good nun's cloak of invincibility." It was advice—given to her when she was still Angela Marie the novice—that Sister Benedict would turn to again and again. To be a nun was to be in a state of perpetual conflict. Discipline and obedience locked horns with compassion and forgiveness, self-imposed poverty was a source of mockery in a society driven almost entirely by consumerism, and chastity and desire could never be reconciled.

The Sister considered herself above base instincts like desire and materialism, but in the end, she was human, and some days, one or the other would tug at her conscience. As a young novice she would mention these things in confession, but the penance was always the same—a few Hail Marys, a few Our Fathers, and her soul was clean. As she grew older, she knew enough to mete out her own punishment, and kept her darkest thoughts to herself.

When she saw her aging face, with its harsh mouth, squinty eyes, and not-so-subtle facial hair on the television screen, the Sister acknowledged the sin of vanity, turned off *Life and Death*, and recited "Hail Mary, full of grace" over and over again.

As was always the case after such episodes of weakness, the Sister approached her canonical responsibilities with renewed vigor.

The next morning, she cajoled Jared Stone out of bed and insisted that he get some light exercise. "The mind is nothing without the body, Mr. Stone," she told him.

"But, Sister, I'm so tired." Jared was too weak and befuddled to remind the Sister that his doctors—her doctors—had ordered bed rest. The crew in the truck, who like the Wicked Witch in *The Wizard of Oz* were watching everything, knew that Jared was supposed to be in bed. But the sight of Jared pleading with the Sister, and ultimately trying to do some light stretching and a few push-ups, made for much better television than just watching the man waste away.

When Jared was safely back in bed, panting and gasping until he fell asleep, the Sister went through the rest of the house to see how else she could help.

***

Glio explored the entire network of Jared's outward-facing nervous system. He rode the brachial plexus to the musculo-cutaneous nerve to the radial nerve to the ulnar nerve to the median nerve in the tips of Jared's fingers, reveling in the cool cottony touch of Jared's pillow. He pushed off from the gusta-tory cortex and traversed the highway of nerves leading to the tightly bunched fungiform papillae on Jared's tongue, nearly exploding with joy at the sensation that was oatmeal. He came as close to the outside world as he dared in the nerve endings at the very edge of Jared's nostril—a flirtation with the termina-tion shock of his host's corporeal being—momentarily repulsed by the smell of disease, not realizing, at first, that he himself was the root cause.

From the top of Jared's scalp to the tip of his pinky toe, Glio had explored Jared like Magellan circumnavigating the globe. There was only one place left to go: the optic nerve.

Glio, having been imbued with emotion from Jared's memo-ries, was frightened. Hearing the world, touching the world, tasting the world, and smelling the world were not, he was certain, the same as seeing the world. But curiosity was a powerful master.

Feeling his way from the medulla oblongata to the visual cortex, Glio arrived at the lateral geniculate nucleus, the point of no return. In the way a six-year-old is filled with terror at the top of a large waterslide, so, too, was Glio at the site of the optic nerve; a swirling rope of ganglia spiraling into the brightest light Glio had ever seen. It was too late to chicken out now.

He jumped in.

A moment later, Glio was looking at a blinding red light with no definition and no form. He realized he was looking at the inside of Jared's closed eyelid. The membrane of tissue was thick enough for its host to experience darkness. But to a being like Glio that had never known real light, it was paper-thin.

Glio desperately wanted to see the *outside* world, only Jared was resting, and thin though it was, the eyelid was an impenetrable barrier. Glio needed a plan.

Having spent months inside Jared's head, he had come to know every twist, turn, and fold of his host's brain. And Glio had grown large. What the doctors thought were twenty-four distinct tumors was really one large organism, the seemingly individual growths connected by strings of microscopic cells. While Glio's attention was focused on the optic nerve, his tendrils simultaneously reached everywhere else. He would force the eyelids to open.

With the flick of his metaphorical wrist, Glio tugged on a packet of neurons that made Jared gag. An instant later, he felt the entire body convulse, and then Jared's eyes opened.

The light was too intense, and Glio had to retreat part of the way up the optic nerve. The experience was painful and exhilarating all at once. Slowly, he inched his way forward again until, at last, he could see the world.

His first vision was shocking: The edges, the shadows, the innate qualities of the image were entirely different and entirely more satisfying than the memories and dreams on which he'd been feasting. Glio found himself looking at the person Jared thought of as "the nun." Her weathered face had a countenance that was both angry and sad, a kind of fierce expression meant to calm but that could only terrify.

"Mr. Stone," she was saying, "are you all right?"

"I don't think so. I can't see."

Glio knew that Jared's impaired sight was a direct result of his own activity on the optic nerve. No matter, he wasn't going to stay long.

As he adjusted to the light, Glio could see that he was in the makeshift hospital room that had been Jared's office. He was sorry he hadn't seen the room before all the medical equipment had been moved in. Jared's office was, Glio knew, a focal point in space that was central to the man's character. And as Glio was subsuming the very essence of Jared's character, it had become a focal point for him, too.

"Try shutting your eyes for a little while," the nun said to Jared.

Jared tried to shut his eyes, but Glio tweaked the packet of neurons that made them pop back open.

"I can't," Jared said.

"That's odd," the nun answered. "Wait here. I'm going to get the doctor."

"Right," Jared answered. "'Wait here.'"

Glio was no fan of the doctors. Twice they had pumped Jared full of morphine, and twice Glio had drifted off in a daze. The drugs slowed him down, and he didn't like it. Not wanting another dose, he fled to the center of the brain, occupying himself with a memory of the night Jared won his first election but already scheming and planning for a more meaningful outing.

***

While Megan tried not to show it, she was annoyed with Ethan.

She'd hoped he had come in his limousine to tell her that she, Megan Stone, was, at least for a little while, going to be the star of *Life and Death*. She knew that with her dad too sick to do much of anything and her mother and sister on strike, now was her chance to step into the limelight.

But that wasn't it at all.

"I want you to do something for me," he had said. "I want you to keep an eye on Jackie and let me know if she tries to make any more movies."

It left a bad taste in Megan's mouth.

For one thing, she and Jackie had grown closer since their father had gotten sick. She knew it was just temporary, that Jackie wasn't going to suddenly stop being weird, that things would eventually turn back to their natural order, but still, if she was being honest, she liked that she and Jackie were talking. Plus she guessed that what Ethan was asking would go against her mom's wishes, and that didn't sit too well.

Megan paused, looking at Ethan, waiting for the rest of it.

"I promise, Megan," Ethan said, sensing her disappointment. "I will personally see to it that you get whatever you want. Better clothes, better makeup, better toys."

Better toys? Megan thought.

"Just tell me what you want."

When she didn't respond, Ethan surged ahead, assuring Megan it was for the good of the show, that in the end, her family would understand.

"I-I . . . ," Megan finally interrupted, feeling stupid saying it out loud, "I thought maybe you would want me to be in the show more."

Ethan sat back and smiled. "Is that all? That's easy, kiddo." He took a deep, cleansing breath. "You help us, and I promise, you'll get lots of screen time. This is how Hollywood works." That was the phrase that sealed the deal for Megan. She was an insider now, in the know. She was Hollywood.

"Besides," Ethan added, "the rest of your family is on strike. If you're the only one talking to us, then you're the only one we can use."

In the end, Megan was able to convince herself—her inner demons drowning out her better instincts—that Jackie kind of deserved it for making that video. At least that's what Ethan had told her.

Megan nodded and shook Ethan's hand when it was offered.

The next afternoon, just after she had given the most detailed, enthusiastic, and altogether saccharine interview in the history of television interviews ("Oh, Andersona, I was just *devastated* at what happened to poor Trebuchet. That dog was a kind of soul mate to all of us."), Megan put "Operation Nancy Drew" into action. Ethan had come up with the name, and even though Megan didn't really know who Nancy Drew was, she played along.

Watching from the kitchen window when Jackie came home from school, Megan took notes on everything her big sister did, and what she did was really strange.

Jackie, who always came in, said hi to Trebuchet (or used to), and then went to her room to do her homework, went instead to the backyard. She made a beeline for The Wall and started picking up different rocks at the base of the fence and shaking them. She had a very serious look on her face, like she was searching for something important. After a minute, Jackie picked up a large, off-color rock, shook it, and smiled. She looked around, like she wanted to make sure no one was watching, and carried the rock back into the house.

When Jackie walked through the door from the backyard, hiding the rock under her shirt, she didn't even notice Megan skulking behind the ficus tree in the dining room. She bounded up the stairs, went right into the bathroom, and closed the door. Megan crept to the door just in time to hear the shower curtain move, like Jackie was taking a shower.

Recording every last detail in her notebook, Megan retreated to the hallway outside Jackie's room and waited. It was a full five minutes before Jackie showed up.

"Hey," she said to Megan.

"Hey," Megan said back. "What are you up to?" She tried to sound casual but could tell by the look on Jackie's face that it hadn't worked.

"Nothing." With that, Jackie went into her bedroom and shut the door.

Megan sprang up and ran to the bathroom. There was no sign of the rock anywhere. Just some cut-up cardboard in the garbage can. She added it to her notes and went back to her own room, where she sat on her bed and tried to figure out what her sister was doing. After a while, her attention drifted, and she dozed off, dreaming about how famous she would become. She didn't think her notes revealed anything terribly clever or insightful, so she never gave them to Ethan.

Later that night, as the family sat gathered around Jared's make-shift hospital bed to watch *Life and Death*, Megan could scarcely contain her anxiety. With the rest of the family on strike, the entire episode revolved around her—her day at school, her wardrobe, and her feelings about her father's illness. Other than Jared's momentary and inexplicable bout of blindness, which was teased in every commercial break and held for the end of the show, this was Megan's hour.

She had hoped Ethan was right, that her mother would see how good it was for Megan to participate, but those hopes were dashed at the first commercial break when no one in her family so much as looked at her. "Mom?" Megan asked. But Deirdre didn't respond.

By the second commercial break, Jared had fallen asleep. During the third commercial break, Jackie had left the room shaking her head.

By the time it ended, only Megan and her mother were watching.

When the last of the credits scrolled off the screen and faded into a commercial break, Deirdre used the remote to turn the television off. She choked back a sob, said, "It's okay, honey, I forgive you," and left the room, too.

"Forgive me?" Megan said out loud, her only company her sleeping father. Her voice tried to sound confused, but her heart was thoroughly ashamed. Megan used the TiVo to roll the show back to the beginning and watched it again in its entirety, never moving from her father's side. By the time it was over, she thought she might throw up.

***

Max couldn't believe it. The plan had worked perfectly. Deirdre had retrieved Jackie's confiscated cell phone on the way out of the house—"If she's not allowed to use it, at least let me try to get my money back," she had told Andersona—and dropped it off at school per Jackie's instructions. Jackie gave the phone to Jason Sanderson, who tucked it inside a cardboard rock he "borrowed" from the school's drama department. That night, while all of America, including everyone in the Stone household, was watching *Life and Death*, Jason rode his bike to Jackie's house and threw the rock over the seven-foot-high fence into the backyard. Jackie retrieved it the next day.

Now Max was looking at fifteen minutes of brand-new footage. He was giddy.

With the crew on strict orders to stop Jackie from filming, capturing footage had become much more difficult, but the assembled group in Azeroth anticipated this. The guild counted among its members two East Coast television editors—one worked at Lifetime, the other at TLC. Using a floor plan of the Stone household provided by Jackie, the two editors analyzed five episodes of *Life and Death*, noting camera angles and edits. They used the information to identify what they believed were enough blind spots for Jackie to remain hidden while filming.

The footage wasn't as good or explosive as the earlier episodes, and it was all taken in a relatively short window of time, but it was enough for Max to work with. The real magic was in the voice-over.

Jackie and Max wrote it together, and she recorded it while she was in the computer lab at school. It was a poignant plea from Jackie to the American viewing public to let her father die with dignity:

> *It's not just the cameras and the microphones. If they were capturing the truth, maybe it wouldn't be so bad. In fact, if I'm being honest, my family—well, really, my parents—signed on for all this when they invited ATN into our house. But they didn't sign on for the lies.*
>
> *The network doesn't want you to know the truth. They want you to see my dad at his worst; they want you to think my mother, sister, and I are helpless; they want you to think we give a shit about Jo Garvin.*

(Jackie, who was something of a prude, didn't want to use foul language. Max convinced her that the soliloquy needed it.)

> *This isn't real life. Nothing on TV is real life. It is fiction. The only part of this that's true is that my dad is dying, and that he is—that we are—being robbed of our privacy and dignity. Think about it. What if your father or mother or sister or brother was dying? What if it was your son? What would you want?*
>
> *If you really care what happens to my dad, if you really care what happens to our family*—Max cut to an

extreme close-up of Jackie talking to the camera—*then*
I beg you, don't watch the lie that is Life and Death.
I promise I will give you updates via YouTube, but please,
get these damn cameras out of my house.

The third installment of *The Real Family Stone of Portland,*
Oregon was posted at three a.m. Pacific standard time, just
twelve hours after Jackie had done the principle photography.
A team of Azeroth guild members based in London was standing
by. The minute the episode was posted, they unleashed a social
media campaign announcing its arrival.

It took each of the first two episodes more than a week to
top one million views. The third episode got there in twelve
hours. *The Real Family Stone of Portland, Oregon* had gone from
being viral to being a phenomenon.

***

Ethan was back in California, asleep in his Malibu beach house
and dreaming about a girl he knew many years ago. For some
reason, every time the girl opened her mouth to speak, a loud
buzzing sound came from the back of her throat. It was
happening in a rhythmic pattern—mouth closed, mouth open,
buzzing, mouth closed, mouth open, buzzing. It took on a
hypnotic quality, almost like a—

The cell phone vibrating on the bedside table buzzed Ethan
to consciousness. He tapped the answer icon and mumbled a
groggy "What is it?"

"It's your ass, Overbee, that's what it is!" The sound of Roger
Stern's voice was enough to bring Ethan into a hyperwakeful
state.

"Roger? What time is it? What's going on?"

"Time is immaterial." This was one of Stern's favorite sayings, though no one was quite sure what it meant. "As for what's going on, check your e-mail. I want a full report on how you've contained this problem before the end of the day." He hung up.

Before the end of the day? Ethan thought, still in a fog. *I'm not even sure what day it is.*

Ethan used his phone to check his e-mail, and he saw it right away. A link to a new installment of *The Real Family Stone of Portland, Oregon.* He paused a beat, then hurled his cell phone at the nearest wall, cracking its screen and leaving a dent just under a framed Andy Warhol original. It was 4:30 a.m. He landed in Portland five and a half hours later.

***

The entire Stone household was abuzz with the news of the latest YouTube posting. The third-shift director, who received a phone call from Ethan at 4:45 a.m. local time, was instructed to have his team go through the previous three days of outtakes to find out how and when Jackie had managed to record new footage.

While a growing number of crew members were secretly rooting for Jackie, their first loyalty was to their paychecks. Besides, they were too terrified of the damage Ethan could do to their careers if they failed him, so they did as they were told.

It didn't take long to find the image of Jackie picking up the rock in the backyard, bringing it into the house, and cracking it open in the bathroom. After that, they watched her disappear into one blind spot after another, always reappearing twenty seconds later. You didn't need Sherlock Holmes to piece it all together. You only had to know to look.

Andersona, also on orders from Ethan, confined the Stone family to the house, not allowing anyone in or out. While Megan, who had become persona non grata with the family, stayed in her room, Jackie took her computer and crawled into bed with her mom. She looked for Max online, but he was still recovering from his all-night editing session and had gone to bed very early.

When Jackie heard Ethan arrive, she considered hiding but knew it was no use. She looked at the camera in the corner of the ceiling in her parents' bedroom—an unfathomable invasion of privacy, she realized—and said, "Tell him I'm on my way down."

"Do you want me to come with you?"

"No, Mom, that's okay. Besides, you can always watch it on TV tonight."

Deirdre was still smiling at the joke as Jackie left the room with her computer tucked under her arm.

Ethan was sitting alone in the living room. When he saw Jackie, he clapped, very slowly. "Smart kid," he said, "but you have no idea how much trouble you're causing." This, more than anything else, made Jackie smile. "Give me the phone."

Jackie expected Ethan to ask for the phone and knew it was pointless to fight. She took the iPhone out of her pocket and tossed it across the room. "The computer, too."

"What?"

"The computer, Jackie." The edge in Ethan's voice was frightening. "We've decided you need to engage more with your surroundings. Burying your nose in your computer screen all day isn't very good television, now, is it?"

Jackie just stood there. Ethan shook his head, got up, crossed the room, and took the laptop out of Jackie's hands. She didn't put up a fight. Ethan went back to the couch.

"You told people not to watch the show."

"I did," Jackie said.

"I'm not sure I care, but curiosity is getting the best of me. Why?"

"You really don't know, do you?"

"No."

"Then I don't think there is any way I can make you understand."

Ethan shrugged his shoulders. "It doesn't matter. Your wings are clipped. You're going to get in line and do what we say, starting tonight. You're going to tell America that you were just lashing out because you're sad about your father's illness."

"No, I'm not."

"You're not what?"

"I'm not going to tell America that I was just sad because of my dad's illness. I'm going to continue to tell them, every chance I get, what a big phony you and this television show are."

"Don't be so sure, Jackie. I've handled some of the toughest people in show business. I think I can handle a fifteen-year-old girl."

It was this moment of arrogance, of naked hubris, that gave Jackie all the confidence she needed.

Later that afternoon when Andersona tried to interview her about how wrong she'd been to post the new episode of *The*

Real Family Stone of Portland, Oregon, Jackie answered every one of the questions with a stream of curse words.

ANDERSONA: It must be hard on you, having to watch your father go through this.

JACKIE: Fuck, shit, piss.

ANDERSONA: The YouTube show was all about you lashing out, wasn't it?

JACKIE: Cock, tits, bitch.

This went on for a full five minutes. When Andersona was done asking the questions she had come to ask, which she read from a prepared script, she left the room without saying a word.

Jackie stayed in the chair and laughed, at first. Eventually emotion overwhelmed her and the laughter turned to tears. She sat there until she was done crying, and then retreated to her room to read a book.

***

The episode of *Life and Death* that aired that night was made especially for Jackie.

The opening scene was Jackie's plea, from *The Real Family Stone of Portland, Oregon*, for people not to watch the show. It dissolved to Jackie listening to Andersona's question: "The YouTube show was all about you lashing out, wasn't it?"

The camera shifted to a view over Jackie's shoulder, showing a concerned Andersona. Jackie's voice-over, plucked and cleaned up from her conversation with Ethan, was made to seem like an answer to Andersona's question: "I was just sad because of my dad's illness. I was a big phony." Only the most seasoned editor could have spotted the fakery.

"How does that make you feel?" Andersona asked. The editors cut to Jackie cursing, with all the swear words bleeped out. Then back to Andersona to ask the question again. This time the camera cut to Jackie, sitting in the interview chair, weeping.

The credits rolled.

After the commercial break, Ethan, who was furious that Megan hadn't alerted him that Jackie had somehow recovered a phone, had a small message for her, too. They showed the entire sequence of Megan following Jackie, and even included a bastardized version of her conversation with Ethan in the limousine. In the version that aired, Megan approached Ethan and offered to spy on Jackie if the producers would feature her, Megan, more prominently in the show. Ethan, in a set piece recorded after the fact, refused.

The actions of the two Stone girls were stitched together to show a family splitting apart over the stress of their dying father. Jackie and Megan were shown to be conniving but pitiable characters, with Ethan and Andersona each playing the part of compassionate benefactor.

It was both a high and low watermark for the power and pull of the medium.

***

Jared watched the episode with his wife and daughters like he always did, but none of it was making sense. He knew that something bad was happening between his family and the producers of the show, he just didn't understand what. And worse, he didn't seem to care. All Jared wanted to do was sleep. Even the pain in his head seemed like it should be someone else's problem.

He found himself wondering about the strangest things. Like what was a nun doing in his house? Was this even his house? The frequent visits from Deirdre, Jackie, and Megan suggested it was, but maybe the television network had built a replica of his house for the show. Maybe they were all in Los Angeles. That was a horrible thought. He didn't want to die in LA.

Jared was increasingly aware that he was dying, and he knew that it would be sooner rather than later. He knew he should be putting things in order, or at least that's the phrase that kept rolling around his brain. *(Intrepid snorting thug.)* Though what things and what order were a mystery.

He'd had three more instances of blurred or lost vision, and the same had happened with his hearing, inexplicably failing and then returning to normal.

Jared Stone was checking out, and he knew it. He had only one foot in this world; the other was already probing for the next, whatever and wherever that might be.

As he maneuvered through the remnants of his faculties, he made a decision. It was the last lucid thing on his mind, and he needed to tell someone before it was gone. He summoned Deirdre.

"D," he told her when she arrived by his side, "come closer."

"I'm here, Jare," she answered, putting her ear next to his mouth.

"I want to end this," he whispered. She didn't respond, and Jared closed his eyes. She was about to go when he added, "Please, help me."

With that, Jared rolled over and went to sleep. Deirdre kissed his head and said, "Of course, my love. Of course."

***

When Max watched the latest episode of *Life and Death*, he knew immediately what had happened. His video-editing skills were growing at an exponential rate, and it wasn't hard for him to spot the handiwork of the ATN team.

"Pizdet!" he barked. He was watching Ethan Overbee's evisceration of Jackie on the ATN website after school the following day. A cold wet rain that smelled of winter was pelting his window.

More than anything, Max wanted to talk to Jackie, to tell her that he knew what the editors had done to her, that together they could make people know it was all lies. But afternoon in Western Russia is the middle of the night in Oregon, and Jackie was not online. Max needed to talk to someone, to do something now.

After the meetings in Azeroth, Max and Hazel had become Facebook friends. Knowing that it was already six thirty in the morning in Alabama, he sent her a message.

Max

Hazel, do you see the television show yesterday? Do not believe this is true! They use editing tricks to make Jackie look bad. We must do something. Meet me by palace.

Five minutes later, he was standing outside the guild head-quarters in Azeroth.

Hazel

Hi, Max.

Max

Oh good! You are here. Did you see this new episode?

Hazel

I did, and I didn't believe it. Jackie told me how heavily they edit the show to create story lines that don't really exist. It's sick, but I don't know what to do.

Max

I am worried about our friend.

Hazel

Me too, Max. But maybe they're just too big and powerful for us.

Max

Nyet! This is not true of American colonists, this is not true of Russian Bolsheviks, and I do not believe is true of Jackie Stone. She is not girl to give up. She beat them step by step. We have Russian saying: "Ispodvol' i ol'khu sognyosh." Anyone can bend alder tree, if they do it little at a time.

Both he and Hazel were silent for a minute.

Hazel

Okay. Let's think about the problem. We know they're manipulating their own footage to box Jackie in.

Max

What means box in?

Hazel

Sorry. They are making it very hard for Jackie to react or take any action against them. They are cutting off her options.

Max

Yes.

Hazel

We know they took her phone, twice. They'll probably take her computer, too.

Max

Yes, I think this also.

Hazel

So Jackie probably can't get us footage, at least not until we figure out how to get a camera into her house.

Max

Yes.

Hazel

So what we need is another way to make an episode.

At that instant, a lightbulb went on over Max's head. Literally. His mother had entered the room and turned on the overhead light to combat the grayness of the day beyond the window.

"Maxi, I wish you wouldn't spend so much time in front of that computer," she said before moving on down the hall.

He barely heard her. The literal lightbulb had, in fact, been accompanied by a figurative one.

Max

I have idea. And I will be needing your help.

***

When Jackie got to school the next morning, her heart fell into her stomach.

Three large ATN trucks dominated the teachers' parking lot. Students gawked at them like they were looking at Taylor Swift's tour bus. Jackie knew what was going on even before the principal—a balding man with a rumpled suit, mismatched socks, and an old ketchup stain on his tie—pounced on her at the front door.

"Good morning, Miss Stone!" he offered with too much enthusiasm. "Isn't it wonderful? Your television show has come to our school!"

Jackie clenched her jaw. "This can't be real. Don't you have to get parents' permission or something?"

"Apparently the ATN legal department worked on that all night, and we're good to go. The few students who didn't want to participate are attending another high school until this is all over."

Jackie locked eyes with the principal, the scowl on her face making him realize the horror of what he had just said. He put a hand to his mouth the way a bad actor feigns surprise and regret.

Jackie rolled her eyes and tried to brush past him. The only thing she wanted was to go to her locker.

"But you don't understand," he said, blocking her way and trying to regain his footing in the conversation. He looked up at the ATN camera suspended from the ceiling like he was starring in a soap opera. "The network is going to build us a new gymnasium, and we have you to thank!" He stood in front of Jackie holding his arm up, palm facing her.

Does he actually want a high five? she thought. *Lame!* This time she squirmed past with force and ran inside.

Everywhere Jackie turned, she saw cameras, and everywhere she turned, students were staring at her. A gaggle of the school's most popular girls had formed a semicircle around her locker.

"Hi, Jackie," one of the girls said. They all wore the same basic outfit, the same hairstyle, the same makeup, and had the same affected speech; Jackie had trouble telling them apart and wasn't really sure which one was talking. "Isn't this exciting? Now we know how special you must feel every day!"

"Why, is your father dying, too?" Jackie couldn't help herself. She knew the smartest course of action was to keep her head down and her mouth shut, but this was too much. Ethan was pulling out all the stops, and it was getting to her.

Before the stunned popular girl could think of a response, a high-pitched whine originating from deep inside someone's sinus cavity was saying, "Let me through; let me through!" An instant later, Jason Sanderson pushed his way into the center of the crowd.

"Hi, girls," he said, grinning like the village idiot.

"Go away, geek," the same popular girl said.

"Congratulations, Brie," Jackie answered, having sorted out which queen bee was which, "you were just a primo bitch on television's most popular show." Jackie pointed at the camera aimed directly at her locker.

Brie's cheeks turned the same color as her cherry lip gloss, and she stormed away. The gaggle followed her.

"Thanks, Jason," Jackie said. "It's really good to see you."

Jason blushed, shook his head, and got right to his point. "Did you see it yet?" Jason asked.

"See what?"

"Oh, boy!" he said. "Come with me!"

Jason led Jackie to the computer lab.

"Hi, Miss Onorati," Jason said.

"Mr. Sanderson, Miss Stone," the teacher answered, unable to stop from grinning.

"Jason," Jackie whispered, pulling his arm, "we're not supposed to be here. I have history now. So do you!"

"It's all right, Miss Stone," Ms. Onorati interrupted. "I spoke to Mr. Egloff a few minutes ago, and he understands that you might need to miss history this morning."

Jackie looked from Jason to their teacher. "What's going on?"

"What's going on," Ms. Onorati offered, "is that the young squire here has a small bit of treasure to impart to Gerald the Generous."

"What?" Jackie looked closely at her teacher. She was a pretty woman but didn't seem to know it. Long but stylishly unkempt brown hair with a touch of gray; bright, hazel eyes made large by a pair of round glasses too big for her vertically orientated face, its long nose holding court over a wide and smiling mouth. She looked like a short, disheveled version of Angelina Jolie.

"Surprised?" Ms. Onorati asked.

Jackie was too surprised to speak. She nodded.

"Jackie, I'm a forty-one-year-old, unattached computer science teacher. Do the math."

"Her name in Warcraft is Onan the Arbarian," Jason snorted. "Isn't that great?"

"Were you at the guild meetings?" Jackie asked.

"No, but when you've been in the game as long as I have, word travels fast. I'm here to help you in any way I can."

"But what about them?" Jackie asked, pointing to the camera in the corner of the ceiling.

"What about them?" Ms. Onorati said. "Let them watch. I think they'll want to see what Jason has to show you, too."

"I'll show you on my computer," Jason said with just a bit too much volume. Jackie realized that everything that had happened to her—*was* happening to her—was actually a good thing for Jason. It was helping him belong, giving him a purpose. It wasn't much of a silver lining, but it was something; Jackie tried her best to hold on to it.

Jackie sat at the computer station with both Jason and Ms. Onorati standing behind her. On the screen, Jason clicked a link to YouTube, and there in the middle of the screen was *The Real Family Stone of Portland, Oregon: Episode IV, A New Hope.*

Jackie knew the title was in homage to the original *Star Wars*. What she didn't know was how a new episode of *The Real Family Stone of Portland, Oregon* could even exist.

"Seriously, what's going on?"

"Just watch," Ms. Onorati said, putting a gentle hand on Jackie's shoulder.

On the screen, the video started. It was footage Jackie had shot more than a week ago, for the second episode. It was a thirty-four-second clip of the Jo Garvin interview, the scene where Jo goes from crying to winking at Andersona's "Honey, you're going to win an Emmy" remark. The image freezes on Jo's wink and fades to black as a voice-over begins.

"This is unedited footage; it's what actually happened." Jackie didn't recognize the voice, but the lilting Southern drawl gave her a good guess as to who it was.

"It has not been manipulated in any way," the voice continued. "It's footage that came directly from Jackie Stone's now confiscated iPhone. Our showing this to you is not meant to influence your opinion of Jo Garvin. We only want you to see the truth.

"If we had wanted you to like Jo Garvin, we might have shown you this."

A scene, back in the interview room, fades in. The footage is of Andersona interviewing someone. Jackie remembered capturing the footage her very first day of recording and knew that the shoulder the camera was looking over belonged to her mother. The shot is framed so that only the smallest wisp of Deirdre's hair is visible. Out of context, it's impossible to tell who is being interviewed.

"Tell me, what has this done to your career?" Andersona asked.

There is a seamless cut back to Jo Garvin, whose tears are already starting to fall. The unmistakable impression is that Jo Garvin is devastated that her career as a television character actor is over.

Max's edits were so good that even Jackie did a double take, feeling, for a moment, sorry for Jo.

"Do you see?" the voice continued. "Do you see how easy it is to fool you? But it's not you who should feel foolish; it's them." The voice said "them" with all the bile it could muster.

"And that brings us to the point of tonight's episode of *The Real Family Stone of Portland, Oregon*. Jackie Stone never apologized; she never acquiesced. Everything you saw last night on *Life and Death* was a lie. You, America . . . no, not just America. You, world," the voice grew in timbre and pitch, "have been duped.

"Jackie and her family are being held in a prison of the network's making. It's up to you to free them. Stop watching the show. Stop supporting the sponsors. Free Jackie Stone."

The screen faded to black.

Jackie leaned back in her chair trying to take it all in. She looked down and saw that the view count on YouTube was 1,340,006.

"When did this go live?" she asked without looking up.

Jason smiled. "Forty-five minutes ago."

PART SIX

Resolution

Thursday, October 29

Glio was ready to go for gold. Replete with almost all of Jared's memories, and emboldened by his experience manipulating the conduits to the outside world, it was time for the tumor to become the host.

The plan was to stretch his mass to each of Jared's sensory centers simultaneously, to use the sum total of the knowledge he had collected, and to interact with the outside world in the first person. And Glio had his target. He wanted to talk to that nun.

Everything in Jared's memories had taught Glio to fear and respect nuns, in that order. He knew that they had devoted their lives to God, eschewing mortal pleasures, but he couldn't understand why. Glio had learned a lot about mortal pleasures in a relatively short time. To reject them, he believed, was to commit a kind of suicide of the soul. Not that Glio really understood what a soul was. But that was the word Jared would have used.

There was one memory in particular from Jared's teenage years that formed the basis of his feeling toward nuns. Jared's first semester in high school was spent at the all-boys St. Leonard's Catholic Academy. (The irony that Leonard was the patron saint of prisoners was not lost on the students. Their sports teams, officially called the Scarlet Knights, were more commonly known as the Convicts.) Jared hated every minute of it. He hated the uniforms. He hated the religious instruction. He hated the complete and total lack of girls. But most of all, he hated Sister Louisa.

Most of the nuns in the school were caring and well-educated, if a bit dowdy, teachers. Sister Louisa was another story and, like Sister Benedict, a throwback to another era. It wasn't uncommon for the faculty at St. Leonard's to use harsh tactics to ensure discipline, the punishment usually taking the form of a yardstick applied with medium force to the transgressing student's knuckles. But Sister Louisa took it a step farther and a step too far.

Beyond the usual litany of high school crimes—talking or chewing gum in class, failure to do your homework, tardiness—Sister Louisa punished independent thought; she did not like students to ask questions. This was an approach that most schools would consider anathema to teaching history.

When one of Jared's classmates asked why the Founding Fathers didn't abolish slavery at the time of the Revolution, Sister Louisa's answer confounded the entire class.

"Because," she said, "slavery wasn't a sin until much later."

There was a momentary pause, which the Sister quickly filled by going on to the next point in the lesson plan.

"But, Sister Louisa," another boy interrupted, "how can that be true? How can something be okay one day and a sin the next? Didn't they know it was wrong?"

When the boy saw the rage in Sister Louisa's eyes, he pleaded for mercy, but it was too late. She advanced on him with violence and relish, like Hannibal Lecter. Her yardstick missed the boy's knuckles and caught the side of his face. She would later claim it was an accident, but every student in fourth-period American Studies knew better.

Even though Sister Louisa was summarily dismissed from her post over the incident, Jared begged his parents to let him transfer to public school after Christmas. They complied.

It was this memory that Glio was examining and reexamining as he prepared for his trip to the outside world.

He started slowly, moving down the nerve endings in Jared's extremities, thinking he would start by wiggling Jared's toes and tapping Jared's fingers. He stretched himself to the full limit of his being, found the contact points, and . . . and . . .

Nothing happened.

He tried again.

Nothing.

Something was wrong.

Glio tried the same with Jared's other senses. There was no taste. There was no smell. There was no sound. He tried the eyes, but they were shut, and no manner of poking or prodding of Jared's oculomotor nerve would make his eyelids open.

Glio retreated to the center of the temporal lobe to ponder his predicament. Jared's brain was still functioning, but barely. As he examined the situation more closely, Glio saw that the medulla oblongata was having trouble communicating with Jared's lungs, which meant less oxygen was getting to Jared's blood, which meant less useful blood was getting to Jared's brain. It was, he knew, the beginning of an irrevocable downward spiral.

Desperate to complete his journey and become Jared, Glio tried to seize total control of Jared's brain, to force his host back to a state of corporeal animation. He used every weapon in his arsenal, massaging, pounding, electrifying neurons, but it was no use. Though not yet technically dead, Jared Stone was gone.

Glio knew from Jared's memories what people thought of cancer, what they thought of tumors, what they thought of him. He knew that they couldn't comprehend the reason for his existence, and he knew that he and those like him were among the most reviled things on Earth. But until that moment, Glio believed with all his metaphorical heart that he existed as a caterpillar, waiting to emerge from his cocoon as something beautiful and new, as Jared. Only now, at the end, did Glio see the tragedy of his life, of all life.

And for the first time, Glio felt sorry. Truly, and horribly, sorry. Maybe if he had become Jared it would have all been okay, but now that he was confronted with the truth, he understood what every tumor comes to understand:

Life—his life, Jared's life—has no meaning intrinsic to the life itself. It just is. Life, he now saw, is only what you make of it. And even though he knew it was through no fault of his own, Glio had spent his life as a thief and a murderer. The realization was overwhelming.

Glio howled in agony as he retreated into himself.

***

"Mr. Stone?" Sister Benedict gently shook Jared's shoulder. There was no response. "Mr. Stone?" she said again, shaking a little harder. "Time to wake up. Time for breakfast." Again, there was no response.

One of the Sister's young novices, Sister Nadine, was attending to Jared with Sister Benedict. "Go, child," Sister Benedict said to her, "find the doctor."

After the young girl left the room, Sister Benedict got down on her knees and prayed.

"Please, Father, bless this man's soul and give him the strength to carry on. Please ease his suffering and help him to recover, to be there for his family."

The Sister, despite her best efforts, could not stop thinking about the cameras watching her as she prayed. All around the room, from every angle, tiny cameras were trained on her and Jared Stone. Later that night, she knew, she would be on television. More people would be watching her prayer in one night than watched *The Duke Hamblin Show* in a month.

Maybe, she thought, *he'll have me on as a guest.*

She pushed the thought away and continued her conversation with the Lord.

A moment later, the doctor entered, looked at the bank of machines monitoring Jared's vital signs, and sprang into action.

"Sister, code blue," he said matter-of-factly but with enough edge to make his point.

The Sister got off her knees and went to the phone. She had practiced this many times. She dialed the number, said "code blue" when the person on the other end answered, and hung up.

Exactly forty-five seconds later, the doors of an ambulance flew open—the network paid to have it staffed and parked in the driveway—and a team of doctors and medical experts poured out.

Exactly forty-five seconds after that, Jared Stone was connected to an extracorporeal membrane oxygenation machine, a dialysis machine, and an anesthetic machine. He was alive, but only in the clinical sense.

There but for the grace of the machines went he.

***

When bad things happened to Ethan Overbee, which wasn't very often, they tended to come in twos.

In the second grade, Ethan was scolded by his parents for tying one end of a string around Taffy, the family cat, and the other to his father's car. His parents saw what Ethan had done in time to save the cat from any harm, but they took away his television privileges for two days. It was one of the few times in his entire childhood that Ethan—a boy both coddled and adored by his parents—had been punished, and the memory stuck with him. To make matters worse, later that same day, when he was playing an aggressive version of "doctor" with Rita Fitzsimmons, the little girl who lived next door, her parents heard her crying and reprimanded Ethan, banishing him from their house and calling his mother. (Having already punished Ethan for the feline felony, his parents elected not to hold him accountable for what was tantamount to grade school molestation.)

On Ethan's seventeenth birthday, he failed the road test for his driver's license, only to have his girlfriend break up with him that same night. She threw a lot of SAT words at Ethan—narcissist, pedagogue, vapid—which made him think she was too much of an egghead for him anyway, but it stung.

During his first semester in college, on the same day he learned he hadn't won a part in the school's production of *A Funny Thing Happened on the Way to the Forum*, his parents called to tell him that Taffy the cat had died. He never really liked that cat, but still, he was starting to see a pattern develop. When one bad thing happened to Ethan, another shoe was sure to drop soon after.

When Ethan learned that Jared Stone, the star of his television show, had slipped into a coma, he was not surprised to see Roger Stern's name on his cell phone. The other shoe. He let it go to voice mail.

As far as Ethan was concerned, Jared's condition was a mixed blessing. He had eight hours to flood the world with *Life and Death* promos—sizzles they were called in the industry—letting viewers know that what they had been waiting for, what they had been ghoulishly hoping for, was finally coming to pass. And, of course, he had those doctors and that nun, the latter of which was turning out to be a better ally than he could have hoped for, to make sure Jared stayed clinically alive as long as possible. From what they told him, he could continue to ride this for weeks.

On the other hand, with Jared—whose moments of confusion, whose physical decline, had made for such compelling television—no longer an active participant in the drama, and with his family causing problems, the ratings would suffer. Ethan knew he would need to get creative, to schedule more celebrity drop-ins, make the show more interactive. He had already sketched much of this out. Now he just needed to put it into action.

Ethan was in his office at the ATN headquarters when he got the news. He conferred briefly with Andersona to make sure that the medical team was in place and that they had what they needed. His next call was to the advertising and marketing apparatus that fueled viewership for the show. From what Andersona told him, they had incredible footage of Sister

Benedict praying by Jared's bedside as the doctors rushed in. They would flood the airwaves with that clip.

Satisfied that the situation was in hand, he listened to Roger's message. It consisted of only two short, clipped words: "Call. Me."

Before Ethan could tap the "call back" icon on his voice-mail screen, a text message popped up. It was from Thad St. Claire, and it had a link to the fourth episode of *The Real Family Stone of Portland, Oregon.*

***

When Jackie got back to her house, the world had turned upside down. That in itself was astounding as it had been upside down for weeks. *Does that mean the world is right-side up again?* she wondered. No, it was more like the world was a Möbius strip, something she had learned about in math class. "Why did the chicken cross the Möbius strip?" her teacher had asked. "To get to the same side," he said, answering his own joke. Jackie, along with the rest of the class, groaned, but for some reason, walking into the madness that was her home, it finally seemed funny.

Medical personnel were everywhere. They were drinking coffee in her kitchen, talking on cell phones in her living room, even smoking cigarettes in her backyard. (Seeing doctors smoke made Jackie wonder if maybe it wasn't so bad for you after all.) And, of course, they were squeezed into the room that used to be her father's office and was now an extension of the Saint Ignatius Hospital.

As soon as Deirdre learned about Jared's condition, she left to pick her daughters up from school and bring them home.

When Jackie saw her mother in the principal's office, she knew the news was bad. She thought maybe the network had seen *The Real Family Stone of Portland, Oregon*, and they were all going to jail. Or maybe her father had died.

Somehow, the coma was worse.

If her father had died, this would be over. His suffering would end, and Jackie's life could get back to something closer to normal. When her dad first got sick, she was certain that the hole created by his absence would devour her. But if she could survive Ethan Overbee and the American Television Network, she was pretty sure she could survive anything.

No one spoke on the ride home. Megan started to say something, but Jackie shushed her. "Remember, they're listening here, too."

All three of them did their best to ignore the strangers and equipment and noise as they walked through the house. Jackie looked up once or twice at the cameras on the ceiling, knowing they were watching her every move. She put them out of her mind, and, trailing behind her mother and sister, made her way to her father's office.

When they entered the room, everything seemed to stop. The air was heavy with the toil and sweat of the medical workers, television crew, and clergy, and dripping with the feeling of death. Jackie felt like she was trying to swim through some sort of foul-tasting milk shake.

The lead doctor gave Deirdre an update while Jackie and Megan listened. Jared had fallen into a coma, and there was little prospect he would come out of it. They were keeping his lungs breathing and his blood circulating, and they were giving him morphine to keep him comfortable, but they had entered the endgame.

"How much longer?" Deirdre asked without emotion.

The doctor looked at Sister Benedict, who seemed to be watching his every move.

"It's hard to say, Mrs. Stone. We're doing all we can to preserve his life for as long as possible." Again the doctor's eyes found the Sister, who smiled in response. Jackie fixed her own gaze on Sister Benedict. She imagined using a World of Warcraft spell to immobilize the nun in creeping vines, and a second spell to blow her head clean off her body.

"All right, everyone," the doctor said, "let's give the family some space." One by one everyone left. Even Sister Benedict moved to go, giving a long look over her shoulder at the tattered mess that was the family Stone.

Megan reached for and found her mother's hand. Deirdre took it, but with no emotion, like she was on autopilot. Jackie saw this and could tell that her mother was distracted. At first, Jackie thought she was grieving for her husband, for the father of her children. But there was something else; Deirdre looked like a prisoner plotting an escape.

Jackie turned her attention to her dad. He looked so small, so breakable. His skin was the color of the Portland sky: gray, hazy, foreboding. His nose, mouth, and chest were covered with tubes and wires. The flight deck of machinery by his bed whirred with an electric hum that made Jackie's hair stand on end.

"Mom?" Jackie started to ask. But her mother shook her head no, raising her eyes to the ceiling.

"Right," Jackie answered, understanding right away.

"But what do we do now?" Megan asked. It was basically the same thing on Jackie's mind.

Deirdre paused a moment before answering. "Girls," she said, "let's go out to lunch."

***

Ethan had to watch *The Real Family Stone of Portland, Oregon* three times to believe what he was seeing. Jackie Stone wasn't working alone. He knew he shouldn't have been surprised, but he was. *Smart little bitch*, he thought.

He listened to the final plea, to "free Jackie Stone," over and over again, and he wondered if he'd been playing this all wrong. He had unwittingly turned a high school kid into a martyr, and if the world had learned one thing over the years, people loved martyrs. From Jesus to Gandhi, martyrs were the shit. Maybe it was time to back off.

That thought rolled around Ethan's mind, but it couldn't find purchase. It was too late for him and Jackie to find some accommodation. Besides, his tactic was working. Ethan knew that the two million people who had watched the YouTube video paled in comparison to the tens of millions watching the TV show. The numbers bore that out: the network focus testing showed that Jackie's approval rating had dropped a full ten points after the last episode. He needed to stay the course.

By the time he picked up the phone to call Roger Stern back, he had the confidence he needed to convince his boss that everything was in hand. Roger's phone rang five times before going to voice mail. Ethan was just opening his mouth to leave a message when the door to his office flew open with a bang, rattling the framed photographs of Ethan posed with an array of the network's most important stars. He jumped.

Roger walked deliberately into the room with an unlit cigar clenched in his teeth. His massive frame cast a shadow over Ethan like the flaming Hindenburg on the panicked rescue workers on the ground. He stopped at the edge of Ethan's desk and looked directly into his eyes. Ethan was inexplicably immobilized.

"Overbee," Roger began, "I just got off the phone with the CEOs of McDonald's and Apple." Ethan worked hard to keep the panic off his face as he waited for Roger to continue. "Do you know what they told me?"

"Listen, Roger," Ethan began. "I know about that video. The kid has been working with other people. But she wasn't even in it. She really has been neutrali—"

"They told me," Roger interrupted, ignoring Ethan completely, "that they're pulling their support for the show, effective immediately."

"They can't do that," Ethan said. "They signed contracts."

Roger heaved a heavy sigh and shook his head. "Right," he said. "Let's tell two of the biggest sponsors we have across all our shows that we're going to take them to court. Good thinking. It took every last cent of political capital I had to stop Apple from suing us."

"Suing us? For what?"

"For infringing on that brat's First Amendment rights by confiscating her goddam iPhone. Did you even run any of this by legal?"

Ethan had not. "Let me call my contacts at both companies, Roger. Maybe I can find a way to—"

"It's too late. *Variety* and *Entertainment Weekly* have already blogged about it. PR will spin it that advertisers come and go from television shows all the time, but the damage is done."

"Okay, so what do you want me to do?" Ethan asked.

"Do? I want you to get that house and that family in order. I don't care how you do it. I want to see a grieving, cohesive family unit gathered around their father's bed, and I want to see them talking to your producers again in twenty-four hours. Or else."

With that, Roger pushed himself back to an upright position and turned to leave the room.

Ethan, perhaps surprised that his boss had given voice to the threat, and in one of the greatest miscalculations of his nearly perfectly calculated career, asked, "Or else what?"

Roger paused for a beat without turning around. Then he kept on walking.

***

From the moment *Life and Death* first aired and Deirdre saw the volume of fan mail arriving at her house—including no dearth of mail from perverts and pedophiles addressed to her daughters—she shielded her girls from the outside world. She or one of the producers took Jackie and Megan to and from school, and to any other destination beyond the borders of the house. The longer the show ran, the fewer extracurricular trips they made.

Since all the madness started, Deirdre, Jackie, and Megan hadn't been to the mall, to the post office, to the supermarket, or even out to lunch.

But the scales had tipped. The danger inside the house was now greater than the danger outside.

When Deirdre pulled out of her driveway, three cars—one also in the driveway and two parked across the street—pulled out and followed her.

"Girls," she said, "are your seat belts on?" Both answered that they were. "Okay, good. Then hold on tight."

"Mom?" Jackie asked, wondering just what her mother was going to do.

"We're being followed, Jackie. And I'm tired of it."

"What does it matter," Jackie asked, her voice flat and resigned. "They're listening to us right now, anyway."

"Right, I forgot. Look around until you see the camera."

"What?"

"You heard me. Start looking."

Jackie, who was in the front seat, checked everywhere. She looked in the glove box and on the visors; she felt around the gearshift and radio; she even felt under her seat and all around her mother's seat. She was just about to give up when she noticed something.

"Mom, did your rearview mirror always have this thing on it?" Jackie pointed to a small sliding switch that moved the mirror from day to night mode. Deirdre, who was driving, did a double and then triple take. The line of her mouth, which for weeks had formed a taut, straight shot across her face, inched up at the corners. She reached up to pull the mirror, but it was glued on tight.

"Can you help, Jax?"

Jackie reached up and pulled hard, but it was stuck. "I can't get a good grip with my seat belt on."

"Then take it off." Jackie looked at her mother, disbelieving. "It's okay, sweetheart, you'll be safe."

Jackie did as she was told and put her full weight onto the mirror, but still it wouldn't budge. She tried banging it with her fist.

"Use your shoe," Deirdre offered. Jackie nodded and then took off her hiking boot. On the third hit, the mirror came free and landed on the dashboard with a thud. Jackie pitched forward, hitting her head against the windshield, but not hard.

"Are you okay?" Deirdre asked.

"I think so."

"Good girl. Now put your seat belt back on."

Deirdre used her side-view mirror to take stock of the cars following her—all three were still there. She was just coming up on a shopping mall whose garage had entrances and exits on four sides. She figured it was her best shot.

"Hold on tight, girls," she said, lowering the driver's side window.

Waiting until the last possible second, and then one second more, Deirdre made an abrupt hairpin left turn into the parking lot. As she made the turn, she tossed the rearview mirror out the window and up into the air.

Only one of the three cars managed to make the turn with Deirdre, and the windshield of that car caught the full force of the impact of the flying mirror. While the mirror made a crack that ran from the top to the bottom of the glass, the real damage was done when the driver, a tabloid paparazzo assigned to cover the Stone family, slammed on the brakes. His sudden stop started a small chain reaction of crashing cars that allowed Deirdre time to slip through the mall and escape.

Twenty minutes later, Deirdre and the girls were seated in a sleepy diner on the outskirts of Portland. There were only two other patrons, and neither looked up when the three Stone women entered. Even the waitress didn't pay them any special attention as she came to the table.

"Can I get you something to drink?" she asked in the monotone of an actor condemned to perform the same soliloquy every day and night for the rest of her life.

Deirdre was taken aback that there were no mobs of people, no grotesque intrusion into her and her daughters' privacy. They had lived so long in the bubble of the television show that she had forgotten life outside went on as it always had. Yes, a lot of people watched the show, but more people didn't. Many more.

It was a sobering reminder that the world had become a fractured place. In her parents' day, everyone watched Johnny Carson and Walter Cronkite. And if they didn't, they at least knew who they were. Today, the long tail of culture pulled three hundred million Americans in one million different directions.

Deirdre regained her composure and said, "I'll have a coffee. And an omelet with green pepper." The girls each asked for a grilled cheese sandwich and a chocolate milkshake.

After they ordered and the waitress had left them alone, no one said anything for a very long time.

Deirdre sipped her coffee and savored the bitter taste. It was the first time in weeks that she allowed herself to enjoy a simple pleasure like a cup of coffee. *This might be*, she thought, *the best cup of coffee I've ever had.*

But then she thought of that first cup of coffee on that first date with Jared. She could still smell the latte, the aroma encircling them, pulling them together. Deirdre realized that since this whole nightmare began, she had not been afforded a moment to grieve. Her Jared was dying. He was already dead.

She started to weep.

Jackie and Megan looked at each other alarmed.

"Mom," Megan asked, "are you okay?"

Deirdre nodded, but couldn't stop the tears. "It's your dad, girls. I'm just sad is all."

Before long, the three of them were crying quietly in the booth of that diner. The waitress looked over once or twice, but let the family be. By the time the food came, the tears had run their course. They ate in silence.

"So what do we do now?" Jackie asked when the meal was over.

Deirdre sized her daughters up for a moment before answering.

"I made a promise to your father, and I need to help him." Deirdre could see that Jackie understood right away. They both, Deirdre and Jackie, looked at Megan, hoping she would sort it out for herself. She didn't.

"Help Daddy how?" she asked.

Deirdre was about to speak when Jackie said, "End his suffering, Meg."

Deirdre looked at Jackie. She was reminded how children never fail to surprise their parents. As soon as you get to know them, understand who they are, they change. She wondered if it ever stopped.

"That's right, honey," she said in a calm and even voice.

"But what if Daddy wakes up?" Megan asked. "Sister Benedict said it could happen."

"There is nothing I want more in this world than for Sister Benedict to be right," Deirdre answered, "but doctors know more than nuns. Daddy is very, very sick, sweetheart, and he's never going to get better. The worst thing for him, the worst thing for us, is to watch him waste away to nothing." Deirdre reached across the table to hold each of her daughters' hands. "It was his final wish that we not let that happen."

"I'll help you, Mom," Jackie said.

"Me too," Megan whispered.

Deirdre sat back and exhaled.

"But, Mom," Jackie added, "there's one thing I need to do first."

"Anything, sweetheart," Deirdre answered.

"I need to get to a computer. Can we go to a library?"

***

Glio was basking in the glow of a brand-new "snow boat." Unmarked, shiny, and red, like a mid-life crisis convertible, the sled was a thing of beauty.

He, Glio, was a baby again. He did his baby dance, running in place and laughing, as he held the sled's yellow string. He didn't even really know that it was meant to be used in the snow, but it didn't matter. It was, according to his scale of the world, huge, and it was his. He felt pure, unadulterated joy.

But wait, this wasn't right. He'd seen this exact thing before. He'd felt this exact feeling before. Something was wrong.

Glio probed his surroundings. He saw his first date with Deirdre; he sang to baby Jackie in the hospital OR; he won Twiggy the giraffe at the Greek festival. He had been there, gone there, and done that. What was going on?

He felt around to every corner of Jared's brain and found nothing but dead, useless tissue. Glio was entombed in a sarcophagus of carbon-based hell. The memories he was eating were now his own.

Glio was consuming himself.

***

Sister Benedict Joan hated the women of the Stone family. She hated them a lot.

The Sister, along with the crew in the control truck, watched Deirdre, Jackie, and Megan's private moment with Jared. She saw how they could barely muster the emotion to grieve for the man who had provided for them, nurtured them, from whose loins they had sprung.

And then, to hear that woman say, "Girls, let's go out to lunch"? Disgusting. Even if they felt nothing, didn't they know the cameras were watching? Didn't they care what America and the world would think?

The Sister, who had at first objected to the ever-watchful eyes of the ATN cameras, had come to cherish them. There was no room for sin when you were watched twenty-four hours a day. She made a mental note to petition the Cardinal for funds to install cameras in the convent.

She supposed she shouldn't blame the Stone girls; they were just children after all. But as much as she tried, she couldn't find forgiveness in her heart. Jacquelyn in particular was a wretched beast. So full of hate, so full of bile. It made her wonder what kind of man Jared Stone was—what kind of man Jared Stone is, she corrected herself—that he could raise such loathsome little brats. It didn't matter, though. Most of the blame, the Sister was certain, rested with the mother. *And now those poor girls will be left alone in that woman's care*, she thought. *Tragic.*

Maybe, if she tried, she could help the younger one see the way of the Lord, maybe someday entice her to join the convent. It would make for such great television.

She let the idea roll around her mind as she used a cool sponge to mop Jared's forehead. *I wonder*, she thought, looking up at the camera, *which side is my good side?*

***

Hazel was so relieved at seeing Jackie's name pop up on the Facebook instant messenger that she let all the air out of her lungs at once and giggled nervously.

Hazel

Jackie! OMG! Are you okay? Where are you?

Jackie

Hi, Hazel. Yeah, I'm okay. My mom managed to sneak us out of the house. I'm at a library. My dad's in a coma.

Hazel

I know. They're already airing promos for tonight's episode saying that something big is happening, and one of the blogs that covers the show got a crew member to talk. I'm really sorry, Jax.

They were both silent for a moment.

Hazel

Did you see the latest episode of the "Real Family Stone"?

Jackie

I did!! Was that your voice?

Hazel

Jackie

It was so great. The network is going to totally freak out.

Hazel

They already have.

Jackie

Huh?

Hazel

Oh! You don't know! It's all over the Internet. Apple and McDonald's have pulled their sponsorship from the show.

Jackie

☺☺☺☺☺☺☺☺☺☺☺☺☺!!!!

Hazel

Can you meet me and Max in WoW later?

Jackie

I can't. We're going back to be with my dad, and they've

taken away my computer. I can't go online.

Hazel

Okay, you may not need to. I think we have a plan for you

to get some footage for the next "Real Family Stone." It's

going to get you in a lot of trouble, though.

Jackie

The more the better. ☺

Hazel typed furiously as she shared the plan she and Max had hatched. It was far-fetched, she knew, but if nothing else, at least it would give Jackie hope.

***

"What do you mean you lost them?" Ethan asked. He had been back at the Stone house only five minutes and already things were unraveling.

"That bitch and her two little bitches," Andersona spat. "She pulled some crazy cop movie stunt in a mall parking lot and lost the trail car." She was overstating the facts for effect, though only a little, mostly to cover her own ass.

"What about the journalists?"

"She lost them, too."

"Pull up the feed from the car," Ethan said, nodding toward the array of screens in the control truck. Andersona didn't say anything; the other three crew members in the room looked at the floor.

"Well?"

"Phil," Andersona said, motioning to the technical director seated in the well-cushioned and ergonomically perfect chair. Phil swiveled around and tapped a few buttons. The largest monitor on the wall came to life. It showed an extreme close-up of Jackie, her tongue hanging out of the edge of her mouth, her eyes focused dead center. Something was jolting the camera every second or two, as if it was being hit.

"This is from inside the car?" Ethan asked.

"Just watch," Andersona answered.

The banging stopped, and Ethan heard a voice—Deirdre's: "Use your shoe."

Jackie disappeared from view for a moment. With her face gone, the rest of the car's interior was visible. Ethan could just barely make out Megan in the backseat.

Jackie's face popped back into the frame. She was so close, and it was so abrupt, that Ethan flinched.

More jolts to the camera, this time much more severe. On the third jolt, the camera tumbled from the sky. There was a jumble of swirling images as the rearview mirror, surreptitious home to ATN's secret eye, was manhandled and eventually thrown out the window. It landed with a crack on another car. The final image was of a journalist Ethan knew—a flack, really—cursing loudly enough to be heard through the thick pane of his windshield's glass.

"That was more than an hour ago. It's the last we saw of them."

"Are you telling me that three-fourths of the family starring in the highest-rated show in the history of this network, the only three-fourths not currently in a coma, have gone AWOL?"

No one said anything because there was nothing to say.

Then Ethan did something he never did. He lost control.

"Holy fuck!" he screamed, the sound of his voice a kind of whiny shriek. He punched the wall next to him and screamed again.

"Holy fuck!" This time it was with the agony of a sprained wrist and broken finger. He went down on one knee and clutched his hand.

No one in the control room moved a muscle.

"Don't just stand there," Ethan whimpered. "Call the staff doctor."

While Andersona was on the phone to the medical team, Phil said, "Look."

Ethan turned his attention to the wall of cameras and saw Deirdre's car pulling into the driveway.

***

Megan was humiliated that ATN had aired her betrayal of Jackie. It would have been bad enough if the network had shown what really happened—that Megan had been drawn into the conspiracy by Ethan, that he had exploited her vanity— but to see it twisted into something an order of magnitude worse left Megan shaken.

When she tried to apologize to Jackie and Deirdre in the car, after the library, she broke down and cried. She was hysterical enough that Deirdre pulled the car over and climbed into the backseat to hug her. For a brief moment, Megan was a little girl again and burrowed her face into her mother's bosom. She had never felt so safe.

"If you're really sorry," Jackie said from the front seat, after Megan's sobs had subsided and her mother started driving again, "I know of a way you can help."

"Anything," Megan said, and she meant it.

Jackie laid out Hazel's plan. It was, on first blush, so replete with points of failure that one of her online friends had code-named it Chernobyl. It involved theft, misdirection, and a bold kind of escape. Megan listened intently as Jackie explained.

"A team of video editors has been reviewing footage from *Life and Death*, as well as the raw footage I shot for the YouTube series."

"A team of video editors?" Deirdre asked. "How many people have been involved in this thing?"

"A lot, Mom. I could never have done this all by myself. But the most important has been my Facebook friend in Russia, Max."

"You have friends in Russia?" Megan asked.

"Just the one," Jackie answered. "But he's the only one I need. Well, him and my friend Hazel in Alabama. The three of us are the core team. But there's a much bigger group working on it, too."

Megan looked at Jackie, then at her mom, and then paused a beat. As sometimes happens with close friends and relatives, the three of them burst out laughing all at once.

"I guess it is a little hard to believe," Jackie offered. "It's just how the Internet works. People, if they look hard enough, can find other people who are like them."

"Okay," Deirdre said, "there's a team of editors."

"Right. This team of editors was reviewing the footage of our house, of the set"—Jackie made quotation marks with her fingers—"looking for any sort of weakness, any advantage we could have over Ethan and the crew. It took them a long time, but they think they found something. A guy named Harrison, a segment news producer from Biscayne Bay, Florida, or someplace like that, found it."

Deirdre, who was zigzagging streets to kill time on the ride home from the library, shook her head in disbelief, muttering, "Biscayne Bay."

"In the footage I shot," Jackie continued, "he noticed that Andersona puts her iPhone on the catering table, just off camera, before conducting interviews."

"That's right," Megan said. "She did that for my interviews, too."

"The cell signal," Jackie explained, "can interfere with the wireless mics, so you're not allowed to have cell phones on the set."

Megan waited for more, but Jackie was silent. "And?" she asked.

"Don't you see?"

"No."

"We steal Andersona's phone and shoot footage for *The Real Family Stone of Portland, Oregon* with that."

No one responded, at first.

"Honey," Deirdre said gently, "I'm not sure what good that would do." Jackie didn't respond, so her mom continued. "First, Andersona isn't going to let you anywhere near that interview room. And even if she does want to interview you, honey, I don't think you should talk on camera. They'll just use it against you. And what if you do get her phone? The cameras all over the house will track the phone's movement, won't they?"

All her mom's questions made sense, so Megan was surprised to hear Jackie laugh. "What's so funny?" she asked.

Jackie explained how she had asked Hazel those same questions and more. And Hazel had answers for all of them. The team in Azeroth had been through every last detail. It would be like hitting the four-meter-wide hole in the exhaust system of the Death Star, but it was doable. The three of them would need to be Luke Skywalker, R2-D2, and Han Solo, but the plan could work.

"Pull over, Mom," Jackie said. "I'm going to need your full attention."

Deirdre did as instructed, and Jackie walked them through each and every detail. The more Jackie talked, the more enthralled Megan became.

The three of them committed the plan to memory, adapted it as they saw fit, and walked through it again.

After they got home, after they and the car were searched like they were terrorists plotting to blow up Seattle's Space Needle, after Ethan yelled at them like they were his children and told them never to leave like that again, Megan looked at her watch and put Plan Chernobyl into action.

***

Jared lay in his makeshift hospital bed; he was utterly still. The only motion came from his chest as it rose and fell in time with the machine filling his lungs with a super oxygenated mixture of air.

His thoughts and memories all but gone, the only flicker of life was a small pilot light buried deep at the center of his brain. It was a still image, a photograph, of Deirdre, Jackie, Megan, and Trebuchet on the beach at Seaside, Oregon. It was a day filled with sunlight, and it was a moment filled with laughter. Jared, who had taken the photo, had told everyone to smile and "say Gruyère." It was a silly joke, but it always made his daughters laugh. Deirdre usually groaned through her smile, but on this one day, she was laughing, too. As Jared's life seeped away, this one happy moment was the last remaining thread connecting him to the world he had known.

The Seaside image was all that was left of Jared Stone.

Glio, not knowing what else to do, ate that, too.

**

Megan found Andersona sitting in the kitchen smoking a cigarette and staring blankly into a cup of coffee. The crew was forbidden from smoking in the house, but Andersona looked too far gone to care.

Megan was delighted to see that something was upsetting Andersona; it could only help their cause.

As Jackie had laid out in the plan, Megan was carrying a magazine.

"It doesn't matter which magazine," Jackie had answered when Megan asked. "Just something that Andersona and Ethan would believe you'd be reading."

She chose *Entertainment Weekly*. Megan was smart enough to know how people saw her, and she knew this fit with their image. Plus, she liked looking at the pictures of the celebrities, especially the women. Sometimes, after carefully studying their every detail, she adjusted her own fashion choices to be more "Hollywood."

"Andersona," she asked, "are you okay?"

Andersona looked up. It took her a moment to comprehend that Megan was standing there.

"What do you want?"

"You just look sad is all."

"Sad?" Andersona barked. "Why would I be sad? You, your mother, and your sister disappear, and I get blamed. I'm going to lose my job. Just like Jo Garvin. Just like lots of people." She turned back to her coffee.

"I'm sorry," Megan said, even though she really wasn't. "But I think maybe I have something that can make you feel better."

Andersona glanced at Megan. "I doubt it."

"Well"—Megan paused, like she had rehearsed in the car— "what if I told you that my mom and sister had kidnapped me and forced me to leave the house with them?"

"I'm sorry," Andersona said, the fog of self-pity starting to lift. "Can you say that again?"

"I can do better. I can say it on camera."

***

Jackie waited for Megan in one of the blind spots identified by the team in Azeroth. It was a corner of the dining room that lay adjacent to the kitchen. Her palms were sweaty and her teeth were starting to chatter with anticipation. She didn't have a good reason to be just standing there against the wall; someone was bound to walk by sooner or later and ask what she was doing. She would either have to make up an excuse on the fly, or go back to her room.

She was holding a book in her hand, *Moby-Dick*, with the insides partially hollowed out. She had used a different blind spot, one in the unfinished basement where hardly anyone ever went, to carve out the pages. It was a receptacle waiting for a hidden treasure.

Finally, after what felt like a week and a half, Jackie heard Megan approaching. She listened as her sister stopped and exchanged a pleasantry with some member of the crew.

C'mon, Jackie thought, *just hurry up and get here.*

Her wish was granted a moment later when Megan rounded the corner with methodical and deliberate purpose. She casually held her magazine out, like she had practiced, and let the iPhone slide into Jackie's outstretched hand. If they'd done it right, the camera would have missed the entire thing. Jackie waited a full two minutes before stepping back into the frame, clutching the book to her chest.

She had to force her feet to move, one after the other, toward her father's office. She couldn't believe their luck. Stealing Andersona's phone was by far the riskiest part of the entire scheme, and Megan had executed it perfectly.

The plan was pretty straightforward. Lay the magazine on top of the phone before the interview, and take both the magazine and the phone on the way out of the room. They all knew that Andersona would spend another few minutes filming reaction shots to edit into the interview later, leaving plenty of time to give Megan a head start.

Jackie entered Jared's office/hospital room, nodding at Sister Benedict and one of the nurses as she did.

"Okay if I read to my father?" she asked.

Jackie did a double take when she saw the Sister talk into her wrist as if she were a Secret Service agent. The nun was also, Jackie noticed, wearing an earpiece. The Sister spoke again and held her finger to her ear, listening to a response. She nodded to herself and then turned her attention back to Jackie.

"It would be better if you read him the Bible," the Sister answered.

"This was his favorite book," Jackie said, holding it up for inspection. Hiding the contraband in plain sight was a specific suggestion from the Azeroth guild. *No one ever thinks that they can be harmed by what they can easily see*, they had told her.

The Sister squinted at the title and grunted. She turned back to a conversation she was having with the nurse, only now they spoke in hushed tones so Jackie couldn't hear. Jackie tuned them out and set her mind to the task at hand.

After she had been there reading for a couple of minutes— she had preserved the first few pages of the book when hollowing it out so she could actually read to her father— she waited until no one was looking, slipped the phone out of the book, and tucked it under her father's mattress. There was some risk in this part of the plan, but Jackie was confident that once everyone back in the control room saw she was only there to read to her comatose dad, she would fade into the background. Again, she was hiding her actions in plain view. It took nerve, but that was something Jackie was developing in abundance.

She couldn't help but think that her father would be proud of her. She squeezed his hand, kissed his cheek, closed her book, and left the room.

As she was heading back to her own bedroom, she saw Andersona rush by, a production assistant in tow. She was barking at him in a whispered frenzy. The only words Jackie caught were: "Find it!"

It look all of Jackie's willpower not to laugh out loud.

***

Ethan needed to regain control. His outburst in the truck was a misstep, and he knew it. After his conversation with Roger, he was starting to think he'd been playing everything wrong. It was this uncertainty, this lack of confidence that caused him to become unhinged.

Bending people to his way of thinking, getting them to unwittingly do his bidding, was Ethan's signature move. He rarely accomplished this through bluster and force. He got what he wanted through charm and guile. It was time to go back to his playbook and stop calling audibles.

The linchpin, he knew, was Deirdre. He should never have tried to deal directly with the younger daughter. With Jared out of commission, Deirdre was the head of this household, and he'd undermined her authority by going behind her back. Both daughters, he had to believe, would follow their mother's lead. Ethan needed to coax Deirdre back into his confidence, make her feel like part of the team.

That wasn't going to be easy. Ethan had dressed the family down—yet one more mistake—when they'd returned from their excursion. He was pretty rough and now he needed to fix it.

There was only one place to begin: with an apology.

He knew from the control truck that Deirdre was lying down in her bedroom. It seemed like too intimate a place to start to heal wounds, but time was of the essence. He needed to get back on course now, before it all fell apart.

Ethan knocked on the door. There was no answer. He had seen on the monitor that Deirdre wasn't asleep. She was reading. He even knew what she was reading. Ethan couldn't figure out why people wasted their time with books. Weren't there enough good movies and television shows?

He knocked again. "Deirdre, it's Ethan," he called out. "Listen, I want to apologize."

After a moment he heard movement, and then the door opened.

Deirdre stood there, her body language and facial expression a cross between tired and agitated.

"Do you have a minute?" he asked.

"Does it matter if I say no?" she responded.

"Look," he began, "I know what you must think of me, and I don't blame you. I've been a jerk, and I'm sorry."

"Thank you," Deirdre said and started to close the door on him.

"Wait. Please, just hear me out for one minute."

Deirdre stopped, the door half open, and leaned her shoulder against its edge.

"I know this isn't going to matter to you, especially with Jared so, so . . ."

"Dying," she interrupted.

"Yes," he said, "dying." This was when Ethan was at his best; confronting difficult truths and somehow making himself share in the pain of others. "Anyway, I know it must seem silly to you with everything your family is going through, but I'm under immense pressure to try to hold this television show together. A lot of people at the network are depending on me, depending on us, to make this successful."

He had Deirdre's attention, but she didn't respond.

"Listen, I could tell you how much America needs to see you and your family, how they've become invested in your lives—"

"You have told me that."

"And it's true. Or maybe it's true on some level. But if I'm being honest, I'm here trying to save my own skin." Ethan paused and looked at his shoes. "Anyway," he said without looking up, "that's why I've been so hard on you and the girls. Hell, that's why I did this." He held up his bandaged hand.

"You told me someone slammed a car door on it."

"I lied about that, Deirdre. I punched a wall in the control truck. I didn't want you to know because I was embarrassed." This was another arrow in the Overbee quiver, own up to everything. "I lost control with you, and I lost control with my crew. I'm going to apologize to them, too."

"Okay, Ethan," Deirdre said, now more tired and less agitated, which he knew was progress, "thank you." Again, she started to close the door.

"Wait," he said, "one more thing."

Deirdre held the door and waited. Ethan was now talking to her through the smallest sliver of daylight.

"I'd like to sit with you and the girls and figure out how we can come to some sort of détente. You want to live your life, and I have a contract with the family to produce a television show. And I have advertisers to keep happy. You tell me what you need, I'll tell you what I need, and maybe we can put the hatchets down, if not bury them. You don't have to like me, Deirdre, but maybe there's some way we can work together. It would be best for all of us, don't you think?" *Always end with a question*, he thought. *Don't let them just walk away; make them respond.*

Deirdre waited for a long moment. He could feel her searching his eyes.

"Okay, Ethan," she answered. "First thing tomorrow. The four of us will meet over breakfast and see what we can figure out. Would that be okay?"

"That would be more than okay. I really appreciate it. And I'm really sorry to have disturbed you. Thanks, and have a good night." *When the sale is done, stop selling*, he thought.

"You too," Deirdre said, and closed the door.

Ethan heaved a sigh of relief. He could feel his mojo coming back.

***

Deirdre knew the cameras were on her, so she was careful not to show emotion, but when she closed the door after talking to Ethan, she wanted to laugh. It was partly from the release of stress, and partly from the joy of knowing she had bought herself valuable time to do what she needed to do.

Ethan was going to back down until the morning. Yes, the control truck would be watching, and yes, she and the girls had to dance a very careful dance, but Ethan's visit was both unexpected and good news.

There was less than two hours to air, and Deirdre was full of adrenaline. It was this spike in nervous energy that made it all the more remarkable that she was able to muster the discipline to lie on the bed and close her eyes. She recounted what had transpired in the past twenty-four hours and drifted into an uneasy sleep.

***

Sister Benedict was enamored of the technology she now wore. She thought of the earpiece and microphone as accessories. Vain women wore lipstick and high heels. Sister Benedict wore sophisticated communication devices, all, of course, in the service of the Lord.

While the Sister didn't watch much television beyond Duke Hamblin, she thought she knew enough about it to dismiss it as ephemera. She was wrong. *I've been wasting my time*, she thought, *with that blog. This is still where America's heart beats.*

The Sister had received nearly fifty pieces of fan mail. A few were not unlike the misanthropic messages posted to christscadets.blogspot.com—mean and nasty people with disdain for God and too much time on their hands—but some were simply wonderful.

A senior citizen in Boston sent her a blessing, thanking her for helping to prepare Jared's soul for the next world. A married couple in Idaho encouraged her to impart some religion to the Stone daughters (a goal with which the Sister heartily agreed). A teenage girl in Indiana called her an inspiration.

Me, she thought, *inspiring young girls all over the country*. It was overwhelming.

She had even been contacted by an agent. Her immediate reaction was to scoff at the idea. She, the Mother Superior of the Sisters of the Perpetual Adoration, should have an agent? Ridiculous.

Or was it?

Yes, an agent, she thought. *I can bring the message of the Lord to people everywhere. It can be my voice that lifts them up.*

"All clear, Sister?" the voice from the control truck buzzed in her ear.

"All clear," she said to her wrist, almost giggling as she did. Young Jacquelyn had left the room a few minutes earlier, and she and Jared were alone. Or as alone as two people can be when someone else is watching their every move.

The Sister thought that maybe she would use the opportunity to change Jared's sheets, but the more she thought about television and her role in it, the more intrigued she became. The sheets could wait. She went to the kitchen to write a letter to that agent.

Sister Benedict Joan had stars in her eyes.

***

The moment had come.

Jackie and her mother and sister filed into Jared's room and arranged themselves around his bed to watch that night's episode of *Life and Death*. Sister Benedict, as she had done each night since she joined the Stone household, sat in a corner of the room, not giving the family privacy, but trying to be as unobtrusive as possible. No one said a word.

The episode began with Megan's interview.

Jackie had to stop herself from chuckling as she watched. Megan had really laid it on thick.

"It was so *awful*," she said, her face showing the emotion of a silent film star. "My mother said that if I didn't leave with them, they would ship me to an all-girls private school and that I couldn't be with my dad anymore. Now that he's so close to the end, I didn't know what to do, so I went."

"What were your mother and sister hoping to accomplish?" Andersona asked from off camera.

"I-I can't say," Megan answered, each word a thick cloud of breath.

"It's okay, Megan," Andersona prodded, "you can talk to me."

"Well," she said, "they wanted to buy Jackie a new phone, this time an even better one, the new Samsung Galaxy phone." The screen showed an inducement to learn more about the phone online.

"Did they succeed?"

"No. The man at the store had seen the show and didn't want anything to do with us. I felt sorry for my mother and sister, really."

The interview went on for a while longer, ending with Andersona telling Megan how brave she had been to come forward.

"I'm only doing this for my father, so that he may rest in peace."

The opening credits rolled.

Jackie reached over and squeezed her sister's hand. Megan permitted herself a fraction of a smile.

The first commercial break was Jackie's cue. She reached over, hugged her father, said, "I love you, Daddy," kissed his cheek, and got up to leave the room. Her voice cracked when she told Sister Benedict, "I need to use the bathroom."

Sister Benedict listened in her earpiece and then nodded.

Jackie, with the iPhone successfully palmed from under her father's mattress, walked into the hall knowing she would never see her father alive again.

***

Ethan watched the show from the truck and passed out compliments and kudos to the crew like they were PEZ. It was his effort to get back in their good graces. Andersona, who had been in a foul mood all day—*Probably on the rag,* he thought—sat huddled in a corner reviewing dailies.

"Loosen up, Andy," he said. "You can worry about tomorrow's footage tomorrow. Enjoy the fruits of your labor tonight."

Andersona didn't answer. Instead, her jaw hung lower and lower from her face, and her cheeks were turning the red of a royal flush, all hearts. Something was wrong.

"Fuck!" she yelled. It was one curt but penetrating bark.

"What?" Ethan asked, both startled and annoyed.

Andersona paused for a moment, but she was too upset to obfuscate the truth. "That little bitch has my iPhone," she said flatly.

"I'm sorry?" Ethan said. The temperature in the room fell twenty degrees. "What did you just say?"

"Today, after Megan's interview, I couldn't find my cell phone. That little bitch took it and gave it to her sister."

"Are you sure?"

"Yes!" she shrieked. "I've been looking at this footage until I'm blue in the face. You can't see her actually take it, but the clues are all there. I'm pretty sure Jackie just took it from under her father's pillow or something."

"Okay, let's stay calm. Phil, tell Sister Benedict to excuse herself quietly from the room and go stall Jackie until I get there. Where is she?"

"The kid just went into the bathroom near the office."

"Just have the Sister stand outside the door and tell her not to let Jackie out. I'll be there in a minute."

"Got it, boss."

Ethan turned to leave the room. As he did, he looked over his shoulder. "Oh, and Andersona?"

She knew what was coming next before he said it.

"You're fired."

***

Deirdre watched Sister Benedict hold a finger to her ear, listen intently to someone on the other end of her earpiece, and then leave the room. Deirdre couldn't believe her luck.

Sister Benedict was the wild card in all of this. Deirdre was going to ask for a private moment with Jared but wasn't sure the Sister would comply. If that didn't work, she had planned to use brute force. Deirdre had sized up the nun and was pretty sure she could take her.

Now there was no need. The Sister's overlords—that was the word that popped into Deirdre's head to describe Ethan and his minions—had called her away. The time to act was now.

"Meg," Deirdre said with as gentle a tone as she could muster, "I don't think you should stay here for this. You can take a moment if you want to tell Daddy good-bye, but it has to be quick. We probably don't have a lot of time."

Megan looked at her father, but she couldn't go over to him. She started bawling. "Good-bye, Daddy." She choked the words out.

"Okay, sweetheart," Deirdre said, pulling her daughter into an embrace. "It's going to be okay, I promise." Deirdre's nerves were rock solid. She didn't know where her resolve was coming from. Love, she figured, can make us weak-kneed and wobbly, but when it needs to, it can make us stronger than steel.

Megan was still crying but managed to get herself under control. "You wait outside the room," Deirdre told her. "I'm going to lock the door. I'm pretty sure they'll try to break it down, but you do your best to stall them. Just get out of the way before they can do anything to hurt you. Okay?"

Megan nodded and hugged her mother. She left the room without looking back. Deirdre was alone.

She locked the door, went over to her husband, took his hands, and kissed his lips.

"This is for you, Jare. I love you."

Deirdre reached across Jared's body, her finger poised on the ventilator, and paused. She had come to the precipice, but she couldn't go through with it. She couldn't stop her husband, the father of her children, from living.

She looked at Jared's face and so many memories came flooding back, as if his life was flashing before her eyes.

She remembered the night they sat on a stone wall high on a hill in some park near where Jared grew up, watching the moon rise. It was fall, and Deirdre was nestled into Jared to keep warm. Ninety minutes passed as the moon traced its arc from the horizon to the sky. Neither one spoke and neither one moved. It was a perfect evening.

She remembered the day Jared took Megan, when she was three, to her first movie. Jackie was in kindergarten, and the legislature wasn't in session. The two of them, Jared and Megan, came home covered in popcorn butter and cotton candy, singing, dancing, and hugging. Until that day, Jared hadn't really seemed to connect with Megan, and Deirdre was beginning to worry. She thought maybe there wasn't enough love in his heart for two children, but Megan, who was persistent, won him over.

She could still see in her mind's eye the day they buried Deirdre's mother. Jared was so full of compassion and so full of strength that Deirdre just let her entire being collapse into him. He was stronger than anyone she'd ever known.

And now, now he was this.

Deirdre took a deep breath and closed her eyes, looking for the courage to do what her Jared wanted, but it wasn't there. She drew her hand back.

Then she opened her eyes and looked up.

The lens of a camera—the crew not bothering to hide the cameras in the sick room—was trained directly on her face. The convex curve of the glass distorted her features, stretched them like a funhouse mirror. On the other side of that glass, she knew, was the rest of the world. They sat there, gawkers at a zoo. It disgusted her. It made her angry.

It gave her all the strength she needed.

Deirdre removed the pillow from under Jared's head, took the pillowcase off, and tossed it over the camera. Then she leaned forward, turned off the ventilator, and put the pillow over her husband's face. A throbbing pain exploded behind her eyelids, but she didn't flinch. Deirdre was prepared to stay there until the end of time.

***

"Young lady." Jackie heard Sister Benedict's voice through the door. "We know you have Andersona's phone. Mr. Overbee is coming here now. You would be a smart girl to just give it back to us."

Jackie panicked. They knew. They knew before her mother had a chance to do what she had to do. Maybe they knew about that, too. Maybe it was already over. She looked at the bathroom window, trying to figure out if she could wriggle through and escape, but she was pretty sure it was too small.

"Is she still in there?" It was Ethan's voice. There was no answer from the Sister, which Jackie thought was strange. Not sure what else to do, Jackie started the video recording on Andersona's phone.

"This is Jackie Stone," she whispered with urgency, pointing the camera at her face. "I'm trapped in my own bathroom with a stolen iPhone. The *Life and Death* producer, Ethan Overbee, and that nun, Sister Benedict, are outside the door demanding I—"

"Sister?" Ethan asked, alarm in his voice. "What is it?"

"NOOOOO!!!!" the Sister wailed. "The control truck . . . they're saying . . . it's Deirdre! She's, she's . . ."

"Fuck, no!" Ethan yelled in response.

Jackie heard them both running down the hall away from the bathroom. With the phone still recording, she opened the door to see what was going on.

***

Megan was overwhelmed. Sister Benedict made it to the door first, with Ethan hot on her heels. The doctors arrived only seconds later. All of them were shouting at Megan to move.

"Out of our way!" the Sister bellowed.

"Megan, please!" Ethan implored.

"We need to get in," one of the doctors said, panic in his voice.

Only they were all talking at once, creating a wall of sound that was indecipherable. The Sister's piercing scream cut through it all.

"Enough!" she shouted. The hallway went silent. "Move, you insolent brat. Your mother is in there committing murder! Move! Now!"

When Megan didn't budge, Sister Benedict slapped her across the face. It was a hard slap, and it stung.

In the wake of the startled silence created by that slap, the echo of hand on cheek reverberating through the house, a noise of movement from down the hall drew everyone's attention. All the heads turned as one, just in time to see Jackie holding the phone out in front of her and pointing it at the assembled crowd. She left the bathroom, ran down the stairs, and raced out of the house.

Ethan ran down the hall in pursuit, faster than Megan thought possible.

When the Sister turned her attention back to the office door, Megan was ready. She landed her right fist on the very end of the nun's nose, making blood splatter and making the woman shriek in pain.

"That," she said, "is for, is for everything." Megan, over-wrought with a tidal wave of emotions, started to cry. A nurse pulled her aside and hugged her while the doctors tried to open the locked door.

Megan buried her face in the nurse's shoulder and let it all out.

***

Jackie held the phone behind her as she ran, filming her pursuer while she tried to narrate.

"My mother is trying to end my father's suffering," she said through heaving breaths. "Sister Benedict attacked my sister, and Ethan Overbee is chasing me. I think he wants to hurt me or kill me."

Jackie was across the yard in a heartbeat. She stopped at the edge of the seven-foot fence they called The Wall.

"Give me the phone, Jackie," Ethan said. He was panting, too. "There's nowhere else for you to go. It's all over."

Jackie looked straight into his eyes. "Almost," she said. She saw the perplexed look on his face, then turned around and threw the phone over the fence. They both watched it tumble end over end against the night sky.

A second later, there was an exclamation of joy from the other side of The Wall. "I got it!" It was Jason Sanderson's voice. He was exactly where Hazel said he would be. What Jackie didn't expect to hear was the cheer that went up from the crowd that had gathered around him.

Jackie turned back to Ethan. "Now," she said, "it's over."

Ethan dropped to his knees, then to his butt, and sat down on the grass as if he'd been shot.

Jackie stepped around him and went back into the house.

***

Deirdre held the pillow over Jared's face for what felt like an eternity, but what the clock on the wall revealed to be only about ninety seconds. That's when he flatlined. Jared never moved, never twitched. Deirdre was still holding the pillow there when the doctors broke down the door nearly four minutes later.

She stepped out of the way knowing she had succeeded. Jared was dead.

Deirdre, understanding the gravity of what she had done, staggered backward and fell into a chair, where she started to cry, and then she cried some more.

***

Glio's life ended a few seconds after that of Jared Stone. But to a high-grade glioblastoma multiforme, a few seconds is an eternity. With no memories to eat, with no external stimuli to occupy its attention, Glio fell into a black hole of nothingness.

Some would say it was just deserts, that it was what a brain tumor had coming, and they would probably be right. But Glio had been transformed. He had become the sum total of Jared Stone's memories. He had grown to love Jared Stone's wife and daughters; he had come to love Jared Stone.

The Glio wasn't sorry to die, only sorry he hadn't lived more.

Epilogue

Later

The final episodes of both *Life and Death* and *The Real Family Stone of Portland, Oregon* aired the day after Jared Stone passed away. The network, having dispatched Ethan and his senior crew without the courtesy of an in-person meeting, elected not to show any of the footage from that harrowing night in the Stone household. Instead, Roger Stern, in a bold move, did a live interview with Deirdre, Jackie, and Megan, during which he apologized for the behavior of the American Television Network and handed a shell-shocked Deirdre the five-million-dollar check she had been promised.

She and the girls were quiet but respectful. They thanked Roger but didn't say much more. The balance of the hour was a commercial-free montage of images and clips of the Stone family in happier times. Much of it had been provided weeks earlier, when Jared had first signed the deal, as background for the producers.

The Real Family Stone of Portland, Oregon was equally simple. It showed Jackie's unedited footage, beginning when she was locked in the bathroom and ending with the iPhone held high over Jason Sanderson's head. The final image was of the assembled crowd—including many of the kids from Jackie's school, along with Ms. Onorati and a few of the other teachers—cheering. There was no commentary; there were no titles or credits, just two words in a plain, unassuming font: "The End."

***

Jared was laid to rest in a small, private funeral, attended only by his family and closest friends. It was, in typical Portland fashion, raining. Deirdre, Jackie, and Megan stayed huddled under a single umbrella and cried as they bid their husband and father a final good-bye.

It was short. It was elegant. It was bittersweet.

Afterward, everyone went back to the Stone house, now completely free of television equipment, and ate lunch.

***

A public memorial, including a solemn march down Burnside Avenue, was staged by the euthanasia lobby, but Deirdre, Jackie, and Megan declined to attend. They'd had enough of the spectacle.

Sister Benedict Joan was there, praying for the soul of the man with whom she had inexplicably become obsessed, and praying for the souls of those who would treat life as if it was disposable. She was largely ignored.

After the media frenzy died down, Sister Benedict was summoned to the office of Cardinal Trippe. The video evidence of her behavior the night Jared Stone died had found its way to the Cardinal. He was speechless. He shook his head in disappointment.

"I'm sorry, Sister," he said.

"You're sorry, Your Grace?"

"To have misjudged you." A golf-ball-sized lump formed in the Sister's throat. "I've carved out a new assignment for you."

"New assignment?" There was dread in the Sister's voice.

It was the last the Lower 48 would see of Sister Benedict Joan. As penance for her actions, the Cardinal assigned her to a convent in Fairbanks, Alaska. Sister Benedict would spend the endless winter nights lamenting her involvement with Jared Stone and his family.

***

Ethan Overbee cursed and swore like a sailor as he drove his Tesla home from the studio, his meager personal possessions in two cardboard boxes. He had been escorted off the premises by security.

The previous sixty hours were a blur. He wasn't really sure what had happened.

As his rage subsided, he started to go through his options. Without knowing or understanding he was doing it, Ethan had dropped back to the bottom of Maslow's hierarchy of needs. He thought, mostly subconsciously, about his safety. Check. Food, clothing, shelter. Check, check, check. His physical desire, however, was unsated. He picked up his cell phone and called Monique.

He got her voice mail.

"Hi, you've reached Monique. I can't talk right now, so leave a message. And if this is my former boss, Ethan Overbee"—she emphasized the word "former"—"I hear they fired your sorry ass. Don't fucking call me again."

Ethan wanted to be mad at Monique, to ruin her, but he knew he was no longer in a position to ruin anyone, which stoked his fury all over again. He needed a way out of this nightmare. It was all the fault of that lunatic, Kingsborough. That was when the whole thing had started to go sour. Why the fuck would a billionaire playboy sneak into Jared Stone's house in the middle of the night and stab the guy's dog? Had the world gone mad?

At least Kingsborough would get what was coming to him. Sherman Kingsborough, Ethan knew, was being held without bail in a secure location, and he would soon go through the nightmare ordeal of trial, conviction, prison. "That poor jerk is in for a hell of a ride," Ethan said aloud.

"A hell of a ride," he repeated. When he went through the scenario in his head again, he smiled for the first time in days. He let out a whooping laugh, the cackle loud enough to be heard by two girls Rollerblading along the boardwalk that bordered the Pacific Coast Highway.

"A helluva ride!" he shouted as he picked up his cell phone again. This time, he dialed the number of a board member he knew over at the rival Global Television Network. *Those guys,* thought Ethan happily. *Now, those guys have no soul.*

But it was not to be.

Ethan Overbee shopped *Busted,* a reality show featuring Sherman Kingsborough, for nearly a year before giving up. No one was interested in Ethan or his show. He was persona non grata in the world of television production, and any project with his name attached was doomed to fail. With nowhere else to go and his tail between his legs, Ethan found his way to the last refuge of industry professionals. He was hired as the chief executive officer of the National Association of Television Executives.

***

Sherman Kingsborough is serving a twenty-year sentence for attempted murder in the first degree. He's writing a book about his experience. It's expected to fetch a seven-figure advance.

***

After the final episode of *Life and Death* aired, Deirdre and her lawyer drove to the main precinct of the Portland police station, where she surrendered herself to the authorities for the murder of her husband, Jared Stone.

The district attorney, a seasoned law enforcement official and a skilled litigator, had contacted Deirdre's lawyer after word of her mercy killing reached his office, and suggested a quiet, benign meeting to discuss options.

He explained to Deirdre that while he didn't agree with it, he had no choice but to prosecute.

Deirdre was processed and then released without having to post bail. Given the nature of her crime, the DA agreed with the judge that Deirdre didn't pose a danger to herself or society, nor was she a flight risk.

She and her attorney rejected all offers to plead to a lesser sentence, each of which would have required her to serve at least six months in jail. Deirdre's defense was funded by the right-to-die lobby, a group that was, thanks in part to Jared Stone, marshaling a significant war chest. They saw Deirdre's trial as a test of both the law and of public opinion.

The trial, which didn't begin until almost a year after Jared's death, lasted six weeks. Deirdre's legal team pursued a unique strategy. She was, they contended, defending the rights of Jared Stone. They freely admitted that Deirdre turned off the ventilation machine and smothered Jared with a pillow, causing her husband to die. (They had no choice, as the prosecutors showed the video from every camera angle in the room save the one covered by a pillowcase.) Deirdre had wanted to keep her daughters out of it, but they were all over the police report, so both appeared as hostile witnesses for the prosecution.

The DA made a simple argument: Deirdre Stone, frustrated by the intrusion of the television cameras—a fact with which he sympathized—had admitted to killing Jared Stone. Doing so was against the laws of the state of Oregon. The state had no choice but to hold her accountable.

Church officials were called to testify about the nature of the care administered to Jared Stone on the set of *Life and Death*. The defense countered that the Church had used its influence to cajole the medical team into artificially prolonging Jared's life, making him an icon to promote their political views.

In the end, the jury sided with Deirdre. She was found innocent of murder. The double jeopardy clause of the US and Oregon State Constitutions kept the DA from filing a manslaughter charge—which he wouldn't have done in any case—and for Deirdre, the nightmare was truly and finally over.

Like Sherman Kingsborough, Deirdre is writing a book. It's called *House of Stone* and is dedicated to the memory of her late husband.

***

When the news stories spread about the events that night in Portland, Hazel was featured prominently. Until then, her parents had known little about her involvement with Jackie Stone. They were aware of her fund-raising effort but thought the matter had ended after that.

Hazel wasn't sure how they'd react, but the Hucks were good people. They saw tenderness and love in their daughter they had never managed to see before. As a reward, they bought Hazel a dog: a pug, whom she named Max.

Hazel drifted away from Azeroth. There were just too many real-world adventures to spend time chasing zeroes and ones in the form of dragons and gold. Her newfound celebrity brought her more attention than she wanted at school. But it also opened up new avenues of friendship. Before long she was dating a boy by the name of Richie McGill. He played drums in a punk band, and he worshipped Hazel.

She and Richie fell in love. Both were accepted to schools in Boston—she at Emerson College, he at Boston University. The following fall, the car loaded with their belongings, and Max the pug, they moved north.

Jackie and Hazel did finally meet two years later when Jackie was scouting colleges. The online friends were each thrilled to be in the other's company, and Hazel delighted in showing Jackie around Boston. But, truth be told, the two young women didn't have that much in common. They kept in touch for more than a year after that meeting but eventually drifted apart. Time and distance, as it often is, was too much to overcome.

***

Outwardly, little changed for Megan Stone. She was the queen bee before it all started, and in the aftermath of the unprecedented media coverage, she was the queen bee still. The other popular girls at school flocked around her, and the popular boys wanted to date her.

But Megan was different. Not only were she and Jackie talking again, they were friends. As often as not, Megan would decline an invitation to a party with the in-crowd to spend time with her big sister. As she looked back on the events of those several weeks, she was in awe of Jackie, of the strength and courage she'd shown in standing up to the network, and in standing up for her father.

And it wasn't just Jackie, it was Deirdre, too. Megan did all she could to be supportive of her mother during the trial. They were, as a family, closer than they had ever been before. And that, more than anything, made Megan miss her father.

***

Maxim Andreevich Vasilcinov went from nobody to rock star overnight. News of his involvement in the Stone family saga—it was the biggest story on the Internet for one solid week—made its way to Saint Petersburg, and to Max's school. Suddenly, everyone wanted to be his friend.

At first, Max was overwhelmed and didn't know how to act. But before long, he realized that he simply needed to be himself.

Three weeks later, when the world was returning to a measure of equilibrium, Max was summoned to the headmaster's office. Max had never been called to the office before, and he racked his brain as he made the walk down the long hallway, trying to figure out what he might have done wrong.

"Ah, Maxim," the headmaster said when Max entered, "please, please come in."

There was a woman in the room, a grown-up. Max thought she was very pretty, even glamorous.

"This is Miss Pretaskaya," he said, "from the Moscow Polytechnic University."

"Please," she said, extending her hand, "call me Luba."

Max shook her hand and sat down.

Luba explained how his footage from *The Real Family Stone of Portland, Oregon* was the talk of the film program at the school, and asked whether Max would have any interest in a scholarship to study film and television when he completed high school.

Max fainted.

When he came to, he accepted. He would go on to be one of the most successful directors in the history of Russian cinema.

***

Jackie Stone went on with her life. A day never passed without some reminder of her dad—a song on the radio, a reference to a card game they used to play, just an undefined scent on the wind. As time wore on, the memories blurred and the pain of loss eased. That's not what Jackie wanted—she wanted to feel hurt, anger, and sadness for the rest of her days. She thought it was the only way to honor her father. But that wasn't how the world worked; while time doesn't necessarily heal all wounds, it does provide just enough scar tissue to allow people to move on.

After the ordeal of her trial was over, Deirdre asked Jackie if she could have anything, what would it be. "The only good things that happened in the last year are because of you, sweetheart," Deirdre had told her. "Tell me what you want."

It didn't take Jackie long to answer.

Three months later, after their visas had been issued and processed, Max and his mother crossed the security barrier at the airport in Portland, Oregon, and into the terminal. Max walked right up to Jackie, who was trying to look around him for the boy whose photo she had so often seen online.

"Solnyshko," he said. Jackie was startled; it took a second to focus her attention on the boy standing in front of her. A bit overweight, unruly hair, a complexion like the surface of the moon.

"Max?" she asked.

"Da." His answer was one of resignation. "I did not know how to say to you that I am not boy in picture."

Jackie started to laugh, and Max hung his head in shame. He was taken aback when Jackie threw her arms around him in a hug that would have made a Russian bear proud.

"I am not understanding," he muttered into her shoulder.

"Oh, Max, I am just so happy to see you."

The two teens spent a week together touring every part of Portland, and even drove to Seattle for a day. They held hands, but they never kissed. It just didn't feel right to either one of them.

When Jackie bade him good-bye at the airport, they both promised to stay in touch and to meet again.

It was a promise they would keep many times throughout the course of their lives.

Jackie followed in her father's footsteps. She majored in public policy at Hood River State College and pursued a career in politics.

She would visit her father's grave every year on the anniversary of his death. For a while, Megan and Deirdre came with her, but after a couple of years, they lost the impetus. Jackie never stopped going, and never forgot her father. He was with her, always.

***

While the high-grade glioblastoma multiforme had no progeny in the traditional sense, its seed had been planted in Megan and Jackie Stone. It was there in the form of a slight but identical variation in each of the girls' DNA. It was a marker waiting to be noticed. The hammer on a pistol, waiting for a trigger.

But not all markers are noticed, not all triggers pulled. It would be many, many years before either girl would find out whether her own dormant Glio would awake.

But those are stories for another time.

Acknowledgments

This book was a long time in the making. The story went through several iterations before it ever reached a publisher's desk. In the first draft, Glio wasn't even anthropomorphized . . . he was just a brain tumor.

I played, I tweaked, I wrote, and I rewrote. And along the way a tribe of friends and family provided invaluable feedback. I offer my heartfelt thanks to the following early readers of the manuscript:

All one hundred students at the 2014 Denver Publishing Institute, Bob Almassy, Carol Almassy, Bobbi Gilligan, Tom "71" Gilligan, Carl Lennertz, Tess Murch, and Matt Strollo.

Thanks to my bookseller friends Janet Geddis, Paul Hanson, Allison Hill, and Christine Onorati for reading the early manuscript, and for their never-ending support.

Thanks to Katya Gonella for providing advice on the Russian phrases used by Max.

A huge thanks to my editor and publisher, Cindy Loh at Bloomsbury Children's, who believed in this project from the start, who treats me like a rock star, and who made this book better. Editors are the unsung heroes of the publishing world. And it's not just Cindy; I owe a debt to everyone at Bloomsbury. Special thanks to copyeditor Wendy Dopkin, senior production editor Diane Aronson, and executive managing editor Melissa Kavonic for cleaning up my mess; designer Jessie Gang and creative director Donna Mark for the beautiful cover; Erica Barmash, Lizzy Mason, Cristina Gilbert, and the entire marketing team for helping this book find its way to your hands; and thanks to eagle-eyed intern Jessica Mangicaro for spotting all of my World of Warcraft mistakes. (I did play the highly addictive game for three months as part of my research, reaching level twelve before realizing I was supposed to be writing, not questing.)

Thanks again to my intrepid agent, Sandra Bond. Sandra has been a stalwart friend and supporter since before I had a career.

And, as always, thanks to my family—Kristen (always my first and best reader), Charlie, and Luke. Without them, this all means nothing.